The Last Maya

The Amazing Adventures
of Rebecca Quinto

Thomas Paul Severino

The Last Maya

The Amazing Adventures of Rebecca Quinto

Thomas Paul Severino

Copyright 2021

Pollywog Pond Communications, Ft. Lauderdale

tomseverino.com

tomseverino100@gmail.com

ISBN: 978-1-7369769-1-3

Cover: Head of King Pakal, as an adolescent. Stucco. Classic-recent (600 - 900 C.E.) Temple of Inscriptions, Palenque, Chiapas, Mexico, Wikimedia Commons, 2014

P. 13: Detail of the Dresden Codex (as drawn by William E. Gates), showing a conversation about the creation of human life between a divinity of maize (on the left) and Itzamná (on the right), Wikimedia Commons, 2006

P. 83: Detail of the Codex Grolier, showing the day positions of a Venus almanac. Wikimedia Commons, 2020

P. 267: Kukulkan, Feathered Serpent Deity, detail of Classic Maya lintel at Yaxchilan, from "A Study of Maya Art" by Herbert Spinden, 1913, Wikimedia Commons, 2016

Also by Thomas Paul Severino

The Amazing Adventures of Rebecca Quinto

The Frozen Diva

The Lost Museum

The Kayne Sorenson Mysteries: The Quartet of Blood

Seed Blood

Tribal Blood

Stage Blood

Ancient Blood

The Kayne Sorenson Mysteries: The Quartet of Evil

The Evil Genius

The Shadow of Evil

The Pearl of Great Evil

The Evil League

Thomas Paul Severino

Men make their own history, but they do not make it as they please; they do not make it under self-selected circumstances, but under circumstances existing already, given, and transmitted from the past.

-- Karl Marx, 1818 – 1883, Philosopher, Sociologist, Economic historian, and Revolutionary Socialist

Out of the dim shadows emerged a vision from a fairy tale, a fantastic, ethereal sight from another world. It seemed a huge magic grotto carved out of ice, the walls sparkling and glistening like snow crystals. Delicate festoons of stalactites hung like tassels of a curtain, and the stalagmites on the floor looked like the drippings from a great candle. The impression, in fact, was that of an abandoned chapel. Across the walls marched great stucco figures in low relief. Then my eyes sought the floor. This was almost entirely filled with a great carved stone slab, in perfect condition... Ours were the first eyes that had gazed on it in more than 1000 years.

-- Alberto Ruz 'L'huillier, 1906 – 1979, Archeologist.

The wolf shall dwell with the lamb, and the leopard shall lie down with the young goat, and the calf and the lion and the fattened calf together; and a little child shall lead them.

-- Isaiah 11:6

Thomas Paul Severino

The Last Maya

For Janet

Thomas Paul Severino

Dramatis Personae

The Americans

- Rebecca S. Quinto; President and CEO, The Fritcher Museum of Fine Arts, Ft. Lauderdale, Florida, USA
- Mark R. Gadarn; Journalist, CBN, Inc., New York, New York, USA
- Diego Friedman Cortez
- Joaquín Cortez
- Thomas "Kick" Sorenson, Vice President, Aerie Industries
- Mitchell Sorenson, MD, President, Aerie Industries
- Gints Bergovic, Security Director, Aerie Industries
- Joshua Walker Strong Bear, Master of Horse, Aerie Industries
- Sheriff Matthew Strong Bear of the Nu Ci Nation
- Capt. Daniella Lamb, USMC (Ret.)

Ciudad de Guatemala, República de Guatemala

- Maria de Flores Benitez Friedman
- Juan Sebastián Sandoval, Restauranteur
- Marc Antonio Rameriz, Chauffer
- Alberto Cruz Captain, Policia National Civil
- Father Andres, La Iglesia de La Remedios
- Tomás Benitez, Coach

Museo de Totonicapán/El Universidad San Pedro

- Guillermo Rios Carillo, Director
- Elyssa Nájera Trejo, Graduate Student

Quetzaltenango, República de Guatemala

- Rosalina Ochoa De Leon, Proprietor, Casa De Flores Tikal
- Jacinto Davide De Leon, a boy
- Carmen Varela-Garcia, Cook, Casa De Flores Tikal

- Cauli De Leon, a Xoloitzcuintle
- Domingo Diaz-Sandoval, aka *El Esquivador* (The Dodger)
- *El Maquinista* (the Engineer)
- Elena, aka *La Shuka* (The Dirty Dog)
- Bartolomé Cabrillo, United Nations Office on Drugs and Crime
- Maria, Teresa, Sancho, and Tucki, "Mules"

Palenque, Estado de Chiapas, Estados Unidos Mexicanos

- Hugo Calavera de Armas, Director of Historical Research
- Yolotli Pacheco, Assistant Director, Museo Alberto Ruz L'Huillier

Tila, Estado de Chiapas, Estados Unidos Mexicanos

- Efraín Trejo, Carpenter and Educator
- Cadmael Santana, Apprentice Carpenter
- Ian Nájera, Apprentice Carpenter
- Mamá Xumucane

Playa de Santa Caridad, Ocos, República de Guatemala

- Nelson Osterman-Diaz, Presidente, Empresas Osterman-Diaz
- Enrique Osterman-Diaz, Jefe de Operaciones, Empresas Osterman-Diaz

La Plantación de la Condesa, República de Guatemala

- Ilia Mercado, Directora de Operaciones, Empresas Osterman-Diaz
- Maria Cabrara-Virella, Equipo de Relaciones Laborales, Osterman-Diaz Enterprises

Olivado Sands Detention Center, U.S. Immigration and Customs Enforcement, Brownsville, Texas

- Albert Matthews, Director
- Sgt. Susan Delborn, Security
- Pvt. James Riser, Security

And

- Eris, The Goddess of Discord
- Ix Tz'akbu Ajaw, the Red Queen
- K'inich Janaab Pakal I, the Shield of the Sun

Thomas Paul Severino

Prologue: Jack

Quetzaltenango, República de Guatemala

"Do not delay after school. We have many visitors, and I need all the help you can give me. Hand me the maize flour in the big container, Jacinto."

Rosalina Ochoa De Leon instructed her sister, Carmencita, on the menu for dinner and how to begin one of the dishes. Usually, the inn's cook handled the kitchen. Still, over the weekend, the regular cook got married, and her employers at Casa De Flores Tikal made adjustments. Carmen Varela-Garcia had offered to help her sister. She checked on her baby in the woven infant wrap. The child was asleep. The busy woman was expecting her second, but her time was still a few months away.

Jacinto Davide De Leon stuffed the last of his eggs-in-a-corn-tortilla-roll-up in his mouth, placed his mini tablet on the table, and went for the plastic flour container for his mother.

"Mom, the WiFi is out again."

At eleven, the boy was a savant at the web, social media, and the internet information sources, way ahead of his parents, his aunts, and uncles.

"Thank you. Finish your mosh, *mi hijo*. Tia Carmen made that porridge herself, just for you."

His Auntie pointed to his bowl and plate. She made her point, saying, "Jack, the most important meal of the day for Guatemalans – *desayuno tipico*. We tell the gringos a 'typical breakfast,' hearty and delicious. Eat up."

"Ay, do not call him that, *Hermana*. It sounds so American. That should be enough chilies. Remember, you are not cooking for the family. They are gringos and have delicate stomachs."

The boy preferred the nickname "Jack." His Auntie was cool.

15

"I need to see to housekeeping. Jacinto, drink your orange juice and do not forget your lunch. Make sure you eat all of it today. Do not give my food to that dog either. Cauli has not finished what is in her bowl. Is everyone in this family wasting food?"

The excited hotelier made the sign of the cross. She pressed her hands together as she said, "There are countless poor children in this city who have nothing to eat. It is a sin to waste food, my son. I put in some of the *pepián* from last night's dinner, your favorite."

"Thank you, Mamá."

The boy gathered up his backpack and kissed his mother and aunt goodbye. His little three-legged dog looked up at him, expecting just one more secret morsel. Jack shrugged, petted his best friend, and said, "See you later, Girl, after school."

The family pet headed over to her basket in the corner. This was Cauli's favorite spot for watching her humans. From her comfy dog bed, the pup's eyes carefully scanned the comings and goings of the hotel's kitchen. She sighed.

Her boy would be home to play in no time.

Jack stopped at the kitchen door.

"Mom, don't forget..."

The woman was taking off her apron. She said, "Yes, yes, little one, I will call the WiFi guy."

She raised her eyes to heaven and said, "Americans without internet access... heaven forbid."

***

The Academy of San Cristobal was only three blocks away, behind the big, crumbling church. On the street, Jacinto De Leon hooked up with his besties, Carlos and Rafaela Maria. They talked about the upcoming math exam and the exciting civic soccer match next week.

Rafaela turned around as they walked. She kept moving, but backward. Lagging just a bit, she returned to catch up and walk between her companions.

"Are those buzzards following us, you guys?"

"Where?"

"The blue van down the street."

"You are creeping me out, Rae."

"Carlos, it's OK," Jack said. "We'll report it to Señora Fernanda when we get to school. No one will get in trouble. They are always telling us to say something if we spot trouble."

In the excitement of beginning a new school day at San Cristobal's, the children forgot all about the men in the dark blue van.

Chapter One: The Inca

Ciudad de Guatemala, República de Guatemala

"Cooo. Cooo. Cooo."

The older woman tossed bread crumbs to the pigeons in Plaza de la Constitución. Rebecca sat on the bench next to her, slipping out of her shoes and massaging her sore feet. *La Señora* chuckled softly.

"You American tourists... it is not like your country does not have enough comfortable shoes. Why would anyone wear heels to see the sights of the capital? I will never understand *los gringos*... Hush up you. I am going as fast as a seventy-seven-year-old can."

She pointed to a fat mourning dove and said, "Just like a male. Not happy unless having it all for himself."

Reaching into her beaded carry-all, she tossed a fist full of white and tan crumbs at the feet of the hooting beauty. The male's wing-flapping intimidated his bird comrades.

Rebecca started to say something, but the woman continued speaking.

"That one... the skinny one with the little *séquito*, his group of females... that is 'Atahualpa.' I named him that because he is an Inca Dove. His bird ancestors survived the Spanish genocide, unlike the humans who share the name, Inca."

Rebecca watched a gray-brown dove with feathers that folded in a scaled pattern. He and his mate had long tails and reddish underwings. The Inca King saluted his two human retainers with forceful cooing that sounded like *cowl-coo* followed by *poo-pup*.

"They are not found in any lands where their namesakes had an empire-- Peru and other South America locations. They are plentiful here in Latin America, however."

She handed the American a handful of feed as more of her *Columbidae* circled, fluttered, and floated to the ground around the two women. A nanny stopped her pram and directed her little girl to watch the cloud of white and grey doves swirling and settling in the late morning air around the new friends.

Rebecca smiled at the very fashionable *dama* and carefully tossed her bounty to the awaiting aviary. She remarked, "Is my Spanish the giveaway?"

"No, my dear, your English. When you sent that dashing young man off to get some water. You have a slight New York accent, I believe. By the way, I do hope he purchases purified. I am sure you are familiar with the consequences of... Ah, yes. Here he is now."

Mark Gadarn stepped carefully among the feeding birds and handed Rebecca a water bottle. The older woman reached for it and examined the label. She gave a nod coupled with a thumbs-up.

Mark extended the second bottle, saying, "Señora?"

"No, thank you, Mr. Gadarn. I have something of my own here."

She reached into her bag and extracted a silver flask. She took off the cap, poured an amber liquid, and offered it to her new American friends.

"Ten-year-old Laphroaig. Good scotch. Taste?"

They both passed. The woman shot back a good slug.

"It's how you get to eighty-three, my dears. And by the way, *Felicidades* on the Pulitzer, young man. Your reporting is well worth the accolades."

"Thank you, but Rebecca, you should not brag on me. "

Mark settled on the bench next to Rebecca. He touched her shoulder with a soft caress. His lady love's expression was one of amazement.

"I didn't, Darling." She turned to their companion and asked, "Are you a spy, Señora, or *clarividente*?"

"No, no. Clairvoyant? No. I read and follow the media, Ms. Quinto. You are often paired with this extraordinary man. You are the President and CEO of the Fritcher Museum of Fine Arts in Fort Lauderdale. I visited during your Native American exhibit last year, but I believe you were out of the country."

"Yes. 'Tribal Blood.' Did you enjoy it?"

"Very well done, my dear. I am Maria de Flores Benitez Friedman. Please call me 'Floria,' all my friends do."

"*Encantada*, Darling. I love your couture.

"Yes, nice to meet you, Ma'am."

"Chanel. Yet another iteration of my friend Coco's 'little black dress.' The shawl is Kaqchikel-woven... from Quetzaltenango. I love the colors."

Rebecca thought, *This woman knew Chanel. How ultra chic.*

She sighed, looked at Mark, and added, "Ahh, if I were fifty years younger. You actually resemble my..."

The boy struck suddenly, scattering the pigeons and the doves. He grabbed Señora Friedman's bag, did a spin, and vaulted over another bench. The young thief sprinted down the lawn.

Mark was up and off in a shot. He snagged Floria's cane as he ran. As the thief attempted his getaway, Mark got three-quarters of the way to the boy and tossed the stick. The hardwood hit the kid in the back of the knees, and the fugitive went head over heels into a flower kiosk. He jumped up and scrambled away into a crowd. Mark retrieved the stolen bag and the cane.

He was smiling as he came back to the astonished women. Floria's birds, now deciding it was safe to return, cooed their approval as they resettled.

"See. The pigeons also appreciate a champion. Thank you, Mark."

"That boy was probably eleven or twelve. A young thief -- so unfortunate."

"Yes, my dear, there is much poverty in Guatemala. It appears you are both quite heroic from what I have read and from what I have just seen. Tonight we will dine together. Please do me the honor. *Por favor.*"

Thomas Paul Severino

Chapter Two: Q'eqchi'

Zona 10, Ciudad Guatemala, República de Guatemala

"What did you think of the Palacio Nacional de la Cultura? Very flashy, yes?"

Floria asked for her table in an alcove on the roof of one of the finest restaurants in the City, Restaurante Q'eqchi'. Wait staff fell over themselves as she entered and was ushered to the Art Deco elevator. Mark and Rebecca had been waiting at the bar.

The panoramic view of the largest city in Latin America was breathtaking. The city sounds and sparkling lights softly wafted up to their dinner perch in the warm night air. The ambiance was very romantic, and the patrons seemed to sway to the marimba's soft music.

Mark said, "I found it interesting that the former grand banquet hall in the Palacio had these ornate panels representing the virtues of good government. Wasn't the famous dictator who built it pretty much of a maniacal bastard?"

"You know what I drink, Ricardo, dear boy. Please tell Chef Diana I am here. The rest is up to her. She will recommend the wine. A lovely girl."

Floria slid back into the conversation with a few asides.

"You should always wear that shade of red, Rebecca. You absolutely smolder in it. Mark, beware. The older version of this afternoon's thievery is on deck. Only these Don Juans are not after my purse. I can see the eyes of the men watching your beautiful woman."

"Not a bit worried, Señora... plenty of practice." He reached over and touched Rebecca's hand.

"Jorge Ubico Castañeda.The dictator you mentioned..."

Floria said it as if she were announcing that someone had leprosy.

Rebecca said, "Ohhh yes, I read that the General's was the only name on the ballot when he was elected in 1931. He has been characterized as one of the most oppressive tyrants ever known."

"You have no way of knowing what life was like in Guatemala back then. It indeed was a military dictatorship. An American journalist described the situation he found here in 1941 as a country that was one hundred percent dominated by one man and one man only. The reporter told of Ubico's spies and agents who were everywhere. The General made himself the sole authority on every detail of daily life. Guatemala, under Ubico, was like living in prison."

Floria stared off as she sipped her newly arrived Rusty Nail. She seemed to remember.

"It was monstrous. Ubico militarized numerous political and social institutions, the post office, the schools, and even the arts. He placed individuals with no experience in charge of many government posts. Ubico demanded total government control of the media. He frequently traveled around the country performing 'inspections' and held political rallies to benefit his vanity."

Rebecca added, "He completely sold the country to foreign companies – control of the port, the import duties, the electric company, and the railroad."

Mark said, "I once researched the pro-democracy uprising of 1944, which led to the ten-year Guatemalan Revolution. The oligarch was out to benefit the upper class, the landowners. Guatemala had a substantial middle class, but it had little representation in the government. Big mistake, it was the democrats that overthrew him. They had had enough."

"The dictator met any resistance with savagery. He tortured and executed his critics and detractors, forcing them to confess under torture. There was much resentment against the president's repressive policies and arrogant demeanor, particularly concerning his desire to extend his term for six more years. My husband was part of the insurrection led by middle-class intellectuals, professionals, and junior army officers. He had Francisco and many others imprisoned and executed."

Mark said, "It must have come as a great relief when he was deposed and driven into exile in October 1944."

"Yes. The nightmare was over."

Rebecca asked, "How did you and your husband meet?"

"I was the only daughter of a coffee baron who thought very highly of education and free-thinking. My father introduced me to Francisco Maria Friedman at this very restaurant, Q'eqchi'. It was called Sabor de Acqua in those days, a very literary and bohemian crowd. He taught at the University – Political Science. I taught primary school. We had one son, Diego. He lives in Miami with his husband. It was they with whom I visited your museum."

Floria inquired about their accommodations. As the server placed beautifully prepared and fragrant dishes, Rebecca responded that she and Mark were staying at the Casa Zaculeu on the El Salvador Road.

The food was accompanied by carefully selected wines. Each dish was a festive pairing representing the region's traditional cuisine: grilled Robalo Fish with fresh tomato and basil, lobster, jocón, Chicken Pepián, and Guatemalan tamales. The presentations were restrained and artistic; the fragrances and tastes sublime.

"Rebecca, please tell me about your art interest here."

"Like most of my projects, it started with an overly expansive vision-- Pre-Columbian Art in Latin America. There are so many beautiful and powerful civilizations from which to choose. Mark, who is my touchstone with reality in most ways – you see, I tend to overthink like an artist... anyway, he got me this, in an art village in West Palm Beach."

She pointed.

Floria reached out and touched the pendant on Rebecca's chest. But a new voice interrupted with an admiring remark.

"*Exquisito.*"

"I beg your pardon. I am Juan Sebastián Sandoval, the owner of this establishment. Before I ask for your review of the dinner, which I know will be superlative, I want to tell you a story."

The Americans were spellbound. The Guatemalan Señora smiled mysteriously. The owner of Restaurante Q'eqchí continued, referring to the image on the brooch.

"This is the moon goddess. My ancestors, the Q'eqchi', say that she is Po, the daughter of the Earth God. She was beloved of the Sun. They slept together. The father swore vengeance and had her destroyed. However, true love is more potent. In the magic that follows her death, the Moon Goddess is reborn. She and her husband represented the origin of human procreation."

Rebecca said softly, "The food was as wonderful as your story, *Cocinero* Sandoval. Our compliments to the chef." She replaced the pendant.

"Muchas gracias." The cordial man refilled the wine glasses. He bowed and exchanged a look with Doña Benitez Friedman. Juan Sebastián consulted with the waiter but hovered nearby.

Floria said, "Then it is to be Maya art, is it? Rebecca, there are many secrets to uncover about the Maya."

"So I am told, Floria darling."

She whispered, "Then you must go to the City of the Snakes and learn of the Shield of the Sun."

Her remarks were not lost on the Maya restaurateur. He restrained his excitement as he looked around for nosy eavesdroppers. As Señor Sandoval gave a short bow and proceeded to take his leave, he turned to Rebecca. He said most mysteriously, "*Tu eres su luna y el es tu sol.*"

You are the sun, and he is the moon.

Chapter Three: Soft Light and Intense Heat

Casa Zaculeu, El Salvador Complejo Vista Real, Ciudad de Guatemala, República de Guatemala

"He said that I was the moon, and you were my sun."

Mark moved his arms around her as he continued...

"Mmmm, I might be up for a bit of a reenactment of some of that ancient erotic legend Señor Sandoval narrated. The light of that full moon only adds to my erotic sense, Beautiful."

The Ruler of the Night Sky was slowly emerging from behind the hills surrounding the eastern side of the Valle de la Ermita. The large full moon seemed ethereal and sacred from their sixth-floor balcony of La Casa Zaculeu, softly caressing the cityscape and the countryside with its sensual light. The curves of the American couple's bodies were washed with the warm caresses of the moonlight and the cool darkness of the night as they moved against each other, stroked by a scented breeze.

"See the rabbit... ohhh, Mark, that feels so good..."

"No, I do not see the rabbit, Beautiful... widen your stance a... yes, that's what this man wants..."

She knew she was teasing and tempting him as she continued her astrology report.

"Sorta curled around the left... ahhh, ohhh, damn, Darling... the left side. The rabbit stands by a cooking pot. The Maya Moon Goddess is often depicted with a rabbit, so..."

Mark put his hand over her mouth for a moment, saying, "End of lesson. I'll take your word for it."

Standing behind her, the very aroused man lowered her teddy's left strap and replaced it with his persistent and moist mouth. He traced the contours of her neck, holding her mane of mahogany tresses off to the opposite side. Rebecca could feel the excitement in his hard, naked body.

With her right hand, she reached back to caress his shoulder, already damp with a sex flush. He moved his attention to her breasts.

In their love dance, physical and emotional clues marked pace, tempo, and intensity. Mark and Rebecca understood each other's sexual chemistry -- scent, touch, movement, and vocals. Screaming, yelling, explicit carnal word imagery, heightening sexual excitement before and during sex play. Like a musical piece, their couplings had risings and fallings, soft and tender persistent motifs, fast and intense scherzos, loud and savage crescendos, and an adagio that either led to afterglow or the coda of the next round.

"Ohhh yeah... just need some time to reload, Beautiful."

"Do not fall asleep, Pagan Boy. This doll needs more – this ain't over, Studly. Let's see if I can help... Ohhh yes, you bastard!"

They made love as equals. In their relationship's totality, it was almost always about what was best for both. That is not to say that role-playing was off the agenda. Dominance and submission were special features that often crept into an evening's or morning's events. For example, this memory:

"What? Am I supposed to wear this?"

"Yes, I think it's hot."

"It's something that a cheap hooker would wear. Why there's not even a..."

"Yep. Makes it hot."

Pulling her close and he growled, "You are a dirty whore, aren't you? Huh?"

"OK, you watch and see, badass. But you are taking this off me with your mouth. Damn, you are strong."

Tonight, Rebecca had started before they got to their room. They held hands and walked through the night gardens of the Casa Zacuela Hotel. She pinned Mark against the elevator's wall in the elevator, opening his shirt and tasting his hard-muscled chest. They both believed sex was meant to be fun, loaded with romance, and very athletic.

Now, in the moonlight, his hands came up under her garment, slipped into her bikini briefs, and down across her firm buttocks, playing with the cleft between them. As he stooped to lower them, he came back up, and his hands came back to move to the front.

Rebecca moaned.

Now, the pace began to intensify. Mark's body decided to drive the action, and she let him as she felt the silk covering drop to the floor. He turned her to face him, hands and mouth, exploring the exciting sensuality of her body. She arched against him and matched his heat, encouraging his feast and working the parts that drove him deeper into savage lust. Somehow, they got to the bed, and somehow, logic and reason gave way to passion and raw desire. They brought each other beyond the limits of indulgence, it seemed, in the sensuous moonlight.

***

"What the fuck was that?"

"Go back to sleep, Darling. Just something out..."

Mark leaped off the bed. A dark figure slinked like a large reptile over the balcony's edge and down.

"Someone's in the fucking room!"

Now Rebecca was awake. She reached for her phone.

"Mark, be careful."

As the young journalist dashed across the room, he stumbled and fell, knocking a table and its lamp to the floor around him. Rebecca turned on the other light.

Mark rolled up and onto his feet, hitting the edge of the balcony and searching for the intruder.

"Gone."

"Darling..."

Rebecca was pulling on her robe and pointing to the obstacle that had tripped Mark.

It was long, black, and broken in two...

A walking stick.

Chapter Four: *La Remedios*

Centro Médico, Ciudad de Guatemala, República de Guatemala

"I am so sorry, Diego. I guess our arguments about your mom leaving this city are over. Our worst fears have come true."

Joaquín Cortez pulled his husband closer to him.

"She is with your father now, D."

Diego Friedman-Cortez was tall and dark, with impossibly long eyelashes and perfect eyebrows on a handsome face. He had inherited his mother's openness of personality and fine features. His twenty-something scruff was immaculately groomed. Right now, he was in shock.

"I talked to her yesterday. She said she was going to dinner with friends. She said Marc Antonio would drive her as usual."

As the private room's five occupants crossed the hall to a small waiting room, hospital staff quietly and reverently dismantled and removed the life support machines. The same healthcare workers extinguished the lights as they exited. After a short interval, when the family left the hospital, another crew would remove the now covered body to the morgue.

A small priest, Father Andrés, said, "She was a good woman of deep faith who cared for many in this city and, in fact, the country. Like the saintly women of the scriptures, she will be remembered for her good deeds and generosity to the poor."

Diego was silent.

"Thank you, Father," Joaquín said softly. We appreciate your words of consolation. I will contact you regarding the…"

The little cleric nodded and waved words away as if to say, "Yes, yes. Much of this can wait until later." Father Andrés raised his hand, murmured a blessing over the two men, and exited.

The taller American helped his spouse into a chair and gave him a water bottle. He eased himself next to the grieving young man.

Joaquín Cortez, he never went by "Jack," was a typical South Beach beauty. Fit, with a killer smile and a $300 haircut, the man was a fitness and couture model, a life guru to the glitterati, and an influencer with a soon-to-be-announced men's clothing and accessory line. He ran a hand lightly through the hair of Diego's bowed head.

"I am so sorry to intrude."

Rebecca and Mark were the only other occupants of the room. She introduced Mark and herself and explained.

"We were with Mrs. Friedman last night at Restaurante Q'eqchi'. Her driver took her home about eleven-thirty."

Accompanying a doctor, a law enforcement officer with a name badge indicating he was Captain Alberto Cruz of the Policía Nacional Civil stepped into the room. He said, "The attack came close to midnight just as Señora Friedman was about a block from her home at Fifteen Calle and 4A Avenida. Two men on a motorcycle forced them off the road and demanded cash. Her driver, Señor Rameriez, said that he gave them a goodly amount, hoping they would go away."

"My mother-in-law had a stash of some cash and old jewelry she always carried in the compartment behind the passenger seat. She referred to it as her insurance."

The officer checked his notes and continued, "Ramirez has stated that Señora Friedman always removed her personal jewelry before traveling. He always placed them in the trunk in her purse. The driver had a handgun taped to one of the compartment's sidewalls and one under the dash. He claims she was unaware of this, and he did not have the opportunity to use either of the firearms. He was pistol-whipped and left unconscious.

The doctor said, "Marc Antonio Rameriz will make a full recovery. I extend my sympathy to your family over this casualty on behalf of everyone at Centro Médico."

Rebecca remembered the name on one of the wings of the hospital's façades, "Centro de Medicina Interna Diego Luis Friedman."

Capitán Cruz continued, "Apparently, there was a second pair of armed individuals accompanying the thieves -- lookouts. They demanded more, and your mother resisted. Ramirez attempted to get out of the vehicle. The assailants clubbed him, shot her, and got away."

"Description?"

"I am not able to share that information, Señor Gadarn."

He paused.

"Your reputation precedes you."

Mark pressed, "I'll answer for you then, Capitán Cruz. They were young, wore black bandanas, and had plenty of blue and black tattoos."

The police officer said nothing at first, nor did his face imply anything. Finally, he warned, "I would advise you, Señor, not to get involved in this. We are very cautious concerning the press these days."

Rebecca's hand on the journalist's arm seemed to whisper, "Not now, Mark. Let's keep everything as low-key as possible." Mark bristled at officious stonewalling and bureaucracy.

As if he were suddenly coming around, Diego looked around a bit and seemed to be trying to explain. His voice was quietly chilling.

"She was fiercely independent. She always said that her staff took good care of her. There was no way she would leave Guatemala City. My mother said that many times. Too many memories. My father is buried here."

He seemed to be drifting as he said, "La Señora Floria was sublimely comfortable with her ghosts of those horrible years through which they both lived. However terrible, not every one of her memories was a specter."

Joaquín stood up and said, "OK, D. Time to get the fuck, Bud. Let's go, *Papi*. Hospitals are bullshit, Kid. We can sign the papers on the way out. We can't do anything more for her now."

Rebecca asked, "When was the last time you both had something to eat?"

"Miami International Airport... coffee and... six hours ago. Yeah, he needs to eat."

Diego said, "Joaquín, we need to go to *La Remedios*."

"Right, D. Perhaps Rebecca and Mark will join us?"

***

"No, no Señores. Solamente dos Quetzales."

The tiny older woman was dressed in a black *huipil* with a multi-colored embroidered yoke and a felt cowboy hat. She carried a basket and held up two fingers. Mark shook his head and gave her 20 USD. He took four candles. The woman appeared shocked, looked around, and stuffed the bill into her bosom. She hurried away.

Across the street, La Iglesia de La Señora de Remedios was a crumbling edifice that was nearly destroyed during an earthquake in the 1960s. A decaying beauty for its Spanish Mudéjar-influenced Baroque architecture, the front façade had been partially restored. Still, one side of the structure, including one of the two towers, was a pile of stone, glass, and tile heaped at one end of the building. As they crossed the plaza, parish members used a side entrance next to the Virgin's statue, which had been rescued from the rubble. The saint looked a bit off-kilter on her column base.

Rebecca tied a scarf around her head and took Mark's arm as they followed their two new friends into the church. He whispered, "You look like the Madonna yourself."

She pointed down. "Better shoes."

Large beams stretched at weird angles between columns and pilasters inside the collapsing central aisle and apse. The dome had a large hole on the left side. The floor beneath showed that rain and birds often poured through. The altar had been moved further into the transept. A large and bloodied image of "The Crucified" and the wood-carved reredos remained at the back of the sanctuary. The tabernacle had been removed.

As Diego passed a flame to his friends, he commented, "After the earthquake, someone stole the tabernacle – actually pried it off the altar. See the empty space where the women are placing the flowers. The priest

34

begged for the return of the holy bread, *El Cuerpo de Cristo.* He keeps it now in his house."

Before the Sorrowful Mother's statue, the young man knelt, placed his candle in the stand, and twisted it in the sand. He prayed. Those who accompanied him followed his example.

"They were married here, La Floria and my Father. I was baptized here." He indicated the bowl of a once elaborate font, now off its stand, cracked, and tipped.

Supplicants knelt on the floor throughout the church, using the backs of a few scattered wooden chairs for support. A rosary clacked against wooden slats. Somewhere, a baby cried and was hushed.

Rebecca said almost to herself, "The persistence of faith."

Chapter Five: The Brigade

Zona 7, Ciudad de Guatemala, República de Guatemala

"This is where you grew up, Darling?"

Joaquín went in another direction. He raised a glass.

"La Floria Friedman -- *Que descanse en paz.*"

Mark echoed, "May she rest in peace."

"*Salud.*"

"La Floria."

"No, Rebecca. I was a prep school kid over on the rich side of town, but my parents grew up in this neighborhood. They met just a few blocks from here at a dance at the community center, El Centro. It is gone now. Not much to dance about in this parish anymore."

Diego was an up-and-coming local broadcast journalist. Careerwise, there were currents about his going national. He and Joaquín often appeared together as one of Miami's power couples in the straight and LGBTQ+ communities. Social media loved their asses – and the rest of their very toned bodies, for that matter.

"Anyway, I kinda love this neighborhood, so different from Nine and Ten, the city's 'fancy zones.' And the food is exceptional."

"I saw your piece on fugitives from the drug wars – ex-pats in Miami. Well done, man. You are definitely on the rise."

"Thank you, Mark. I am honored to receive praise from one of the media's best."

The young journalist sighed and said, "It's all right here -- heaven and hell in the same place. Inequality and privilege live side by side in this country. You can be sitting in a chi chi outdoor café sipping *horchata* in '*Zona Viva*' and smell the garbage odor wafting over from a landfill in Zone Three."

Restaurante D'Alejandro was a dine-in-or-out hole in the wall featuring *antojitos*, "little cravings," very popular here and in Mexico. They ordered tacos, tamales, gorditas, quesadillas, and delicious local stews. It was mid-afternoon and time for the main formal meal of the day. Their table in the front window tempted passers-by with the restaurant's savory fare.

The sights and sounds of Zone 7, the city's neediest, surrounded the Americans like an old overcoat. Ramshackle stores lined pot-holed streets between crumbling houses and low apartment buildings. There was some traffic, but not much. Pedestrian travel included pushcarts, dogs, running children, basket-laden marketers, and tool-bearing laborers.

Diego pointed and said, "That woman is a doctor. She sets up under that tree with those canvas stools to see her patients from the neighborhood. Some of those kids who almost knocked us over were brought into this world by *La Merced*, that woman over there. She is the midwife. See, she is giving advice to those three new mothers on the park bench."

Rebecca asked, "I am still in the dark about the attack on Floria and our break-in. Our hotel claimed that our midnight visitor was in it for robbery. I mean the cane.. your mom. Darling, we need to connect some dots."

"So, I will try to put this in some sort of context," Diego said. "While you are in Guatemala, you must be very vigilant. This country has one of the highest violent crime rates in Latin America, one of the world's highest homicide rates, and a very low arrest and detention rate. Most incidents of violent crime are drug and gang-related."

Mark said, "We'd be lying to you if we didn't say we knew what we were getting into when we came here. We were contacted by folks in the U.S. Department of State with a Travel Advisory, indicating that we should exercise increased caution due to crime. It's not that we are super badasses. It's just that we have been in war zones together before and, well, there are good people here too."

He passed a plate of something savory.

Rebecca said, "Yes, Mark and I both knew this country had a significant amount of corruption. We realize there is an inadequate justice system and a lot of gang and narcotics activity across the country."

Joaquín chimed in, "No purse, good move. But dress more down and do not rent a car. You are too gorgeous, too rich. The most common crimes against tourists are theft and armed robbery. Many robberies occur during daylight hours. Do not rent a car."

"Back to your Mom, Darling – she looked like a modern character from an Isabelle Allende novel in her Paris couture the day we met in the park."

"Yes, she was quite a woman. Took no shit. Try this, Bud. Better than what we get on South Beach."

He went on with, "When I was in school here – an elite academy run by the Jesuits in Zone 10, San Ignacio, there was a scandal. I was 'favored' by my football coach, and it got out. My parents were approached by members of a crime syndicate for payment to keep the matter away from the press. My father, the owner and president of Black Gold Coffee, immediately went to the newspaper, 'Diario de Centro América', and demanded an interview. 'My son is gay, and we love him.' No blackmail payments, bitches."

He tapped the table.

"The crime bosses have been after the family's business for two generations. We do not give in."

"And the coach, prosecuted for rape?"

"No, Mark. I was sixteen when all of this began. Legal in this country."

Joaquín cocked an eyebrow, "And?"

"OK, OK, I was the instigator in the situation. He was my *Cielo* – sixteen... what did I know? Anyway, my parents... well, they accepted it all, although the no grandchildren thing was a sore spot. I was sent to live with relatives in Kansas City – went to UMKC, by the way."

Rebecca tenderly touched the hand of Diego Friedman Cortez. She said, "Darling, I asked you what time it is, and you are building me a Swiss village. It is not that we are not interested, but – Floria? Last night?"

"Right. My mother and Marc Antonio – just what you heard back at the Centro Médico."

"The police will not apprehend them. Law enforcement is a farce here," Joaquín said.

Mark commented, "Cruz really shut down, especially when I mentioned black bandanas and lots of tats."

"How did you know?"

Mark explained the attempted purse snatching and the late-night intruder at Casa Zacuela at 1 AM.

"The kid in the park -- the walking cane. La Brigada de Salvación, 'The Brigade of Salvation,' aka BDS-13. They wanted to make a point – get ballsy with all of this."

He looked at Rebecca.

"I am concerned that they know who we are, Beautiful."

Rebecca looked out at the street. She said, "We will be careful, Mark. We have been up against tougher outfits than this, Darling."

Mark continued, "This gang was actually born in Los Angeles, California, in the eighties. The members were deported to Guatemala. Most of them are minors forced into membership. The group targets mostly women and children, but they are known to wipe out entire families."

Diego said, "Many of them are trying to get into Canada, given the Republican policies on immigration. Latin American gangsters believe the countries of El Norte will not deal as harshly with them as police here."

Rebecca could not hold back. She spoke with conviction.

"I am a huge critic of Trumpism and its policies in my country. Latin American gangs have been a large part of the political discourse in our Presidential campaigns and ongoing debates on immigration. Republicans have called for draconian immigration policies to deal with groups like BDS-13.

"Politicians have argued that sanctuary cities, those jurisdictions that do not prioritize immigration law enforcement, bolster gang activity like BDS-13 activity. However, they are ignoring studies on the relationship between sanctuary status and crime. Report after report shows that sanctuary policies do not affect crime, nor do they decrease crime rates."

Mark said, "The bullshit flies. Since 2016, BDS-13 has become a top priority for the Department of Justice. On multiple occasions, the Trump White House claimed that they had deported 'thousands and thousands' of BDS-13 gang members. They used that fear to justify implementing a family separation policy for migrants accused of crossing the border illegally. U.S government officials claimed that child migrants were being used by Brigada members to cross the U.S.-Mexico border. There appears to be some truth to this."

"Sources?"

"I'll text them to you, Diego. You will be amazed. I did a series of media pieces for an independent immigration watchdog group, La Comisión de la Verdad, about two years ago. They were lobbying with the United States Justice Department members to correct the Republican-based policies on violence in Latin America."

The Miamian sneered, "I'm not surprised. His White House had little use for research and facts. It appeared that the current administration is moving away from the right wing's call for concentration camp policies. They are harsh, and they do not work."

Mark continued, "According to the FBI, Brigada de Salvación accounts for less than one percent of total gang members in the United States. There is no hard evidence to back Republican claims that there is a surge in BDS-13 gang members and that weak immigration enforcement contributes to more significant BDS-13 crime activity."

Rebecca closed with, "This is the age of the politics of fear and blaming everyone else. Meanwhile, families are divided, and they suffer cruelty and life-threatening treatment."

Chapter Six: A Bag of Oranges

Quetzaltenango, República de Guatemala

"Arf!"

The little dog was dancing by the kitchen door.

"Hush, Cauli, be still. We have guests. Jacinto is home. I know, I know. *Paciencia, por favor.*"

The kitchen door opened, and the pup scrambled up, almost knocking down the boy. Jacinto was in the midst of turning to his friends.

"Yes, I will be there. I just gotta convince my mom. See you in a short time. Good-bye."

Stepping inside, he dropped his backpack and went down on one knee to receive dog kisses and wiggly nuzzling from his best friend. Cauli got petting and scratching in return.

"Did you miss me, girl? Were you a good watchdog today for Mama'? Yes, you were. I know you were. Are you still my best buddy? Hello, Mama'."

He reached up and handed his mother a paper from his school books.

"Hay, *Dios mío.* Your teacher gave you an "A" on your arithmetic test. Excellent, my son." She kissed the top of the boy's head. "Please take her out, like a good boy."

He took the leash from its peg by the door and snapped it on the collar of his dog. "OK. Come on, girl."

They dashed across the lane and into the small park, Cauli's bouncing gait matching Jacinto's scramble. She checked him at the nearest grassy spot for a squat. He used a plastic bag to clean up and tossed it into the nearest trash.

"What happened to your dog, Kid?"

Never, never, never talk to strangers.

Jack looked up at the man— a young guy, a bit older than the big boys at school. Cauli got between the two and started a low growl.

"Watch out. My dog is really mean," the boy said. "I don't know. She was like that when she found me."

"Bet she was in a dog fight. You ever fight her? She doesn't look too bad-arsed, though."

The guy reached for her with a heavily tattooed hand, and Cauli went vicious. Jack pulled her back. The stranger backed up but was unafraid.

"Still got some fight in her. You live around here?"

"I gotta go."

"C'mere, Kid. I need you to help me with something. Wanna earn some money? Don't be afraid. I won't hurt ya."

Jack could see behind the scary guy another man hurrying up to them.

He panicked and dropped the leash. Cauli faced the thugs, a wild thing on three legs. The second guy went for the dog and got bitten. She latched onto the arm of his sweatshirt and tore back and forth. As the lowlife turned, trying to shake her off, she bit again into his Achilles tendon. He screamed. Jack stumbled and rolled to the ground as the first guy zeroed in on him.

BAM!

"*Vete, pésimos cabrones.*"

Another Bam! Followed by two more.

Carmen Del Gado had stepped outside the kitchen door when she saw the commotion beginning in the park across the street. She immediately knew what was happening. This was becoming more and more a way of life in this town.

She ran as fast as a woman pregnant with her second child could and snagged a net bag of oranges from a fruit stand. The woman let loose like an Amazon. The old guy who sold the fruit oranges joined her, swinging a similar bag of potatoes. Together they yelled and clobbered the would-be kidnapper. The thug was down, turning, and trying to ward off the hard fruits and root vegetable blows with flailing arms.

"Leave the boy alone and leave this park. We do not want you here."

Off to the side, Cauli was threatening to take a piece of the other scum bag's ass. Some guy in a cable service uniform jumped in to scare the bleeding tough away. A woman ran up from a food truck and used a bat on the bitten attacker. She cursed while her young assistant blew a police whistle. More neighbors joined in the fight.

"Leave our children alone, *piojosos bastardos!*"

"Get out. Leave! Go away."

"*Malditos traficantes de drogas.* We do not want your poisons."

Shouts brought onlookers and more defenders. The two bad guys managed to escape and drive off in a blue van. A woman had Jack up off the ground and was dusting him off.

"You OK? Hey, you are Rosalina's boy. Did they hurt you, Little One?"

Jack rubbed his dirty face, determined not to cry in public. Cauli jumped up against him, licking wherever she thought would do some good.

"Thanks, Señora Rivera. Down girl. No, I'm OK, thank you."

He sniffed.

"Jack, did they hurt you?"

"No, Auntie. I am fine. They wanted Cauli for fighting."

The old guy with the bag of potatoes said, "Brave little dog, you got there, Amigo. Drew some blood. She is loyal and true."

Jack did not say anything. He stooped to cuddle his three-legged buddy.

Aunt Carmen caught her breath. She returned the oranges and told the produce man to come by for a reward.

"C'mon, Chico, I will walk you across. We must calm down your Mamá when she hears."

***

"All over, Rosie. Jack is not hurt."

The proprietress of Casa De Flores Tikal knelt to embrace her son. Jack was still a bit dizzy from all the excitement.

"*Barrio en Guardia* - Neighborhood on Guard, my sister. Scared them off." Carmen pointed to the family's pet. "This one gets steak tonight. She is one tough mutt." She held her abdomen, saying, "*Dios*, I gotta go sit down."

Rosalina was softly weeping as Jack told her it was all fine now. She held him away from her. Both mother and son were pretty scared. The boy's mother took a deep breath and stroked her little boy's hair.

"I will call the police, Jacinto. We must report this."

"OK, Mamá. The WiFi guy was pretty cool in the fight, but Tia Carmen was the best. And of course, Cauli." His little buddy wagged her unbalanced rear end so hard she had to sit down to keep from falling over. She did another Jack-hand-lick.

Señora Rivera, the fruit and vegetable man, the women from the food truck, and more neighbors came into the hotel lobby to update each other on the incident. The chatter was excited and loud.

Conscious of her guests' reaction, the hotelier invited the heroic group into her office and extended her thanks. She gratefully reimbursed the produce man for his defensive weapons. One of the bellhops brought a platter of fresh pastries from the kitchen. Pushing to the front, Carlos and Rafaela Maria joined in, checking in on their pal.

The girl shouted, "Was those guys who followed us to school this morning, Jack. Told ya."

"Someone want to tell me what happened out there? "

A police officer squeezed his way into the small, crowded office. He was answered by animated, loud remarks from everyone in the room except Jack.

Within thirty minutes, the story had been recounted at least a dozen times, complete with embellishments. The neighborhood residents went back to their homes, chores, and businesses. Wagging index fingers at the policeman, the folks made many suggestions for how their children would be protected in this portion of the town. Jack's two schoolmates lagged behind.

"Mamá... football... Carlos' brother said he would take us, and..."

"No, Jacinto. I need you here to help. Tia will have your supper for you in the kitchen, and then I will meet you in the lobby. Remember, you promised to help. Besides, with what happened..."

Jack pouted, and Rosalina asked one of her staff to accompany his friends up the street to their homes.

She addressed her son, "I have a new plan for when we let Cauli out, my son. You can bring her through the lobby on her leash from now on and go out the front, where José, on the door, can watch. Stay in front of the hotel, OK? Do not go far into the plaza. And remember to always ask me when you want to go out and play with your friends. Yes?"

"Did I do something wrong, Mamá?"

"No, my child. We must keep each other safe, that is all."

Chapter Seven: Ab Work

Gimnasio Urbano, Ciudad de Guatemala, República de Guatemala

"Not going for a South Beach pump here, Kid. We are reducing the weight, and you are going to show me a better form."

"Yeah, nothing but pecs and bis at those clubs. I try to hit all areas, but... I am a body fascist, I will admit."

Mark straddled the head of the bench as Joaquín lowered the bar to his chest.

"Lifting is all about form. Breathe, Kid. Exhale on the effort move. Slowly, there ya go."

Back in the parish, Mark had whined. Yes, literally begged for some gym time. The Miami boys suggested an upscale fitness club in Zone 12. Rebecca was sure that her comment about thongs and dancing in San Francisco at Pride last summer had sparked some primal interest. Her gays were so deliciously physical.

Now, Rebecca was on the floor with Diego. She dropped one knee on his chest and, with a yell, faked a chop to the throat.

"Damn, girl. No one's gonna mess with you."

"Correct, Darling, Wonder Woman comes to *me* for advice."

He chuckled, and she helped him up.

"Here's how you would break that, Darling. I am going to come from behind and grab you by the throat this time."

She demonstrated the defense move, coaching him through it. Diego asked for a couple of redos until he finally mastered it.

"Not bad, Darling. You pick this shit up quickly."

She tossed him his towel, saying, "As long as we are both down here, let's work on our six-packs."

She started, but continued talking.

"Kansas City, is that where you two met? Please don't hold my ankles so tightly."

Diego did not miss a beat as his exercise partner started her sit-ups.

"We met at a human rights fundraiser in New York. Chita Rivera..."

Joaquín flopped down next to them and interrupted with a smirk.

"Yeah. Chita introduced us. And we all went to the Hamptons with Kander and Ebb. They needed advice on a New York opening. D, you are such a star-fucker wannabe. He tells everyone that story. Sometimes it's Sônia Braga. His attempt to be pretentious somehow never gets far away from his obsession with 'The Kiss of the Spider Woman.' Go figure."

The gay "Teller of Tall Tales" completed his set of ab crunches and kissed his husband. Mark was doing his sets with a twelve-kilo plate held behind his head.

"The truth is, we met at Pride Rio four years ago. I was dancing on a float... um, tossing beads."

Diego finished with a nod to his love, who gave him the index finger warning.

"One too many *caipirinhas*, Papi."

The younger man held up his phone. "There are pictures of you in that gold thong, Bud."

"Ouch! One thousand American, 'Señor *Culo*,' and that is my final offer," Diego joked with hands of surrender in the air.

They all laughed. Rebecca thought that Diego was doing pretty good considering the recent tragedy. Mark was sweating and smiling. *These guys are pretty cool.*

"We need to go, Mark, Darling. The gays really know how to party on Ipanema Beach."

She looked at the couple. "No brag, but we both look great in a thong, Darling."

Mark stood up and whipped off his t-shirt.

50

"Just gimme about thirty minutes on the body bag, and I'll make the plane reservations."

Joaquín did a jaw-drop; Diego played it cool at the sight of the sweat-slicked Gadarn washboard.

"Come on, Darlings, drinks are on me."

Diego walked with her towards the smoothie bar and hitched a thumb in the opposite direction.

"I think we got some boy/man crush action going on, Rebecca."

She looked back to see Joaquín heading back to the martial arts area where Mark was gloving up for his training.

"One gets used to it, Darling, and Mark just loves it."

***

"We work for a secret society."

"Deep State?"

"Ha! Nothing like that, Rebecca… behind the scenes, maneuvering plots and politics… like that. We are known as *Les Gardiens*. We are an undeclared affiliate of the Alliance for Justice and Humanity. This group serves as a go-between among governments and NGOs. We help people find a home – to live in peace, find some bit of prosperity when they have nowhere else to go…"

Rebecca stared intently at her new friend. "Tell me more, Diego."

"A few years back, we were recruited to help with advocacy and logistics specific to the migration of people in Latin America. As I said, *Les Gardiens* prefers to fly under the radar. In the last year, it has ramped up the network so that information comes to us from all sectors of the developing world. Our agents intercede for the lost and disenfranchised in ways that can skirt the corruption of oppressive regimes."

"Which means to say, you guys are a bit sketchy, right, Darling?"

"We get the job done, Rebecca. Not loud but effective. And just this side of illegal."

"Interesting."

"Joaquín has connections in the business world that put us in conversations with the U.S. border agencies. With the immigration crackdown in the United States, our group has moved its focus to more sympathetic democratic nations, Canada, and the EU.

"I have influential connections to the commerce and governments in Guatemala, Belize, Mexico, El Salvador, and Honduras. These are unofficially connected to my family's business."

"Coffee?"

"Yes. Black Gold Commodities, Inc. Money talks... it can buy a lot, Rebecca."

They sat quietly for a moment at the refreshment bar of the fitness center. Mark and Joaquín were finishing up and coming over to join them. They pulled up stools.

"Hold it. Give us a chance to catch up. I'll get us a couple of..."

Joaquín smiled, "I got this, Mark. You never know what you might get hold of. Strange concoctions and big stomach problems. Indigenous dietary supplements are an acquired taste."

He shot back to the counter and ordered.

"You were getting quite an audience, Darling. As usual."

Mark was glistening with sweat. His brown-gold curls were plastered to his forehead and neck. He toweled off a bit more and shrugged. "Dunno what the big deal is. It's a fitness club. Guys exercise — strength and endurance. What's the big..."

He shot her a gunz-up pose.

"... fascination?"

She towel-swatted him.

"Such a showoff."

In reality, Rebecca found his humble and somewhat self-conscious appreciation of his own male beauty so very attractive. His fandom seemed to increase wherever they went, among women and men. Fit and handsome with a brilliant mind and matchless bravery, Mark Gadarn was an incredible journalist and an astonishing lover. His romantic moves complemented her own virtues as a woman of power, intelligence, and beauty. She had the eye of an artist, a profound love of magnificence. Also, they both stood for a compassionate embrace of the goodness of humanity.

Rebecca and Diego brought Mark up to snuff.

"The group we represent is most concerned with addressing the many horrors of human trafficking in the region, the poverty, the gang violence, the drug trade – all interrelated. There are children in the border camps. Migrant kids separated from their families, our group, the Alliance for Justice and Humanity, sees the issue from the big picture and sends in *Les Gardiens* to alleviate specific cases.

"The world governments need to become allies to address the root causes of these evils. The UN cannot do this alone. It will take many people working together with clear heads and a fearless dedication to humanity's rights to rid this part of the world of evil and corruption. It's coming together. We have seen some victories amid the many setbacks."

Joaquín returned with tumblers of thick yellow stuff.

"An ancient and potent restorative... Did you enlist them?"

"Getting there, Joaquín."

Diego continued. "Mother was a big supporter, but I fear that with her death, the board of my family's business will resist involvement in our work. Mark, you can raise awareness of the Alliance's work on the global stage. Rebecca..."

"Get to the good part, D."

Diego Friedman Cortez looked at the art curator and museum CEO. He said, "Rebecca, the people of this land need pride. Poverty has a way of eviscerating the cultural spirit. Eventually, the oppressed believe the oppressors. They see themselves as barely human. The result is nations upon nations of victims unable to take destiny into their hands and rid themselves of the forces that keep them enslaved."

Joaquín took up the narrative.

"People with no sense of history have little hope. The Maya spread their civilization from the Caribbean to the Pacific – a strong and accomplished people. Their culture has been beaten back to tourist sites, exotic cooking, and oppressive syncretistic religion. Since the time of the colonial powers' mass exterminations, this civilization cries out to find a new liberation based on ancient glories."

Rebecca said, "I'm not sure I follow, Joaquín Darling."

"Enterprise, entrepreneurship – capitalism can be reformatted to raise these people up from oppression."

Joaquín Cortez continued with increasing passion.

"It's about cultural treasure – your stock in trade."

He shifted and looked around.

"Secrets – we have heard of them, on the fringes of conversations. Olmec, Maya, and Aztec civilizations had secrets that all but died with them. Treasure and beauty not seen yet by the world -- rightly belonging to a downtrodden people, must be recovered and showcased."

Diego nodded.

"And all that wealth can be used to increase national esteem and fund a total elimination of the death and destruction that plagues the people of Latin America. We are talking about an end to cultural genocide, a massive rebirth of civilization, and a restoration of the value of indigenous culture."

Diego Friedman Cortez added, "My mother advised you to seek the Maya in the mountains to the northwest – Palenque. Before you leave Ciudad de Guatemala, there are some people you should meet."

Joaquín said, "Some are living, and some are long dead."

Chapter Eight: Museo de Totonicapán

El Universidad San Pedro, Ciudad de Guatemala, República de Guatemala

"You must concentrate on the work that has been assigned to you. The Museum is not paying you to research your private interests, Señorita. This is not the first time I have had to reprimand you. We may have to look at dismissal."

"I'm sorry, Director Rios Carillo. It will not happen again."

"Enough. You have made promises in the past, and today I find you again off task."

"My assignments are on your desk, Sir. I completed the analytics for the exhibit on the hieroglyphic texts from the dig at Kaminaljuyu."

"Then move on to the polychrome ceramics from the Early Classic Period at Teotihuacan – Aztec, not Maya. The program is loaded and waiting for your input."

The Director added, "Señorita Trejo, if we do not have enough work here to keep you occupied, then perhaps your fellowship with the museum is at an end."

Rebecca said, "I apologize, Señor Rios Carillo. We can come back at a more convenient time."

The Director switched gears. He took her hand, saying, "No, no, Señorita Quinto. I am ready for you, and this must be Señor Gadarn -- an absolute pleasure."

Mark shook hands and then said, "If you don't mind, Ms. Quinto is the art business half of our partnership. I'll let you both continue without me."

"May I arrange for a tour, Senor?"

"Please do not trouble yourself, Director. I only want to grab a smoke."

Mark winked at Rebecca and turned around as the two of them went into the Director's office. As he passed Elyssa Trejo's desk, Mark did a flat-palms-on-the-desk lean-in and whispered, "How about a tour?"

Guillermo Rios Carillo shook his head with sadness.

"Oh my, yes. Señorita. La Floria, so tragic. She was a major donor to Museo de Totonicapán. I hope that Señor Friedman Cortez and his husband will remember us when they dispose of their collection. How nice of them to send you to us. In this business, collaboration is everything."

The Director continued, "As you are aware, Señorita Quinto, Museo de Totonicapán is known throughout the world for its notable collection of Maya pottery. We also curate an extensive collection of stone sculptures, wood carvings, mural paintings, writings, and ceramics. Organic materials do not survive very long in the tropical world of the Maya. Still, the stone, ceramic, and gems are in excellent condition. Did you have a specific focus on the period for your exhibit?"

"I usually leave the specifics to the Fritcher's other curators. To be honest, I am still in discussions with them. I believe we would like to encompass the entire Maya Civilization timeline. So, a sweep across thirty-seven hundred years from the Archaic Period to the European Contact and the Spanish Conquest."

"Excellent. I will send you the standard business agreements, the cultural documents from our government to yours, etc. If these are suitable, I will send our illustrated catalogs indicating objects that may be loaned."

"Thank you, Director. I will tell you that my mission here is to find more than one partner for our exhibit. Here is the shortlist of institutions I hope will receive our officer of collaboration."

Rebecca touched her phone. Señor Rios Carillo tapped his computer keyboard and opened the file.

"Most impressive, Señorita. Please allow me to open some doors for you."

"Thank you. Although these museums have agreed to discuss the project with me, your assistance will be most appreciated. Are you familiar with the Fritcher?"

"Yes, yes. I have viewed your online offerings and virtual tours. It is easy to see what a marvel the 'Seed Blood' exhibit was. I particularly liked the 'Golden Age of Opera' exhibit, also. Including non-Western compositions was a remarkable feature. Your sources for that program must have been outstanding."

Rebecca now put on the charm. If Mark were in the room, she would have caught hell for her "Playing the *femme fatale* card, Beautiful... getting all bosomy with the batting of the eyelashes and the killer smile." Mark, however, was not here, so she fluttered.

"Director Rios Carillo, I have a tiny favor. *Muy pequeño.*"

She made the thumb and forefinger sign for small.

"Tell me, Señorita, how may I help?"

"As the CEO and Head Curator of the Fritcher Museum of Art, I have big ideas regarding our exhibit, the vision that will announce us to the world, and bring in the public. I am the one who chooses the signature piece- the artifact that will brand the exhibit on all publications. It must be a spectacular wonder that excites the world into coming to the Fritcher."

"I understand entirely. You want to inquire about the availability of one of our big treasures, yes?"

"Señor Director, I would like the jade mask and funerary jewelry of the Maya King, K'inich Janaab Pakal I, the Shield of the Sun. Can you help me get it?"

***

The young woman spoke reverently. "He ruled for 68 years, one of the longest verified reigns in history."

"So, he was King of the Maya in... lessee..." Mark read the banner alongside the doorway to a prominent wing of the museum.

"... the seventh century of the Common Era."

"Almost, Mr. Gadarn. The Maya is a collective term that refers to the peoples of the region. The indigenous populations did not identify by that term because there was never a shared sense of identity or political unity among the distinct city-state communities.

Think of it this way: if you went back in time to ancient Athens or Sparta and referred to the people as 'Greek,' they would not know what you were talking about. They understood themselves to be Athenians or Spartans or Trojans. 'Greek' is a relatively modern term."

Mark nodded.

The woman continued, "So it is with the Maya. Throughout the history of Mesoamerica, the Maya civilization encompasses almost four thousand years of people connected to city-states in southeastern Mexico, Guatemala, Belize, western Honduras, and El Salvador."

"So what unites these groups through thousands of years?"

"Culture, religion, language, genetic material… There are twenty-eight surviving Mayan languages spoken by nearly six million people residing in almost the same area as their ancestors, Yucatan, Southern Mexico, Belize, and Honduras."

Elyssa Trejo indicated the components of the exhibit. "The ancients developed agriculture some four thousand years ago, growing maize, beans, squashes, and chili peppers – still the staples of the Maya diet. The Maya built monumental cities with gorgeous palaces, sweeping plazas, astrological observatories, and elaborate temples, many with ornate stucco façades. Some of these complexes are still around today."

Mark said, "Architecture, astronomy, writing?"

The young doctoral student gestured to a section of the exhibit.

"Yes, theirs is the most sophisticated writing script in pre-Columbian America, which continued until the Spanish conquest of the Maya in the sixteenth and seventeenth centuries."

"They look like Egyptian hieroglyphics."

"Both forms are logosyllabic, but actually, Maya writing is closer to Japanese. These are called 'glyphs.' Linguistic science has made significant headway deciphering the Maya records."

She pointed to a stone pillar in a protective case.

"Writing in stone and ceramic... unfortunately, the Catholic colonizers destroyed Maya books by the thousands. So we lost much knowledge of Maya writing."

They entered a darkened room with spotlights on preserved manuscripts. Details indicated that these were replicas, as the artifacts were too delicate to exhibit.

"There are only three or four books in existence, all from the Postclassic period, circa one thousand of the Common Era."

Mark moved between cases showing the Madrid Codex, the Dresden Codex, and the Paris Codex. He read aloud, "A few pages survive from a fourth, the Grolier Codex, whose authenticity is disputed. Oh, hey, Beautiful. How was your meeting?"

Rebecca seemed to emerge from the dim lighting in the room like an enigmatic spirit. She kissed him lightly and smiled at the young woman. Mark made the introductions and explained their interest in a partnership project.

"Did you survive the scalding from the Director, Darling?"

Elyssa smiled ruefully. "Independent thought scares Director Rios Carillo. He insists I remain on task and, if you will allow me, the work I do is relatively menial and easy. I try to do some research on my own, but he doesn't like it. He is somewhat of a control fanatic, I am afraid."

"Quite unfortunate. It must not be easy, Darling. The business of the arts must allow for change and creativity."

"It just requires some maneuvering. Some days it works. Sometimes, not so much."

"Darling, please take us to see the King."

Chapter Nine: The Altiplano

Above El Estado de Chiapas, Estados Unidos Mexicanos

"Diego was great about loaning us the corporate jet. Did you get much pushback from your Director?"

Elyssa shook her head.

"How did you do it, Rebecca? Guillermo Ríos Carillo does not embrace independent thinking or innovation. On second thought, I think he is happy to be rid of me for a while."

"This proposed partnership between the Fritcher and the Totonicapán will mean big profits for both institutions. He does not want to stand in the way of this venture. I merely suggested he release you for a while to serve as our field guide -- paid sabbatical, Darling. He also suggested we include the Museo Alberto Rus L'Huillier in Palenque. You can get us there."

The young woman nodded enthusiastically and went back to her laptop.

Mark was like a kid in a candy store. He had commandeered the co-pilot's seat and was translating the pilot's tour up into the high plains of Chiapas State.

"We've crossed over from Guatemala into the southernmost Mexican state, Chiapas. Captain Pablo is saying that the... hey yeah, I guess we all speak Spanish, huh?"

Rebecca laughed. "Seriously?"

A warrior-journalist with a passion for adventure, Mark was thrilled to be high above the rich vistas of Meso-America with its mountains, lakes, and jungles. The man thrived on wonder and exploration. His eyes glistened with excitement.

"Man, look at those volcanoes."

Captain Escobar waved a hand over the blue-green vista before them. "This is actually the Chiapas Altiplano, Señor Mark. The Sierra Madre de Chiapas to the west cuts the plateau off from the Pacific. The rain rises up over the mountains and waters these plains, creating fertile agricultural highlands filled with rich volcanic soil. Bananas, corn, beans, and other vegetables... also cacao. See, there is the curtain of a morning storm there off to our left."

The pilot continued, "Those are the Tumbalá mountains, and you can just make out the modern city of Palenque. The ruins are slightly to the southwest in all that green."

"Looks like a lot of waterways."

"Yes, my friend, lakes and rivers fill the plateau. Chiapas has excellent wild fishing on both its coasts as well as a nascent fish farming industry that is beginning to catch on in the freshwater lakes and rivers."

He put the jet into a wide banking.

"The dense wilderness of jungle below us is the Montes Azules – the Blue Mountains – monkeys, tapirs, exotic birds like the Mexican Sheartail, and many snakes. It is a lost animal kingdom ruled by the jaguar and the quetzalcoatl."

"Outstanding... the feathered serpent god?"

"No, the Captain is referring to the bird. Actually, Quetzalcoatl is the Aztec name. As a Maya deity, the god of the wind and rain is known as Kukulkan and Gukumatz. He is 'serpent of the precious feathers,' aka 'the wisest of men,' Darling."

Rebecca had stepped into the cockpit of the HondaJet. She spoke into Mark's ear from behind him. She twirled a lock of his brown-gold hair on one of her index fingers and lightly tugged. Behind her, Elyssa was tapping at her laptop. She was totally absorbed in a project that was best kept from Director Rios Carillo.

He ran a hand up and softly pulled her closer.

"How can you be so sexy and smart this early in the morning, Beautiful and at ten thousand feet?"

The mists of valleys and mountains below them seemed to shimmer in the rising sun, lifting up from the Gulf of Mexico in the east.

"Let's take a closer look."

Captain Escobar began to descend to the small metropolis nestled in the green valleys -- Palenque and the hidden City of Snakes.

***

The plane continued to roll eastward over a depression between the mountains. Elyssa stuck her head into the cockpit.

"There. The ruins rise up from a limestone escarpment surrounded by the mountains and the heavily forested foothills. Imagine you were among the founding chiefs of the city. You'd want a place where the topography forms a natural barrier from your enemies – the steep mountains. Still, the people can come and go to their cornfields on the fertile plains and valleys. See those blue-green ribbons? They had many streams of freshwater near the site. They built aqueducts to bring water to the metropolis."

She became the lecturer in the sky as she continued, "The farmland of the ancient community is believed to have been there in the Tulijá Valley, off to the south and below the escarpment shelf, where the runoff from the rain comes from the mountains. It is very fertile and was most likely the base of their agricultural economy."

Elyssa pointed.

"If you look closely, you can see the footpaths. The highlands are crisscrossed by footpaths and go up and down from the urban center to the farms. The routes for farmers, settlers, and armies run up and down the slopes and into the forests. Many of the ancient trails and irrigation canals are still used."

Rebecca said, "The proximity to the rainforest would give them wood for building, animals for food, and clothing. Nice set-up."

"Quite an infrastructure. It would seem the Maya were knowledgeable urban planners," Mark commented. "A Mesoamerican Shangri-La, hidden, defensible, and prosperous."

The plane straightened out and continued to soar over the rough terrain. Below, white and gray rock formations interrupted the flowing green land. They were square and rectangular monuments reaching skyward, all that remained of the hidden city. A paved road crossed the north side of the plateau.

Elyssa said, "That way goes to the contemporary town. Can you see the red-roofed structure through the trees? That is the Palenque Site Museum Alberto Ruz L'huillier. We can start exploring the ruins from there."

Escobar said, "Unless you want to see more from up here, I am going to head to the northeast and land at the municipal airport closer to the modern city."

At the small regional airport in southeastern Chiapas State, the three travelers rented an SUV. They drove up Federal Highway to just outside the Village of Palenque and the archeological site. Palenque Site Museum, named for the archeologist Alberto Ruz L'Huillier, offered ample parking only a short distance from the ruins.

As they stepped from the SUV, Rebecca was aware of the timelessness of the surrounding jungle. Folding up the valleys and hills, enveloping the traces of all human endeavor-- roads, buildings, and pastures, it was a tremendous and eternal green canopy, drawing all to itself and hiding the secrets of many thousands of years.

Chapter Ten: Gods, Warriors, and the Hitchcock of Archeology

Museo Alberto Ruz L'Huillier, Palenque, Estado de Chiapas, Estados Unidos Mexicanos

"I envision part of the exhibit as an entire room of masks and effigies – 'The Faces of the Gods.' I like the idea of scrolling information on broken pieces of walls, but it must be designed so as to not detract from the artifacts. I see them floating in semi-darkness, mysterious and hypnotic.

"Outside, on the buildings surrounding the Museum Plaza, we will create projections of the jungle and the ruins. Ancient Mayan deities, peasants, athletes, and animals will swirl over and around the Museum during the exhibit. A Meso-American light show in downtown Fort Lauderdale."

"You are a masterful artist, my girl."

Mark seemed entranced by a large pair of figures. He commented, "It is like you are seeing the ancient people in these stone and ceramic works. The headdresses and the jewelry are so ornate. Many of these look like they were painted at one time. The eyes are crazy. It is as if they saw the world from a different perspective – perhaps a world about to crash and burn."

Elyssa came back to them after checking with the administrators of the Palenque Site Museum, Alberto Ruz L'Huillier. Yolotli Pacheco, Assistant Director of the Museum, broke into the spoken thoughts of the two Americans.

"I like to think that they did, Mr. Gadarn. These figures in clay and limestone, the treasure pieces of the Site Museum, manifest the ancient people's artistic tradition's sensitivity and vigor, which radiated its influence into other Maya cities, from Yucatan into Guatemala, and clear to the Pacific coast."

The woman had the striking features of the indigenous people. Señorita Pacheco was very professional with a tendency not to smile.

"I am Tzeltal. We are a community of Maya. Most of my people live from the highlands of Chiapas and all the way to Yucatan. In addition to our communities in the *ejidos,* Mexico's state farmlands, we also live in neighborhoods outside Guatemala's urban centers.

"I am sorry to say that the Director is not here to meet with you. Acting on his behalf, perhaps I can help you with your proposed collaboration."

She stepped forward to the piece on which Mark had commented.

"These are the Hero Twins. The matching set of stone carvings comes from the palace ruins and is from the reign of the Hix Queen, Sak K'uk, in the seventh century of the common era. Their names are Hunahpu and Xbalanque. Their story is told in one of the only surviving Maya manuscripts, The Popol Vuh."

"Yeah, these guys look pretty fit."

"The Twins were honored ballplayers in the courts of the gods. They attempted to avenge the murder of their father by the Lords of the Underworld, Xibalba. They escaped the tests the Dark Lords set for them and defeated the forces of chaos and darkness. They then attempted to resurrect their dead father, Hun Hunahpu, but he could not return to the land of the living. Hun Hunahpu became the Maize God, who seasonally dies and is revived.

"So, the twins, Hunahpu and his brother, Xbalanque, were very popular among the Maya. They are often depicted in artwork throughout the region, usually playing their famous game. Most likely, there were many tales concerning the hero twins that have been lost. This stele shows the brothers climbing up the World Tree and into paradise, becoming the sun and the moon. Hunahpu, the moon, is the evening god who restores the stars to the sky after his brother's daily journey as the sun.

"Dr. Pacheco," Rebecca asked, "Please tell us more about the Museum."

"We curate what is considered one of the best archeological collections representing the religious beliefs, ritual practices, and forms of political organization prevailing in this region of ancient Maya culture. Our artifacts exemplify the aesthetic expressions generated by the dynastic power of the ancient city and the culture of the people who built and maintained it."

From the main corridor, the Assistant Director guided them to the exhibitions. She used a wall map of the facility to point out the highlights and explained each feature.

"This is the South Acropolis Room – artifacts from monuments like the Temple of the Sun, the Temple of the Cross, and the five other buildings that represent the ceremonial heart of the city. Through that door is the exhibit on the Abode of the Dead section. Ceramic pieces, masks, and ornaments from the tombs of the La Calavera and the Red Queen. In this section, you will find the exhibit on the tomb discovered by Dr. Alberto Rus L'hullier, the Temple of the Inscriptions' riches. The final two rooms of the Museo are dedicated to the history of the Palace and its structures. The collection of figurines, liturgical pieces, carved incense smokers, and the elite class' regalia is set out near the household goods and other objects from ordinary folk who lived in the monuments' vicinity. From all of this, we hope the viewer will get a glimpse into the daily life of the city and its people.

Rebecca asked, "The architectural artifacts -- have they been removed from the buildings?"

"In these exhibits and at the site, you will find many carvings connected to the buildings. Unless they have fallen or needed extensive repair, they have been left *in situ*."

As they viewed the galleries, Elyssa and Yolotli Pacheco provided more information as a picture of a very advanced civilization began to emerge from the jungles, plains, and mountains centuries ago. Mark was particularly interested in the warcraft of the people and the class distinctions. Rebecca was caught up in the mythology, the sacred rites, and the dynastic treasures.

Mark observed, "For four thousand years, the Maya established a very advanced written language, built and defended impressive city-states with intricate social systems. They developed a series of three calendars, constructed a complex cosmology, invented sophisticated mathematics, and ruled this land from the Gulf to the Pacific. Outstanding. Man, look at these warriors and their armor – fantastic."

He moved from terra cotta renderings of the soldier class to an arrowhead display and a stone carving of a battle lord offering captives to the king.

"They practiced a unique system of war. Rival captives were the objective, not the slaughter of non-combatants -- human sacrifice, bloodletting was done to please the gods' bloodlust. Generals and officers who were prisoners of war were sacrificed. Ordinary soldiers were impressed for labor."

"You almost have it, Mr. Gadarn," Yolotli said. "The Maya thought and lived in cycles of cosmic time. They believed appeasement of the rival gods enabled creation to continue – the sun to rise each morning, the rain to fall, the dynasty to beget descendants, and prosperity to allow the people to thrive."

She continued, "The overarching question for contemporary observers is 'who were these people?' Our research is based on archeological evidence and what writings remain. Since the 1940s, science has changed our understanding of the Maya from innocent stargazers to a nation of big business, big government, and big problems. They were a civilization that ritualized war as divine appeasement. For millennia, the Maya elite fused art, architecture, and politics into a unified cosmic vision."

"Tell us, please, about Alberto Ruz L'hullier, Rebecca asked.

"He was of Cuban and French descent. He was born in Paris and was a socialist. He specialized in pre-Columbian Mesoamerican archaeology and is well known for leading the National Institute of Anthropology and History excavations here at the Maya site of Palenque. Señor Ruz L'huillier is the discoverer of its most significant treasure."

"The Tomb?"

"Yes, Ms. Quinto. Ruz L'huillier found the tomb of the Maya ruler, Pakal the First. In the 50s, the world turned its eyes here to Mesoamerica. L'huillier's was a discovery filled with suspense and wonder and featured his unique, almost cinematic style."

The Assistant Director led the way into the gallery of the great king's burial effects. The artistry of the curation suggested a unique portal into a wonder of the ancient world.

Dr. Pacheco's voice was almost reverential as she said, "To best appreciate what you are about to see, you must visit the actual chamber of the death and resurrection of the king in the Temple of the Inscriptions."

She gestured.

"Ms. Quinto, Mr Gadarn – after you."

Chapter Eleven: Niño and the Doll Boy

Zona Arqueológica Palenque, Estado de Chiapas, Estados Unidos Mexicanos

"Are you sure it is the two, *Esse*?"

"Fuck yeah, Bitch. Look at my phone. He got that red-gold hair like a *puta* boy, and he's rocking a bod like some big-dicked football star. It's the journalist bitch that kicked Ricky's *culo* in G City before he and Hime killed that old *bruja*. Of that I am sure."

"How about that one?"

"Hmmm, yeah, *Güey*. We gonna have some fun with that piece. Look at the tits on her, man. *La mujer es muy fresa, amigo.*[1] I get first-ups on that one. 'Cause I found 'em. Shit, I will do her good."

The thug rubbed his crotch as he shared his phone with his *compadre*. The younger hoodlum laughed.

"You start getting your nut on him, Bra. I know you like that. *Verdad*? No shame, Felix, man."

Felix made an obscene gesture and said, "They tipped us out right, man. I saw those two. Those two just went into the *pinche museo, Niño P.*"

"We need more than us, *Güey*. That blond *pendejo*, he look strong, Bra."

He chuckled and said, "Couple of us gonna haveta hold him down for when you..."

Now, the dude known as "Niño P" or "Little Patricio" made a two-handed finger gesture accompanied by a series of obscene sounds that were rude but precisely expressive. His wiry buddy put a hand in the big guy's face – he was not small by any means and pushed him away.

---

[1] The woman is very fine, friend.

"Get the locals to come in on this, Shit Head. They are only down the road in Palenque. Four is enough. We do not want to stand out. There will be a crowd in the city by the time they get here, and we can quickly strike. *Tu sabes*?

"*Ay, si, Muñeca*. We gonna get it done."

"Do not fuckin' call me that, *Puta*. I am nobody's doll boy."

The little gang member got rough with his bigger buddy. But the effort was almost comic. At 6'4" and 225#, the hulk called 'Niño' looked like he was swatting off raindrops.

"*Chinga tu madre*, Felix man. What is your plan for getting them back to G City?"

"Right there, that big ass SUV — their own fuckin' car. Once we truss them up, we can drive those rich gringos to wherever El Pálido wants."

"I bet Osterman-Diaz wants them across the border where he can get his hands on them."

"OK, so make like you are selling water and shit. Open that cooler and blend the fuck in. I think I see them coming out."

"Aye *Güey*, we cannot grab them here on the main road, *Esse*."

"No, *mierda para cerebros*[2]. Yo, we can better nab them in the ruins or, better yet, in the forest. *Tú sabes*?"

---

[2] Shit for brains

Chapter Twelve: The City of Snakes

Zona Arqueológica Palenque, Estado de Chiapas, Estados Unidos Mexicanos

"That was spectacular, but I am chomping at the bit to see the ruins."

"Me too, Darling. Lead on, Elyssa."

Locals sold souvenirs, food, and water along the roads and sidewalks outside the museum. Elyssa led them past the vendors to the trails marked "*A las Ruinas,*" To the Ruins.

The jungle was everywhere with its exotic foliage and primitive sounds. Information huts and rest stations were surrounded by invading greenery, interspersed with signs directing visitors to comfort stations and painted maps of the site posted beneath protective overhangs.

"The uncovered fortified city we are about to visit was abandoned in pre-Hispanic times. When the Spanish came, only a few peasants lived in simple huts around jungle-covered stone monuments – a city covered over by nature. This lost metropolis has had many names, like Lakam Ha, 'Big water', and Xhembobel-Moyos, 'Place of Fallen Stones'. My favorite is Na Chán, 'The City of Snakes.'

"Ah, here is Hugo."

Elyssa stepped forward to embrace a young man who appeared to be in his twenties. He stood blocking their path. The man was casually dressed and had an open and welcoming face.

"I checked you both out on Google. This is indeed a pleasure, Señorita Quinto and Señor Gadarn. Welcome to Zona Arqueológica Palenque."

Elyssa introduced Hugo Calavera de Armas of the Instituto Nacional de Antropología e Historia. "Hugo is the Director of Historical Research on the site. He is a graduate of Arizona State University's School of Human Evolution and Social Change."

Mark made an I-have-heard-of-you gesture, tapping the side of his head at the temple. He said, "Yeah… You're pretty famous. Doctor of

Anthropology at the ripe old age of twenty-two – whiz kid. I read where you turned the research on its ass regarding some theories connected to the Aztec city of Teotihuacan."

"Yes... I am afraid I upset established theorists and received my banishment to the jungles of Chiapas. Such is the fate of smart-assed academicians."

He spread his hands wide and sighed.

"Former head of the Center for Archeology and Society at ASU," Rebecca said. "When we were mounting the Egyptian project, 'Alexander in Egypt,' last year at the Fritcher, you advised one of my curators. I remember you were an excellent scholar and collaborator."

"Yes, I heard the exhibit was a great success. Speaking of controversial scholarship. I'll bet you got a lot of pushback from the historians. And now, Elyssa tells me of your interest in the Maya for a joint curatorial perspective. Ready to cause more trouble?"

It was readily apparent that the graduate student and the archeologist had a history. They seemed to pick up where they had left off. The Americans and the Mexican academic were on a first-name basis as they stepped into the tree-shaded autumn sunshine. The sounds and smells of the dense tropical forest were carried by a soft breeze. Far off, the details of the surrounding highlands crystallized as the landscape dropped its covering of mist and clouds.

Hugo said, "Let's take this trail away from the beaten path, as it were. It's my secret way down. Be careful of snakes."

They crossed the road and followed barely visible steps into the overgrowth. Rushing water could be heard, peppered with the soft cry of a bird.

Hugo pointed to the small river. "This is the Arroyo Otulum, a tributary of the Usumacinta. It is the source of water for the ancient city."

The jungle stream gave way to a series of limestone cascades and crystal clear pools covered with mosses, ferns, vines, and assorted plants. A suspension bridge hung between squared-off arches on either bank. They crossed the swirling river among the cool and tranquil shadows of the rubber, kapok, and mahogany trees. An amiable group of Keel-billed

Toucans seemed to cheer their arrival on the river's opposite bank, wagging their green bills with red tips and orange sides. Soon losing interest, they each ruffled black feathers with one blue foot in an attempt to act casually in the eyes of these visitors to their jungle.

"These are the Sombrillas Waterfalls. Up ahead is El Baño de la Reina, the Queen's Bath."

A pair of orange, yellow, and blue macaws screeched and flapped as the humans approached the water cascade. Limestone steps brought the crystal-clear water down into a rock-lined basin secluded by the rainforest's dense flora. A dragonfly examined Rebecca's nose before darting into a patch of sunshine. A snort and rustle of undergrowth suggested a tapir was also interested in the four intruders' antics.

"This place is heaven, Darling. Imagine Her Royal Highness, surrounded by handmaidens bathing in these pools. I am sure many suggestive glances were shared between her ladies and their muscled-up armed guards here in this jungle of desire. What savage love-making was common among the dense cover of greenery and flowers?"

Mark chuckled, "You sound like a romance novel, Beautiful."

Rebecca gave him a rather lascivious wink.

Mark pointed up to an overhanging section of a strangler fig. A black wooly monkey straddling the horizontal branch on her belly was taking her morning snooze. Her four appendages dangled down as she watched the humans with sparkling dark amber eyes. The little forest queen's prehensile tail curled around the branch to keep her from falling. There was stirring across her furry back as another set of small eyes and a button nose peeked out from his mother's lush coat at the tourists.

The forest had been cut back to reveal an acropolis of three pyramid structures, each topped by a temple-like edifice in ruins. Hugo pointed to the buildings, which seemed to reveal themselves through the rainforest canopy as they approached.

"That is called 'El Groupo Norte.' Let's climb up and go around to the south-facing side," Hugo said. "I think it is the best vantage point for the entire city."

The large rectangular building screened the sloping plain of the ruined city. From the front, one could see that the city's limestone piles seemed to grow from verdant lawns stretching across the valley and into the jungle. A few tourists, wanting to beat the crowds, walked the grounds and climbed stairs to graduated platforms and towers.

"That is El Templo del Conte, the Temple of the Count, on the right. From here, our position is opposite the Ball Stadium – Pok-A-Tok. Have you heard of it?"

"Sure. Jai alai."

Elyssa smiled as Hugo resumed his instruction.

"No. Jai alai comes from the Basque people. Pok-A-Tok is much older. We find evidence of this ball game played by the ancient Maya as far back as 1400 years ago in the Maya countries. The Toltecs and Aztecs played similar games. There are ancient ball courts throughout Mesoamerica."

Mark said, "The sport of the mythic hero twins."

Just below El Grupo Norte was El Juego de Pelota, the Ball Court. The rectangular stadium was 100 meters in length, featuring a level playing field between the ruins of two parallel stone walls. Outside the court were the sloping grass and stone remains of the spectators' sections.

Elyssa said, "Do either of you play football?"

Rebecca said, "Mark does a bit. Right, Darling? We have a nephew in San Francisco who is an absolute phenom. Unlike the rest of the world, Americans call it soccer."

Hugo pointed to the site and explained, "There would have been sloping end walls from which the stone goal hoops could extend as high as 20 feet above the court. The ball was made of rubber, and teams consisted of two athletes. Think of a sport that has the strategies of soccer and basketball. You could only pass and shoot the ball using your thighs, knees, and hips. No hands, no feet. Pok-A-Tok games would last many hours, sometimes days. It was a rough sport with no helmets or elaborate protective gear.

Rebecca asked, "Wasn't there a wider religious and sociological context to the ball game for the Maya?"

"Ball games were used to settle conflicts during times of war. The game is symbolic of the life-and-death battle — another of the many creation/destruction themes in Maya society. The court's floor represented the earth's platform, separating the human world from the Underworld. The gods determined the ball game winners, just as they decided who would be victorious at war. Losers in sport, as in battle, were often sacrificed to the gods."

Rebecca added, "It appears that for the Maya, death, the afterlife, and human sacrifice were seen as fundamental aspects of existence. Blood rituals appeased the gods. The ancients believed human sacrifices and sacred blood-letting provided nourishment for the divine beings."

"A defeated athlete," Mark added, "would have been the ultimate offering."

Elyssa said, "Pok-A-Pok is still played in parts of Mexico where the people call it Ulama. With ball courts having been dated to 1400 BC, Ulama and Pok-A-Tok are the oldest continually played team and ball sport in the world."

They descended to ground level and walked between copses of trees into the southern compound of the site. Here, the breadth of the site widened.

The hills rolled forward, fringed by the rainforest and framed by blue-green highlands anchored by purple and gray mountains. Flocks of Collared Araçaris and Yucatán Jays soared up and over the ruins' campus into the far canopy of trees. The landscape was dominated by the long-abandoned temples and palaces of the City of Snakes.

The Americans paused to catch their breath.

Thomas Paul Severino

Chapter Thirteen: Ninety Minutes

Quetzaltenango, República de Guatemala

"Please, Mamá, I promise I will be careful. Carlos Sibaja's big brother, Mateo, is going. He will watch us. Promise."

"Jacinto Davide De Leon, you listen to your Mamá. You narrowly escaped those evil men in the park in broad daylight. I want you home where you will be safe."

Jack whined, "But the match is this afternoon in the light — no school on Saturday. We will be home before dark."

"You are all I have, *mi hijo*. There is so much violence. No, it comes even during the daytime. When you get older, we will talk about more freedom and safety. You have your computer, and the signal is fixed and strong throughout the Inn. Why not spend the day studying, reading, and playing some of those games you love so much, eh?"

The boy hung his head. Cauli, sensing her boy's disappointment, lay down and put her head on her paws. *This was not going well.*

"I can always use your help. There are other chores besides the ones you have finished."

Jack said nothing. He sulked.

Rosalina tousled his hair and said, "At least let us give it a few days, my boy. You will not be a prisoner of this place for too long."

The boy remarked, "I will be in my room. C'mon, girl."

"Jacinto, Tia Carmen made *buneulos*. You know how much you love those..."

Jack grabbed a handful of kibble, deliberately ignored the yucca fritters, and sauntered towards his bedroom. He tossed his buddy some snacks as she followed him out the back, across the gated courtyard. The Inn's airport van took up most of the enclosed space. The boy and his dog made their way to Jack's room in one of the outbuildings that front the street across the property's back. Aunt Carmen and Rosalina each had a suite on the ground floor.

The boy lowered the shade of his room's window on the balcony and scooped up his dog.

"In you go, girl. We sure are gonna get it for this."

Cauli settled into her compartment in Jack's backpack. Only her head stuck out, and he pulled his arms through the satchel's straps. They were both comfortable with this very familiar arrangement.

Jack raised the window at the back of his room and sat on the windowsill. Cauli sniffed. Before he leaped into the arms of the blue jacaranda tree, Jack looked over his shoulder. He caught the look of Deadpool, the rascally, Bad Boy of superheroes, mugging from a poster on the bedroom wall.

Go for it, Kiddo. Learn to fly.

***

"What are you doing here? You are usually under house arrest, *Chorro*."

"Came to watch the game, *mi Entrenador*. Everything is good at the Inn, so here I am… brought my security, too." Jack turned and pointed over his shoulder.

Cauli yipped and licked the Coach's hand.

"Sit near me, *Niño*. I'll show you how *Los Asaltantes* win a football game."

Jack watched as Coach Tomás Benitez gathered the older boys from the neighborhood for the opening huddle. The town's law enforcement association founded the team to neutralize the youth gangs' influence in Quetzaltenango. The boys wore their team shirts with the Maya Raiders logo displayed proudly. Some of the youth of the neighborhood looked on in envy. Each game against the town's policemen and women brought a few more young people into the program, curious and eager to belong.

The soccer match was an exciting event with a big turnout. Benitez was delighted with the positive effect community-sponsored sport had on the youth. A girls' squad had been started last year, and they were quite skilled.

Jack took Cauli out of her cubby and placed her next to him. They watched together. Settling alongside him, she put her head on his thigh. Her alert eyes followed everything. Jack petted her.

"Ninety minutes. That's all. We'll be back up that tree in no time, Girl."

After an opening goal, the retired police officer saw a few questionable characters off to the side. So many tattoos and bandanas...

Trouble.

Chapter Fourteen: The Patroness of Warfare

Zona Arqueológica Palenque, Estado de Chiapas, Estados Unidos Mexicanos

"Amazing," Mark said. "What a place! No one could dispute the power of the people who ruled from this city."

They walked toward the stately Acropolis, which rose up on the eastern side of the plain. The structure was a precise pile of six platforms, interlaced with stairways, ornately sculpted loggia, corbelled galleries, tiered walkways, and planted courtyards. The connected group of buildings included the royal apartments and the king's prison. Doorways, stelae, and facades were covered with stone reliefs depicting many of the numerous Mayan deities. Thousand-year-old kings and queens joined with lords and ladies of the elite class to peer out at the visitors with dispassion, forever imprisoned by the stone. Stone gods embraced their earthly representatives – the kings, the elite, a dynasty graced by a heavenly mandate.

We were here. There was none greater in the entire universe. We thrive with heaven's blessing. Behold the power of the gods.

Near the center of this compound was a four-storied, squared-off tower believed to be the King's observatory. It featured wide, open porticoes and a missing roof. From high above the ancient city, sentries could see an enemy's approach, and priest astronomers could chart the heavens and calendar time. It was here that the team met another guide.

Elyssa and Hugo introduced Maria Alvarez y Acha, the Instituto Nacional's Archeological's astronomer. She led them to the courtyard adjacent to the tower. A staff person brought backpacks of food and bottled water. They sat and ate lunch on the palace steps.

Rebecca introduced the topic of ancient cosmology by saying, "I have read that the Maya believed that the Earth was the center of all things, fixed and immovable. The stars, moons, sun, and planets were divine. Their movements were interpreted as gods traveling between the Earth, the underworld, and other celestial destinations. Much of this is recorded in the few writings that have survived."

"And on the stone calendars," Mark added, "Right?"

Maria began, "The planet Venus, of all the heavenly bodies, greatly interested the Maya. Of all the world's civilizations, they knew her best. They recorded her movements across the sky, relative to the sun, with incredible exactness. Remember, the priests made their observations with only their eyes. In addition to the Sun and Moon, they could see Venus, Mars, Saturn, Jupiter, and various constellations. The cosmology of the Maya created social and cultural dynamics that joined religion to everyday living and the nation's governance."

The scientist rose and climbed three steps to one of the tower's walls. She pointed to a stone carving – circles, triangles, lines, and glyphs near the entrance passageway.

"This stela shows the inferior conjunction when Venus is between the Sun and the Earth. The planet cannot be seen for about eight days during this time. When Venus was at its dimmest magnitude, the people most feared what terrors would come upon them."

Maria moved her finger counterclockwise around the circle of the Sun's image. "Here, when she emerges from behind the Sun, Venus becomes the morning star. This is the heliacal rising because it is ascending with the Sun. The Maya considered this the most important position of the planet. Their fear was replaced by the promise of good things to come if they got the rituals right."

She tapped the image and continued. "In this position, after rising, Venus will be at her brightest, and she will move off to the west as if leading the Sun across the sky."

She traced the arc in the sky above them and off to the west.

"For about two hundred and sixty days, her creative energy fills the universe. Fueled by prayers and offerings, the goddess will bring abundance and prosperity for the people."

She tapped the diagram again, saying, "Until this point, the Sun is hidden between Venus and the Earth, the superior conjunction. The Goddess now becomes a mere follower of the Sun God, moving off to the east. Now is the decline in celestial energy. The brilliance of the planet is replaced by a dimness. Destructive powers will have prominence. The liturgical practices will result in many sacrifices to stave off the hard times that have returned to the people."

The Americans and their guides were enthralled by the presentation. When the Astronomer spoke again, it was with a slight touch of solemnity. She said, "The calendars are proof, however, of universal rebirth. After Venus dips under the horizon."

Again, she referred to the carving. Pointing, she said, "There. Venus appears on the opposite side of the Sun about fifty days later."

On the platform above them, Maria again used the azure sky as her presentation canvas. She seemed to channel the ancient astrologers who mounted these steps with clear eyes to map the heavens and divine the people's destiny.

'With great mystery and ritual celebration, the priests ushered in the rising of the planet as the Evening Star. Venus would remain in the night sky for two hundred and sixty days until it went furthest to the east. There it attained its most incredible brightness, and reached the inferior conjunction again."

Elyssa partially finished her lunch and tapped on her laptop. She asked, "How was Mayan society integrated into the celestial movements?"

"Cycles – creation and destruction. Venus had a psychological effect on the Maya and other Mesoamerican cultures. War was waged based on the stationary alignment points between Venus and Jupiter. Crops were planted and harvested when Venus was in her brightest phase, bestowing success and prosperity. Dynasties rose and fell. Nobility married, copulated, and gave birth. Captured heroes were sacrificed on Venus' first appearance after the superior conjunction. Written Maya almanacs of the celestial cycles of Venus survive to this day."

Hugo took up the narrative, saying, "You are overemphasizing from a twenty-first-century feminist bias for the goddess planet. The male cosmological entity was equally, if not more important."

The archeologist pointed to a round carving above a doorway into the palace. The mask was partially in disrepair, but the face and its surrounding rays were still identifiable. The deity wore a feathered crown, large, circular earrings, and an ornate necklace. The god's expression was serene and timeless.

"Venus was the planet associated with the most powerful god in the pantheon, Kinich Ahau – the sun god of the Maya. The importance of the Sun cannot be overlooked. While the Maya made detailed observations of Venus, archaeologists theorize that they structured their governments to track the Sun's movements.

"As one of the creator gods, Kinich Ahau, would shine in the sky all day before transforming himself into a jaguar at night to pass through *Xibalba*, the Mayan underworld. The king and his priests joined with the gods to continue the great cycles of the universe. They were charged with the creation and destruction of all existence. Rituals conducted by the priests, the king, and the nobles brought about the sun's return to the morning sky each day after its journey through the underworld.

"Those codices you refer to, Maria, also record solar phenomena such as eclipses, solstices, and equinoxes, as well as determining when the sun reached its apex. "

The astronomer smiled, "Yes. You probably guessed I did my dissertation on the importance of Venus in the Maya civilization. But the Maya cosmology is rather quite complicated. Venus, the Sun, and the other observable planets brought a profound depth to their astronomy, their astrology, and the associated cultural implications."

The scientist turned and gestured to the left.

 "Some excellent archeological evidence behind the rituals and the Maya gods lies only a few meters south of where we are sitting. The Southern Group contains the great ritual centers, the Temple of the Sun, the Temple of the Cross, and a few more sanctuaries. Remember, in the classical age, the people who lived here possessed a pantheon of about two hundred and fifty deities."

Rebecca walked to a stele. She turned to the group, seated on the steps like students in a kiva, watching a professor or a doctor elaborate in a lecture. It was at this time that Yolotli Pacheco joined the group, slipping in to hear what the American curator had to say,

"There is little mention of treasure. What happened to it? The museum has some artifacts, and the conquering Europeans made off with quite a bit. Still, *Na Chán*, this capital city, was ruled by generations of a mighty dynasty. Where are the pottery, the jewels, and the valuables?"

She gestured to the surrounding buildings and royal chambers.

"Pakal the Great's city has very little to show for its conquering power and plunder."

She stepped forward to emphasize her point. "Gold... the tears of the Sun God, the mandate from heaven, anointing the king, his descendants, and his court. Where is i? The treasure? Where are the ancient gold, jade, and silver mines?"

"When the Spanish came in the sixteenth century," Hugo said, "They came for the gold of a great civilization. Instead, they found a small community of indigenous folk gathered around the ruins of whatever buildings had not been swallowed up by earthquakes or devoured by the jungle. *Na Chán*, The City of Snakes, had been abandoned for hundreds of years by then, like the other Maya city-states of the Yucatan, Belize, and Guatemala. There was very little Maya plunder to send back in the treasure galleons of the court of Madrid."

Dr. Pacheco asked, "Do you seek the Maya version of the Lost City of El Dorado, Ms. Quinto. If you do, like the exploiters who came here over centuries, you will not find it. The ancients, the Inca, the Toltecs, the Aztecs, and the Maya took their secrets with them when they were exterminated or when they vanished in the mists of the jungle."

She stood as if to emphasize.

"No secret mines, hidden caches, treasuries carved deep in the mountains, nothing... only the people. What the colonists were unable to steal has never been found in more than six hundred years."

The Assistant Director turned to leave.

"I'm afraid you seek in vain."

Chapter Fifteen: The Shield of the Sun

Zona Arqueológica Palenque, Estado de Chiapas, Estados Unidos Mexicanos

"I don't think that woman likes me."

"She means no harm. Come. There is much more to see and to understand."

As they crossed to the west side of the site, Elyssa explained, "About thirteen temples and the palace complex are all that have been uncovered so far. You are seeing only 10% of the city's total area. About 1,400 structures were documented by LiDAR, laser scanning. Most are still covered by dense jungle. The people rebuilt these buildings whenever the city-state went to war."

She indicated the temples and palaces as they walked.

"The Temple of the Inscriptions is the highest on the site."

Mark asked, "Can you speak more about the significance of the design of the temples?"

Elyssa explained, "The architectural feature of stairs and gradient layers had cultural meaning for the Maya. Like a great Jacob's Ladder, they link heaven to earth.

"Everything was built as a grand rising up to the sky as if bringing the elite up into the heavens and the gods down to dwell among the people. The massive pyramids' architects favored a layer cake construction of stone platforms crowned by roofed sacred enclosures, most in good condition. Those grand staircases allowed a procession of priests and kings to ascend to the gods to offer sacrifices for gratefulness, victory, and prosperity."

Hugo added, "What survives is Palenque's refortification by K'inich Janaab' Pakal, Pacal the Great, perhaps the greatest of the Maya. During his reign in the seventh century, this city rose to prominence over the rival cities of Calakmul and Toniná, even eclipsing the great city of Tikal. The art, architecture, and artifacts found at Palenque represent the Classic Period of the Maya civilization. "

The quartet stood at the base of the largest pyramid.

"Magnificent," Rebecca said. "Nine levels. Looks like a hundred stairs." She smiled at Mark. "Race to the top, Big Guy?"

Mark held up his hands.

"No, Beautiful. You'd win. The leg works when I fight, but climbing kicks my ass."

Mark took a bullet about a year ago in Yemen. Every so often, it acted up on him. Never when he was showboating for his man-buds. Heroes were a lot of work sometimes.

They ascended to the five openings in the summit of the temple. Elyssa stopped to point out the entrance piers bearing elaborately carved images. "The surrounding hieroglyphic texts in Maya script give the name to this building. This is the Temple of the Inscriptions."

She continued, "They were once brightly painted – blue for the heavens and the gods, yellow for the underworld, the realm of the dead. These images are of the king's family. The reliefs are a documentation of the family's legitimacy, validating the divinity of the one buried here.

"A god?" Rebecca asked.

Elyssa smiled with a secret expression as she traced a figure on the first vertical panel on its plexiglass shield.

"A great *Ajaw*. That means a warrior lord. K'inich Janaab' Pakal, Pakal the Great, ascended to the throne of Palenque's great city-state when he was twelve years old. He died as king of a powerful 'empire' at eighty in 683 CE. One hundred years after him, the Maya's culture would begin to collapse, the great cities fading into the jungle. The society broke up into a dozen warring states that militarized the landscape and may have destroyed the region's ecology."

She turned and swept a hand over the immense sea of space out over the landscape to the horizon.

"And with the decline of his city-state, so many treasures were covered by the deep layers of the rainforest – a great impenetrable tangle watched over by cedar, mahogany, and sapodilla trees."

Rebecca said, "Many secrets shrouded in the aftermath of war and destruction..."

The scholar moved to the second pier. "This is the child-god K'awiil, the divination of the King's son, K'inich Kan B'ahlam, and family patron. At the King's inauguration, the god promises the people many years of abundance."

She tapped an image.

"You see, K'awiil carries a sack of grain – maize or cacao and holds the King in an embrace. That is a declaration of the legitimacy of Pakal's son, lest the succession be questioned. The tomb of Pakal the Great puts all disputes to rest. Kan B'alam is blessed by heaven to be the next ruler of the Maya.

She stepped to the third pillar.

"Also resolved in this artwork are any issues concerning Pakal's bloodlines. Look here. This is the Lady Zac-Kuk, Pakal's mother. She ruled as queen for three years after the death of the King, her husband. Pakal followed her to the throne as the legitimate King."

Mark drew closer.

"She looks like an important woman. The anchor of the dynasty."

"Yes. Look at this important feature of the figure, please."

Elyssa pointed to a hollow in the stone that went into the interior and into a lower chamber.

"The tomb of Pakal lies beneath. Do you see the stone band that runs down into the pyramid?"

"Almost like an umbilical cord," Rebecca said. "Connecting the dead king to this figure of his mother."

"Yes. It is the architectural reference to Pakal's royal bloodline, and the doorway formed by this pillar aligns with the spring rising of the planet Venus."

"The planet associated with the god Quetzalcoatl," Rebecca said, "The astronomers kept records of the appearances of Venus for the purposes of divination. It is as Maria, the astronomer, described."

Mark commented, "Elyssa, what are these? They are everywhere."

He pointed to a series of oval shapes that seemed to collect in clusters around the images and glyphs.

"Actually, Mark, we just don't know. A royal decoration, it is thought. The shapes resemble storage urns, and they are unique to this pyramid. We find them only here in the city of Na Chán."

Inside the temple, they descended the once-hidden stairway into the monument's center, the tomb of K'inich Janaab' Pakal, Pakal the Great, lying at ground level. A modern exhibition space had been constructed respecting the original structure at the heart of the pyramid. Bulletproof glass separated the opening to the crypt. A guard stood on each side. As they entered, a pull-up banner showed the King's blue-green jade burial jewelry as it was found, now arranged against an orange background.

In situ, the royal mausoleum's presentation was total museum theater – soft lighting, ancient music, and spectacular regal artifacts created an atmosphere of royal wonder and sacredness. This was a grave, and it was a holy space to be respected on all counts.

Against the western wall was a bas-relief of the warrior King in a feathered helmet and full battle dress. The figure presided over a stone slab set tabletop-like over a lower alcove containing a replica of the jade mask and jewelry that once adorned the King's remains. On either side of the chamber were carved members of the King's honor guard.

Elyssa pointed and explained, "The people knew this building as the 'House of the Nine Sharpened Spears' because of the warriors' images that guard the gravesite of the King. The tomb was discovered by Ruz L'Huillier in 1948.

"The body of the King beneath the slab was oriented to face the east, into the rising sun that would bring immortality to the dead ruler. Pakal's remains were covered with a jade mask and bead necklaces, as you saw back in Ciudad Guatemala. The slab is original, but the precious adornment is a copy. As you saw, the rest of the regalia has been relocated to the Palenque Museum."

They moved closer, and Elyssa directed their attention, saying, "The tomb's stone cover depicts the ruler's transformation to a god, joining figures from Maya mythology. On this edge, the hieroglyphics have been worn away; they are barely discernable."

The academic moved close to one edge of the slab. Elyssa spent some time examining the broken script and made some notes on her iPad.

"What is it, Darling? I can tell when someone has a great secret on her mind." Rebecca spoke softly.

Elyssa stopped staring at the set of glyphs and looked up at the corbelled archway that formed the chamber's ceiling. "At the spring equinox, the rising sun sends a shaft of light down the umbilical duct. Remember, I showed it to you when we were on the top of this monument?"

"Yes."

"The rising sun on that day, with Venus as the morning star, illuminates this tomb, and the shaft of light falls there."

She pointed to the corner of the tomb cover.

Mark asked, "What does it say?"

"That's the problem. It's gibberish... meaningless to modern researchers. More of those urn images, but here they are paired with the glyph for the Pleadies. That missing section could be the key, but it is lost. We may never know. Scholars have dismissed this as completely undecipherable, but what if it is some sort of code?"

"But look, that part of the stela, above the lost passage, has a strange monogram. It appears to be K'awiil, the god who brings abundance for countless generations, the divine boy."

"Is it a prayer?"

"No, ritual prayers have a distinct style. There is astrological 'science' here. The script is technical. This seems to be connected to the Maya Calendar."

Elyssa pointed to the large disc, a stone calendar on the western wall. Their young graduate student explained how the priests predicted present and future events using calendars like this.

"Here, you can see the glyphs for lunar eclipses. Those indications are the phases of Venus. This area shows the stars' movements with a particular importance placed on the Pleadies. The birth of the dead king into the afterlife..."

Elyssa grew silent for a moment as she studied the calendar, the broken inscription, and the shaft of light.

"Countless generations... a connection of past and future – people yet to come... until the great destruction."

She looked up at her friends.

Rebecca pointed to a symbol on the calendar.

Elyssa said, "That is the glyph of the jaguar... the deity is Ek Bahlam, one of Pakal the Great's signatures."

Rebecca asked, "Elyssa, what is different about it?"

"Well, the ancients often stylized..."

The graduate student looked at her device and flipped back and forth.

"It's black. The paint has disintegrated mostly, but it is definitely black – all of them."

Rebecca said, "For the Maya Kings, the jaguar represents power, ferocity, and bravery. It was a symbol of the aggressiveness of the ruler. The black jaguar was associated with a knowledge of things to come. He can see during the night and look into the dark forebodings of the future, the great destruction.

"That glyph of the black jaguar would also have been here on the coffin where the equinox light hits, adjacent to the vision serpent, except, Yaxchilan is on his side."

Elyssa, "Yes. Here on the calendar, also. It is a coda, a repeat."

"It is a message, Darling. The ancients are foretelling a time that would come after them.

"Quite complicated. These are instructions regarding the King's legacy, an eschatology – the Maya of the end time. For them, a world yet to come."

Chapter Sixteen: The Red Queen

Zona Arqueológica Palenque, Estado de Chiapas, Estados Unidos Mexicanos

"You spoke of the treasure of the City of Snakes, Rebecca, and I know that you are aware that you are not the first to wonder. When the Spanish military came here in 1786, they tore down the walls searching for gold and hidden valuables. They found no royal tombs.

As they came to the next ruin, Elyssa turned to her colleague to take up the tour.

Hugo said, "Not until 1994, when a young Mexican archeologist, Fanny López Jiménez, found a hidden door leading to a burial chamber in this pyramid, did the secret of the Temple of the Red Queen emerge. Please allow me to show you."

A green metal sign set near the base declared in English and Spanish, "Temple XIII. The Temple of the Red Queen. A step pyramid, twelve meters high, mounted by a broad stairway leading to the sacred shrine on the top."

"This sanctuary had crumbled over the centuries, and the debris blocked access to the interior of the structure. Like the rest of the city, it declined, was gradually abandoned, and reclaimed by the jungle."

The archeologist stopped on the second level. He pointed to a doorway, almost hidden by the stairs.

"Lopez Jiménez' secret stairway."

At the end of a long corridor inside the pyramid, the three descended a flight of stairs into the burial chamber with its stone walls and vaulted ceiling. They stepped aside to allow fellow tourists to climb past them and to the outside. A partition just inside the stairs prevented further access. Just to the left was a guard. Electric lighting was a twentieth-century addition to the site.

Unlike the King's tomb in the Temple of the Inscriptions, there were no decorations on the walls. Beyond the plexiglass divider, a stone sarcophagus was covered by a limestone lid. On top was a carved incense burner with masks of the gods as decoration.

Hugo indicated specific places in the room as he described the discovery in 1994.

"They found the skeleton of a boy on that side of the coffin and the remains of a woman, just about where we are standing. Apparently, they had been sacrificed to accompany the royal occupant's journey into *Xibalba*, the Maya underworld."

Two locals came down the entry stairs, and the guard went up. The new visitors stood close to listen to Hugo's speech.

Rebecca asked, "How was the body presented?"

"When Jiménez discovered the tomb, the coffin was intact. Like Pakal the Great's remains, the skeleton was covered by an extensive collection of jade and pearl objects, necklaces, ear spools, and bracelets. On the skull was a headdress made of flat jade discs and a funeral mask of malachite. The upper body was adorned with more jade beads and four obsidian blades. The entire contents of the stone coffin, the skeleton, and the regalia, as well as the inside of the sarcophagus, were coated with a bright red dusting of cinnabar, the ground ore of mercury."

"Who was the Red Queen?"

"It is believed, Ms. Quinto, that she was Ix Tz'akbu Ajaw, the wife of Pakal the Great and the grandmother of the last Mayan ruler. We have not yet found the tombs of the sons of K'inich Janaab' Pakal. When they are found, DNA tests of the royal children could confirm the identity of the woman who was buried here."

"Where are…"

"After the remains of the Queen and her two attendants were exhumed, they were taken to the Mexican National Institute of Archeology and History for study. They were returned here eight years ago and buried in a different place, away from curious tourists."

Elyssa continued, "She was a member of the elite and a religious person. Someone, her perhaps, authored the prayer that is carved in stucco on the wall..."

She attempted to translate.

"Something... something... most likely the creation gods are invoked here... OK... 'When the great destruction comes upon us, and the jaguar roams no more... and the corn is parched, and rots... at the drying up of the river... (something) turns to dust... he will arrive at the end... the last Ajaw... the Last King... forged in the darkness and blood of Xibalba... take my hand, O king forever... reveal the timeless secrets.'"

Mark said, "The urn-things. See there at the end?"

It got very quiet.

"Hey, I got a question."

Rebecca, Mark, and Elyssa turned to the shorter of the two men, the only other occupants of the chamber.

"Anyone want to die here with the Maya Queen?"

Felix was holding a gun.

***

Poor Hugo fainted. The abductors left him in the tomb. The SUV was parked on the service road, not too far from the Temple of the Red Queen. There were four seats in the large rear compartment. The exit from the depths of the Temple had been carefully orchestrated. The two thugs took the women by the hand, guns barely concealed, and followed Mark up to the waiting escort of four more gang members. Outside, in the maintenance area, they would be hidden by the forest should they decide to harm their captives.

Felix smirked as he patted and then fished the keys out of Mark's shorts. No need to hotwire again. *Sexy man has a lot going on down there.* He saw his buddy's smirk.

The young criminal came away with the keys and brought his hand up and down forcefully to pistol-whip the journalist. Mark collapsed to his knees.

"That's for Pedro the Mouse, *pendejo* bitch. You should learn not to interfere with BDS-13. The Brigade means fear and death. "

Mark came up, fists clenched, ready to rock the house. Felix moved closer, the gun at the ready.

Rebecca spoke as if she were admonishing a child. She said in Spanish, "Ohhh, Darling, you should not have done that to him. No, no, no -- It will end up badly for you. Definitely not good."

Felix kept the gun on Mark but turned to her and snarled, "You keep your mouth shut, bitch. I am going to hurt you good before this is over."

"Darling, just don't say you were not warned."

At gunpoint, the captives were bound at the wrists to the armrests and around their chests to the back of the SUV seats with duct tape. The big hulk, known as Little Patricio, instructed his buddies from the local gang to accompany them to the border in their pick-up truck.

Mark and Rebecca exchanged a look. Elyssa was terror-stricken.

"Hugo?"

"Probably the safest of us all, Darling. All those tourists. Try to remain calm. Believe me, we got this."

The SUV hit the main road in the lead and took Highway 307 to the southeast and into the Chiapas mountains. One of the local thugs took the seat next to Elyssa behind Mark and Rebecca.

As the road began to twist and turn, climbing into the highlands, Rebecca continued to talk about how this abduction would end in nothing but tragedy for the gang members.

Chapter Seventeen: The Laws of Motion
Frontiza del Sur Highway, Estado de Chiapas, Estados Unidos Mexicanos

'Carlos, man, tape that bitch's mouth. I am tired of hearing her shit. You should have done that in the first place, *cabron.*"

Felix looked in the rearview and then waved out the driver's side window.

"Damn, why they gotta follow so close, man?"

As the road came up to a mountain rise overlooking a beautiful lake, the general sequence of events followed the classic laws of motion – momentum, force, and energy conservation. The action occurred as follows:

In the back passenger's side seat, Carlos leaned over and rifled along the floor for the roll of duct tape. He was becoming frustrated.

"This shit's rolling around back here, bro. Water bottles and shit... Yo, why you speeding up, Dollboy?"

Mark shouted something in Welsh.

He and Rebecca went head down, snapping their bodies forward while twisting their wrists up and out. The silver tape ripped like wet paper.

Now free of restraints, Mark used the momentum to push, twist, and vault over the center console into the front compartment on his back. He was propped against the dashboard, facing the stunned driver and his thug mate.

"Hey, fellas. *¿Qué pasó?*"

Rebecca ducked under Mark's flying legs and landed a haymaker on Carlos's jaw. Roll of duct tape in hand, he was in the process of returning to an upright position. The woman's attack shot caused him to roll forward against the door.

Kneeling on her seat, Rebecca reached for the door handle and, with the help of Elyssa's kicking, sent the semi-conscious gang member tumbling onto the road.

The resistance of the open door and the human projectile made the speeding van swerve. Felix fought to gain control of the careening vehicle and slammed the brakes. The vehicle fishtailed.

Felix's gun compensated for the change in velocity and direction by sliding from his lap and into Mark's hand.

On his left, Mark kicked into Little P's gaping mouth while, in the other direction, he brought Felix's gun up to the driver's head as the SUV spun out on the highway.

Behind them, the pickup hit the tumbling Carlos at an oblique angle. It swerved, zig-zagged, and careened into the opposite lane, facing backward into oncoming traffic. The combination of high speed and the driver's lack of control smashed the truck against the guardrail. Impact and momentum – the truck and its three gang members vaulted up and over the precipice.

Back in the SUV, Rebecca grabbed the open door and pulled it closed.

In the front seat, Little P was sputtering and spitting blood, his face and the side of his skull having rebounded off the passenger's side window. Arms and legs flailing, he pointed the weapon in the direction of his attacker.

Mark pulled at the wheel, and the SUV went up on two wheels and rocked back into the proper lane.

Totally out of control, Little P shot Felix in the head, temple to temple.

Behind the killer, Rebecca used the back of his seat for leverage and reached for the front door latch. She shoved, and the shooter went airborne out into the ditch. She called after him, "You guys should learn to use your seat belts."

The SUV slowed as the dead driver's feet slipped off the pedals. It coasted off the road to the right, hanging up on a savanna grass-covered berm.

Elyssa stopped screaming.

Chapter Eighteen: The Ch'ol

Frontera Corozal, Estado de Chiapas, Estados Unidos Mexicanos

"They do not speak Spanish. Most of our ancestors did not. I spoke to them in *Lak T'an*, our language.' May I have the keys? Thank you."

"So, Darling?"

"My nephews will drive back and pick up the bodies. They will never be found."

"Are we doing the right thing, Elyssa?"

"No police, no government means no gang recriminations. We are in Frontera Corozal, my home community. The Lacandon Jungle... as you saw back at the City of Snakes, the rainforest hides everything."

She went on, "My people, the Ch'ol, are Maya people. Here, along the banks of the Usumacinta River, three Maya populations live in harmony. Ironic no? Our ancestors made war and sacrificed each other to the gods. Now we live in harmony on the *ejidos*, the government's collective agricultural lands."

On th river's edge, at the town's embarcadero, long, narrow, pointed boats were lined up on the shoreline with large outboard motors slanted up off the sand. The Usumacinta River was swift and sparkling in the lowering light. Community members attended the rivercraft, the passengers, and the products traversing this vital waterway.

"There is no bridge across the Usumacinta in the whole southern part of the Chiapas State. These boats, *las lanchas*, are the only transport." Elyssa said.

Mark read the names of the colorful boats, "The Jaguar 11, Fundada, Yaxchilam... cool."

Elyssa pointed across to the opposite shore and the soft glimmer of town lights. "That is Guatemala. We are still in Mexico. The customs authorities on both sides of the river get along very well. It is relatively peaceful here.

As night came on, they walked through the village of quaint wood, stone, and adobe houses and shops, many with peaked tin roofs. Streets varied from crushed stone to asphalt to dirt paths and even wood planking. There were few cars, but the trucks of this agricultural community were many. Trees and vines competed with electric poles and wires, creating a combined overhead infrastructure, both natural and somewhat high-tech. A family of monkeys traveled above street levels using wires, vines, and branches.

The people were friendly but slightly cautious of strangers. They were busy doing those things families do just as night comes on – returning to the village from the fields, hurrying home with groceries, and calling in the children. Here and there, lights went on inside a house or a shop. Street football scrimmages ended as a final play was completed and cheered.

As the sun was setting over the blue mountains in the west, flocks of birds, their brilliant colors turning to black in the dying light, circled the streets and houses preparing for their night roost. Chickens, ducks, and geese quieted their bustle in pens, in small paddocks, and under porches. Their allies, the family dogs, would keep the night predators at bay.

Somewhere, soft music was playing – a quiet voice sang to a plaintive guitar. A mother called to her children, and their playmates ran up the street, anticipating their own curfew. The golden light of candles spilled through the open church doors as the sexton pulled each of them to shut out the coming darkness.

"My family is from the neighborhood known as Tila. We can walk there. I'll bet you are hungry, and I have many questions."

***

Restaurante Witsul-Há was a sizeable eatery featuring open dining under a large thatched roof supported by massive wooden beams. The place was decorated in the colors of the Mexican flag: green, white, and red. Tables and chairs were set for ten and twelve patrons.

"The food here is *Comida Regional*, local cuisine. The chefs use only the food we raise here in the fields and pastures," Elyssa said as she pointed to the large tables. "Served family-style. Most of the regular patrons are the workers from the river trading companies."

A waiter came forward, and Elyssa ordered for the group.

Some of the restaurant's walls were illustrated with renditions of ancient Maya mythological figures, warriors, kings, and queens. The long-past characters from the history of a proud people. Rebecca and Mark were sure that fascinating stories went with each painted human, animal, and divinity.

"Frontera Corozal gets a fair share of tourists because of the ruins. In addition to being close to Palenque, the town is near the once-great city-states of Yaxchilan and Tikal." She pointed to a gigantic feathered serpent that seemed to slither down the wall directly to Rebecca's seat at the table.

"An attempt to represent Tepeu Q'uq'umatz, mentioned in the Popol Vuh, writings. He is the Maya creator of the cosmos. I hope he does not ruin your appetite."

"Not at all, Darling. I like his couture, scales, and feathers, very chic."

"So, how did you get out of those bonds when we were being abducted. You made it look so easy?"

Rebecca said, "It actually is. There is a technique."

"We have a friend," Mark said, "Big dude in international espionage. We spent some time with him not too long ago, and he taught us how to escape a variety of kidnapping situations. Ran us through a bunch of scenarios."

Rebecca used a paper napkin as a prop. She explained, "Duct tape is strong if you have a resistance that goes along the length of the tape, Darling.

"But with a sudden snap and twist movement, you can tear it crosswise. So, twist and pull up."

She made the motion with her wrists.

Mark did a pantomime in his chair, snapping down and forward with a twist in his upper body. He said. "We just combined both sets of moves and poof – rock and rolla."

A pair of servers approached the table with trays of food and drink. One of them nearly collided with the athletically exuberant journalist.

Elyssa signaled that the Americans were OK and not acting weird. She pointed to the dish of a familiar, thick, green, buttery salsa.

"We invented Guacamole. You've never tasted better, my friends."

Baskets of still-warm chips and corn tortillas accompanied bean and rice dishes with a heaping pile of golden chicken wrap-ups.

"Tamalitos — like tamales but different. They are spicy. The corn is ground up and stuffed back into the husk with the shredded habanero peppers and the chicken. Then it's roasted."

"Wow, that's hot!"

Mark's eyes and nose were watery on a red face as he reached for his beer.

Smiling, Elyssa said, "I should have told them 'gringo.' That is *Xni Pec* — Dog Snout Salsa. The habanero is a sinus cleanser, to be sure. Not the *cervesa*, Mark. Eat one of the tortillas. It will take away the sting."

"And that dish is my absolute favorite, Cochinita Pibil."

"It smells delicious, Darling. I'd say peppery with a hint of nutmeg."

"So, its name means 'buried.' You marinate the pork in the juice of a Seville Orange and annatto spice. That pretty orange color and the heavenly smell come from the annatto, which are the chiote tree's seeds, right out there in the jungle. The marinated meat is wrapped in banana leaves and placed in a pit with coal at the bottom. The cooks cover it with dirt while it cooks for hours."

They dined and talked further.

"How about it, Elyssa. Have you recovered from our abduction?" Rebecca asked.

"Yes. Somehow, I always feel safe when I come back to Tila. So much violence... what were they after?"

"A little incident in Guatemala City that caused us to be a part of bringing the Brigade to the attention of the police?"

It was a question, and Mark shook his head.

"Don't think so, Beautiful. I'd say the ransom thing. They're after cash. We need to keep a low profile from here on out. Whoever is running these goons is going to be pretty pissed off with the body count."

Elyssa thought for a moment and then said, "The Ch'ol will close ranks. They will not find us here."

Because his mouth was full of delicious fare, Mark said one word but made it a question.

"Corn?"

Elyssa nodded and explained, "Maize is huge in Latin America. We call it *ixim*. The ancient people worshipped it. There are corn gods and festivals of prayer and thanksgiving for the cornfields even today."

Rebecca said, "When I first came on board at the Fritcher, the museum was doing an exhibit on maize. It is fundamental to the cuisine of Latin America, with an immense number of dishes. Likewise, there is an enormous variety of types of maize, around sixty. They all originate from one plant, a Mexican type of grass from which the Maya cultivated maize as far back as fourteen thousand years ago. So, the ancients turned this weed into an edible plant, and maize then spread among all the indigenous peoples in South and North America."

Elyssa nodded and said, "For us, *ixim* is more than a food product. It is sacred. According to the Maya creation story, humans were created from maize/*ixim*. The plant still plays an important religious and spiritual role in the lives of the Maya people."

An entourage of about fifteen people came through the door and straight to their table. They were representative of four generations with dark colorings and unmistakably indigenous features.

The group was dressed in the working class's simple outfits but with touches of traditional local flair – woven belts, sashes, skirts, collars, and sleeves. It appeared that news got around Tila of the returning scholar and her friends. Everyone was interested.

Elyssa received them with hugs, kisses, and chatter in *Lak T'an* and smatterings of Spanish. She made introductions and laughed as she explained.

"My grandmother wants to know why we are eating at a restaurant and not at home. I am explaining that our visit was unexpected and that we will not stay long. She also says that lodgings at the Tila Inn are out of the question."

Elyssa turned back to her relatives and seemed to agree. Grandma nodded and pointed up. On the subject of their accommodations, Rebecca and Mark seemed to be assigned to a second floor. It looked like that was the plan.

A tall, handsome man reached forward and took the graduate student into his arms. He was dressed as a laborer and appeared to have come from working with lumber. They conversed in Spanish as Elyssa picked wood shavings from his shirt.

"My friends, this is my husband, Efraín Rodriguez Sanchez."

The smile was genuine and pleasant. The young man pulled up a chair with the rest of the family and said.

"It is an honor to meet you. I hope we may have time to discuss why you put my wife's life in danger.

Chapter Nineteen: Chocolate Whiskey

Tila, Frontera Corozal, Estado de Chiapas, Estados Unidos Mexicanos

"Apparently, the Mexican State Troopers got to the accident at the lake. They found only the truck upside down on the scrabble. Alas, the lake is bottomless. Ramon and Diego put the bodies of the other two into the water not far from the wreck."

Efraín thanked his two brothers-in-law and handed Mark the keys to the SUV. He gave his relatives another instruction in the indigenous tongue.

The light from the fire pit cast shadows in the overhanging trees. Family cottages and a small barn encircled a central courtyard. Rebecca and Mark could see Elyssa's family members going about their night chores. Settling the children, preparing food for tomorrow's workers in the field. Here and there, they could see a youngster working on schoolwork beneath a lamp. A few of the family dogs settled close to the fire.

Elyssa's grandmother brought a tray with some refreshments. As she served the two couples, she spoke in *Lak T'an*.

"My grandmother is known as Mamá Xumucane. She is eighty-seven and very well respected. She served in the government offices of the collective farms for fifty years. She understands Spanish and even English, but refuses to speak them in Tila. She is explaining the Xocolatl – chocolate, food sent by the gods to give power."

The drink was strong, bitter, and intoxicating. But quite delicious. The Americans were entranced.

Rebecca expressed their thanks, and the elder replied with a shake of her finger and a knowing wink. She settled near the fire and accepted a cigarette from Efraín.

"What did she say?"

The older woman interrupted and surprised her granddaughter by speaking in English.

"I spoke a warning. Do not take the gods for granted. The dark liquid has powerful effects that must be respected."

Elyssa said, "It can be a hallucinogen and is definitely an aphrodisiac."

"Mamá, where did the Maya go?"

The older woman smiled. The wrinkles of her face appeared to deepen in the firelight. Her dark eyes danced. They seem to match those of her two relatives on either side of her, dark and full of mystery.

"You are looking at them. The people, for we are the people... everyone else is 'not the people,' you see. We still live on the land, in the mountains and forests. We are here and have been for over a thousand years. We keep our traditions and customs. We worship at the ancient sites. We pray the old prayers and tend the sacrifices that keep the universe in balance."

She raised her glass to whatever divinity inhabited the moon, off in the distance, rising above the silver and black river.

"The Spanish padres think we worship their saints. How foolish. They are our gods. Only the names are different."

Efraín said, "Throughout Central America, in Belize, Honduras, El Salvador, and parts of Mexico, but mostly in Guatemala, this is most true. We adapted our religion to that of our Christian conquerors. Today, the Maya number about six million people, making them the largest single block of indigenous peoples north of Peru. The culture and people persist."

Mark said, "Bud, you sure know your history."

Efraín chuckled, "I am a disgraced professor of sociology. My advocacy for economic justice in Chiapas State was viewed as a threat. I was forced out of the University. Now I am a carpenter for this community of the Ch'ol. I leave academia to my wife. She does it far better than I."

"You will soon see what he builds."

Efraín smiled and continued, "Centuries ago, before the Spanish, the Maya people of the southern lowlands most likely suffered overpopulation, which caused the fields to be overworked. So, combine this environmental degradation with possible drought, and many died of famine. There were also the effects of constant city-state warfare, shifting trade routes, and extended droughts. However, what is certain is that the Mayans didn't disappear in the aftermath of the collapse of their civilization. They survived."

In the fire's glow, Mamá Xumucane seemed to give off a soft light of her own. She spoke with the whispering voice of the community's memory keeper.

"When the Spanish came, many of the old cities had been swallowed by the forest gods. What people remained lived simply. The elite class faded into the mists of time. Peasants now, we farmed, wove, loved, bred, lived, and died of the diseases the foreign invaders brought with them. But to the west... the warriors fought. Yes, bloody wars until they were killed or enslaved, the land was stolen, and the last remaining cities destroyed. The gods cried and withdrew."

Now the grandmother spoke in the indigenous tongue. Elyssa said, "My Grandmother has invoked the 'great day of destruction.' What she said refers to March 13, 1697. The calendars foretold the fall of the last Maya city, Tah Itza, to the Spanish on that day."

Rebecca said, "Archaeologists and historians argue over whether or not the Maya had a written history. Yet, there are the hieroglyphs that the ancient ones used to record their religious stories, history, and astronomy insights on buildings and stela. What happened to the texts?"

"The Inquisition."

The term hung out there in the darkness.

"We believe there were hundreds of thousands of books," Elyssa said. "Priests, astrologers, historians, mathematicians, bureaucrats in every one of the great cities kept detailed records. With the authority of the Church, they were destroyed, all but a handful. The people were forced to abandon the worship of non-Christian deities under pain of torture and death."

Efraín jumped in, saying, "Don't be fooled by the Christian symbols you see here. The Maya's fundamental beliefs continue to be an ancient Indigenous religion with a skin of Catholicism."

Mamá Xumucane cackled and shook her head as if a great joke had been played. But she said nothing. In the firelight, she stared at the two Americans as if expecting something to be revealed.

Her granddaughter continued. "The destruction of the writings by the authorities changed how the people handed down their history and culture. Now the memory keepers, the shamans, and the daykeepers — those who kept the calendars, they became the bearers of history."

The professor-turned-carpenter took up the narrative.

"The Maya people revolted many times throughout history against the Spanish and the Mexican government. The final struggle for independence was between 1847–1930. This is called 'The War of the Castes.' The Maya people, armed with little more than machetes, drove Mexican troops from Yucatan to establish a short-lived country called the 'Empire of the Cross.'

A small group of children approached the fire circle with a few other extended family members. At a signal from the elder, they sat close to the group. They did not interrupt. They listened with open ears and large, sparkling eyes.

The professor added more wood to the fire, and the embers sparked with upward movement. He concluded, "Neither the Conquistadores nor the subsequent Latin American governments have destroyed the Maya, though they have tried, and it's my opinion that nobody ever will."

Rebecca said, "Unconquered."

"That is what our people say."

The ancient memory keeper held out a hand and asked. "You. What is your story? Do you seek to steal the gold and jade of my people? Treasure?"

Efraín placed a hand on Mamá Xumucane before she could emphasize her remark by spitting in the dirt. He addressed Rebecca.

"It could be that you are one of many capitalist institutions that have sought to exploit the Maya and our world. Dr. Ruz L'huillier had the Rockefeller Foundation, and now we have the Fritcher Museum of Art. Are you just another American tomb raider, Mr. Quinto?"

He nodded to Mark.

"... complete with your very own marketing office. Or have I misjudged you?"

Mark thought, *Man, talk about an attitude change. I will admit I have seen this before when people are oppressed.*

Rebecca responded, "Yes, you have, Doctor. My museum seeks to save the lost cultural riches of ancient civilizations from destruction and abandonment. In doing so, we endeavor to resurrect the glories of a lost civilization. We can remember and memorialize the people who created a vast empire of knowledge, architecture, and science. Our exhibits and associated programs teach pride and respect for those who created these wonders, maintained them, and gave them meaning and importance. I am talking about a cultural significance that later generations have overlooked or denigrated. We want present and future generations to know, learn, and respect. Time and again, the Board of the Fritcher has affirmed our organizational purpose as an educational institution."

Mark scratched his head. He took up the conversation, saying, "As a partner in this project, I have to tell you, my media company and I are in it with an eye on the social justice aspect. You have helped us see that the Maya still exist today despite countless attempts throughout history to wipe them out. The European conquest of indigenous populations in the Americas brought humiliation, subjugation, torture, and death. The colonists brought the destruction of indigenous wisdom, science, technology, and an insistence that their religious beliefs and practices be abandoned and even denigrated in the name of the Christian God of mercy and love."

"The world needs to be reminded, Darling. Reminded of the evils of colonization, subjugation, and slavery, so that it will never happen again. Throughout history, on every continent, the fate of indigenous people at the hands of their colonizing masters has always been the same: genocide and suppression. We must replace that model with one that fosters respect and partnership."

Elyssa nodded. "Yes. It is an injustice that continues -- the genocide of past centuries in a slightly different form. Economic inequality breeds many social evils – misery, crime, ignorance, hunger, and violence. And this part of Latin America has much of that. People across this land have resisted moral humiliation and fanaticism. The surviving Maya people still maintain an incredible spirit of resistance. The Maya, my people, are not a lost civilization. We remain -- living, laughing, loving, and dancing, but also believing and fighting back."

Rebecca said, "These children and young people and the parents and grandparents who raise them – the human family has the responsibility to honor their ancestors' greatness. Our work, our reporting, and our advocacy attempt to restore their rightful heritage and cultural property legacy."

Mark agreed, saying, "So the real treasure becomes the scientific, technical, artistic, and philosophical knowledge of the ancients. What we are trying to do for the indigenous people is restore their faith in themselves. Hopefully, we can help empower communities to address their present and build their future with the same serenity, strength, perseverance, and wisdom of those who came before them. Fighters – Hell yeah.

The former professor traced with a stick in the dirt as he said, "My previous students... even these, the youngest Maya." He pointed to a tall boy of about sixteen. "This is my work, apprentice, Cadmael. He is an excellent example... Social media is everything for them. In some ways, it has a lot of young Maya focusing on their identity."

Efraín counted off on his fingers.

"They do Instagram, Facebook, and YouTube to share their culture with one another. I see them teaching one another to read the ancient hieroglyphs. They construct Maya memes and games, and there's a lot of Maya symbolism in their music lyrics."

The young builder spoke up. He looked intently at Mark as he said, "Dang, Boss. When we get the WiFi signal, that is. At least the youth center has some regular service."

Rebecca thought, *I have seen this before. They are filled with secrets, especially this boy. He looks forward to the day he can leave this place. But, like Elyssa, he will take it with him.*

Chapter Twenty: The Kapok Tree

Tila, Frontera Corozal, Estado de Chiapas, Estados Unidos Mexicanos

"It is the World Tree, *Yax Imix Che*. And we built it."

Rebecca and Mark looked up at the project, which rose not too far from the family compound. They were amazed.

The trunk was enormous, reaching about 150 feet above the forest floor before stretching out its spreading canopy as if to touch the Milky Way. Arching buttress roots were taller than 6 feet, and a small lift in its ground position was tucked in a hollow formed by these natural braces.

Resembling the basket of a hot air balloon, the elevator's car was of open construction, affording a complete view of the forest as the occupants rose or descended. It docked at the level of the living quarters. Its mechanisms were cables that ran from a braced housing attached to supports on branches above the treehouse's roof.

There were lights above.

"Solar," Efraín said. "You cannot see the rainwater collectors, but they are up there. The treehouse is environmentally beneficial. Nothing about it harms the tree. And it is also meant to have religious and social meaning. Here in Tila, it is becoming a ceremonial center."

The man was very proud of his work.

"It's a Kapok of the genus *ceiba*. This is Ian, another of my husband's apprentices. This project involves how many?"

"Twelve, Sir."

"Cad and I made some of the wooden sculptures like those birds. See?"

"Dude, the water monster. That is the coolest. Fucker is going right down the trunk into the underworld. Cool, right?"

Efraín cuffed the young man with the trashy mouth.

"What, Boss. They say, 'fuck' in America all the time."

The boy got 'The Look.' He cast his eyes groundward as he apologized.

"Ok, sorry, I swore."

Rebecca turned from gazing upward to ask the young men.

"Tell me what this means."

Ian spoke, "The house up in the branches is built in the four directions of the compass, called the… umm … oh, yeah, the cardinal points of the universe. The trunk's spiky bark represents the skin of an upright caiman – lots of them in that river over there. That one there at the base is the cosmic turtle, and the carving on the lift is the bird-god Itzam-Ye, who knows a lot of secrets. I made that one. Cool, yeah?"

Cadmael interrupted, "The tree represents the Maya *Anus Mundi*. Ouch, Boss. I mean *Axis Mundi*. It connects the Underworld, this world, and the heavens, up there in the stars."

Elyssa asked the Americans, "Where have you seen this before?"

"Easy answer, Darling. On K'inich Janaab' Pakal's sarcophagus at the ruins in Palenque. It figures principally in the mythology of creation and cosmology."

"The Temple of the Cross, also," Mark said. "Near the bas-relief of Pakal's son, K'inich Kan B'ahlam, the successor to the throne."

"Pretty smart, dude. Hey, you fight, right? I Googled ya, and…"

This time, Cad ducked, and Efraín swatted the air.

Mark laughed.

The older Maya said, "It is also a guest house. Tonight you sleep between earth and heaven."

***

The interior of the thatch-roofed guest house was beautifully designed. Mahogany planks and other hardwoods were crafted to create elegant spaces. There were no solid walls or windows; the living area was open to the jungle on all four sides and divided by bamboo screens. Separate rooms, each under its own roof, housed a cooking area, a storage chamber, and a washroom, respectively. They were steps up from the

118

main area, out on sturdy branches. A smaller lift hung just outside in the branches beyond the kitchen.

The entire house was enclosed by open balconies providing 360-degree views of the forest, the village, and the river from the tree-top aerie. Under the thatched roofs, solar-powered lamps provided soft, flickering illumination.

As the group settled in the sitting area, Efraín pointed to the canopy beyond the encircling veranda. He said, "Wildlife. Snakes, birds, bats, and monkeys... They were here first. We are intruders. Be kind to them should they stop in to inspect you."

The furniture was also hand-crafted and very comfortable. A large mosquito net wrapped the bed like a shower of white mist, fanning out from the sturdy ceiling beams to the wooden floor. Mark popped open his tablet at the plank-constructed table.

Elyssa said, "You will have to hurry. The village does have one communication tower, but internet service up here is sporadic, I am afraid, especially at night."

Mark got busy. He opened his mail and tapped an icon called "Moneypenny." He entered a series of passcodes and did an eye scan with the device's camera.

"Darling, do not think of doing what you are doing."

"Rebecca, it's a machine. Relax, beautiful."

"Oh, good evening, Mark. It is nice to see you again."

The image on the screen was of a very voluptuous woman in very kinky leather attire. She pointed a riding crop at the viewer.

"Do you wish to resume?"

"Business, please, Eris."

The image dissolved as if melting in hot rain. Eris reappeared as a very conservatively dressed professional in an office, ready to take on an assignment. Her blonde hair was in a tight chignon, and she wore a very chic dove grey suit. She was Kim Novak in Hitchcock's "Vertigo." She was attentive and very respectful.

"Please extend my regards to your ahhh... to Ms. Quinto."

"Yes, I am here, you artificial sex bomb. Pull up your tits, and get your fake ass to work."

Elyssa was speechless. Mark explained that Eris was artificial intelligence, a program customized for his journalism work. She was the latest generation of cyber spy, a gift from a grateful foreign head of state.

Rebecca quipped with an arched eyebrow, "And she is known to do a few other things."

The reporter ignored the remark and fed Eris the information, including the images from the Temple of the Inscriptions. He explained the celestial markings and the missing text. He included the prayer found in the Queen's Temple.

"That's part one. Eris."

The feed sputtered.

"I am losing you, Mark. Please proceed quickly. What else?"

Rebecca interrupted, "Get us some intel on the death of Maria de Flores Benitez Friedman. Also, profile our Miami gays -- Diego Friedman Cortez and Joaquín Cortez. Finally, provide an executive summary on La Brigada de Salvación in Latin America."

Eris looked for Mark's approval. He nodded to the image, and Eris' fingers flew across a fake keyboard -- Mark's own version of MI6 at his service.

"Mark, I will have..."

The screen went blank. Then, "*Servicio de Internet descontinuado.*"

Pulling at her top to show more cleavage, Rebecca batted her eyelashes and mocked in a breathless voice, "Ohhh, Mark, I will have your results in 4.3571 hours, Double Oh Seven, Sir."

Mark chuckled softly,

"You are out of control, Beautiful."

Chapter Twenty-One: Golden Eyes

Tila, Frontera Corozal, Estado de Chiapas, Estados Unidos Mexicanos

"It's like me being jealous of your vibrator."

Rebecca knew exactly what she was doing. All of the elements were there, the spacious treehouse ("So Swiss Family Robinson, Darling."), the night forest's exotic sounds, the sultry, steamy temperatures, and the very perceptible heat from her sexy young man. And her emotions – edgy and provocative...

"Lower your voice, please. Elyssa and Efraín are just one tree away."

She continued and hissed, "When you moved in, you made me throw them all away, Big Boy."

She did her best girl-pissed-off smirk...

He slugged a native whiskey brew.

"Damn right. I provide all the vibration you'll ever need, My Girl."

Mark stretched his athletic body in the semi-darkness, relaxed but ready to pounce.

He knew that shirtless, he would fire up her lust for him, so he unbuttoned his Tommy Bahama all the way and let it fly further apart in the soft, scented breeze. Mark hit an assertive stance, feeling his body respond to her chemistry. He dropped a hand to the front of his cargo slacks while stepping out of his running shoes.

"An action man like me has needs that are explicitly primitive, urgent, and intense. Hard-wired for rough play... and relief sometimes takes many intense dimensions. And you, for one, should know. I'd say you have been one pretty satisfied babe since I met you."

Again, the man-grope, this time with the top button slipped.

She turned from sipping a spicy chocolate concoction at the insult, very ready to fight. Then she caught a dark glimpse of Mark's sweaty chest.

This is getting scorching…

She crossed the wooden floor and reached up to slap his cheek, but he caught her. It was going to be a bit rough tonight – jungle vibes and savage rules.

With the other hand, she pushed one side of his floral-print shirt off his muscled shoulder. It slid down and took the rest of the garment to the floor. She locked on Mark's smoldering eyes.

The Man in Charge ran his strong hands up her back, unfastening whatever held her clothes on. She emerged as a naked goddess of the night in his embrace, enthroned between earth and sky.

This was gonna be fuckin' fantastic.

"Tell you what, hotshot. You give it your best, and I promise not to fake this time."

"Ohhh, you…"

Rebecca snarled as her tender face caress moved up to grab his bronze curls. Her kiss was almost a bite. He reached up to pull her head into a submissive posture, His hard body demanding respect and satisfaction – a warrior lord claiming his prey.

Somewhere, a big cat roared in the night.

***

Mark seemed to devour her.

Rebecca's taste was like nothing else in the universe – an addiction he had to have… over and over. Tonight, he starved for her. Waves of pain/pleasure made her arch up against him. Her tongue and mouth found new places of pleasure on and in his hard male body. His strong hands guided her to his biceps, chest, and lower reaches.

Mark worked her body to satisfy both their lust. He raised her to ecstatic physical heights, unreached and forbidden, covering her mouth when Rebecca screamed. Their passion rose as a unity. Together, they surrendered to the cascading rushes of tremendous desire and yearning like the fever of wind that now tossed the branches of the tree.

The bed could not hold their pagan energy, so they stood and lifted and rolled on the floor. They pressed each other against the railings and posts high above the jungle floor in the hot darkness.

They were wet. He was hard and powerful. She was soft, round, and scorchingly insistent. They gripped, entwined, and slapped. She clawed at his back and buttocks. He pulled her closer, going deep inside. Rebecca's eyes were wild and fiery. Mark's were dark and brutal.

Sensations were electric and extreme. They gasped, cursed, growled, and profaned in three languages. They called up gods and devils, forces beyond the physical, conjurers of the fires of lust.

... deeper and harder and rougher and hotter and more and more and more...

... a besieging hunger... irresistible and penetrating torment... and... and... and... a scream of ecstatic release... the gasp of savage passion... the echoed cries of iniquitous abandonment... and then...

Oblivion.

Sleep.

***

The intense frenzy in the House of the World Tree stopped. A stillness seemed to descend over the world. The branches gave over to the gentle sighing of the night breeze. Off in the near distance, the velvet black of the river reflected the moon and the stars. Venus began her descent over the western hills.

A jaguar stepped carefully along a thick branch. She made no sound and little disturbance to her cover of foliage. Her sleek, black fur seemed to shimmer in the starlight. As she came to a crotch in the tree, the cat lowered her haunches and rested her head on her front paws. Her golden eyes were like small lamps in the darkness as she watched the two exhausted lovers entangled in the sheets and each other.

Chapter Twenty-Two: A Bolt of Fire and Light

Tila, Frontera Corozal, Estado de Chiapas, Estados Unidos Mexicanos

"Darling, I am far too big for you. Sorry."

The snake tasted the air between them with her forked tongue. She blinked her black and sapphire eyes and kinked her body, rising back up and away from the opening in the mosquito netting. The reptile with the green and blue scales obviously agreed with the human's assessment. She slowly made her way back up and out through an opening in the thatched roof.

Rebecca turned and reached toward Mark's side of the bed, but he was gone.

Fine. So much for the morning after the night before. Just like a man.

Someone had brought a tray of fruits, hot coffee, and juices up and left them on the broad wooden table. Bath towels were set out on a chair. The main lift was in the treehouse dock. She had slept through "room service."

Propped up on pillows, she pulled at her mane of lustrous mahogany hair. Rebecca watched the colorful birds in the near branches hop, fly, and do their bird things, chasing each other and soaring in and away. Rebecca was lost in a rewind of the previous night's lovemaking. Her body ached with memory and a yearning for more.

Once upon a time, she had explored the physical and emotional power of love at first sight with her bestie's husband, Nick. The Bronx boy spoke of being "hit by the thunderbolt."

In her reverie, she remembered: "Yeah, Girl. Happens to me a lot to tell the truth. But then again, I'm Italian American. Yeah, well, you're a sexy Latin, so you get it too — genetic friskiness. Hardwired for the racey and passionate."

"Ok, so, you see this guy and BAM! He's hot, and he knows it, and baby's gotta get some. The whole thing is sudden and hottern fuck. Afterward, nothing is ever quite the same — romance, romance, romance

... sexing-up like pagans... moonlight dinners... music... more romance. And even quiet times together where no one is talking and shit. But that is totally comfortable too. You know, just wanting to crawl into his back pocket and stay there. That's the way it was with Kayne and me-- sudden and totally electrifying. And... and... long-lasting. You know, Kiddo, I have loved and lost with the best of them, but 'the thunderbolt' changes everything. This one did, anyway."

Yes, life totally changed when she met Mark Gadarn, looking like a hunky man-boy in his black tie and formal wear. Uncomfortable yet willing to do the glamor thing. It was at a museum opening, and the world tilted. She was totally swept up in his charms, his intellect, and his smoking hot body.

She and Mark turned heads. Rebecca caught the women's envious glances (*Look at them. You know he's younger, right? Yes, I say good for her),* the alpha-to-alpha nods of the straight men (*Sup, Dude? What's good*), and the shamefully disrobing looks of the gay men. (*Total spornosexual... this doll definitely needs some hot jock. Please, queen, straight men are a hell of a lot of work.*)

Rebecca chuckled, remembering the way Mark's admirers got that glazed-over look of mentally undressing him. The eye fuck coming from all corners, straight, gay, and whatever.

She remembered a line from an old movie.

Leave something on him, Darling. He'll catch cold.

The first time they made love was the entire weekend after the opening of her exhibit, "Seed Blood." Total abandonment... talking burning down the house lovin'. Mark called that Sunday night, and the adventures began.

Mark was sensuously physical -- light-hearted and easy-going but heroic when he "got his Welsh up" about a cause. An award-winning journalist, he was comfortable in her world of fine arts and international adventure. He looked dashing, whether in high fashion, military khaki, or jock chic. Mark Gadarn also possessed a pure and genuine soul. A no-bullshit man, he spoke his mind and used his impressive intellect to make a statement for the voiceless.

126

She was his "Beautiful," and she just adored him.

His laptop on the table pinged. Eris.

He's busy. Sorry.

She got up for the coffee and heard laughter and shouting from the ground. Leaning out over the balcony, she saw the three of them.

***

"Come down for a swim, Beautiful. Bring me a towel, please.

"Ow! Ya little bastard, not cool."

Mark turned from calling up to the treehouse to Cadmael, who had kicked him in the ass. He pulled up his fists in an automatic response to the very sketchy attack.

"Yo, Cad, it's not *fútbol*. It's kickboxing, Dude. C'mere."

The boy walked over.

"Put your body weight on the pivot leg and twist into the motion with the opposite shoulder going down. If you do that, you can lift the kicking leg to strike higher on the opponent. See?"

Mark demonstrated, stopping his bare foot an inch from the side of the boy's head. He held it there in a fantastic extension. His body was bent at the waist so that his head, shoulders, and trunk were no higher than his hips. In that position, he continued speaking, "A kick in the butt is a wasted move, Dude. Too much muscle to get the guy down. Here... right here..."

He moved the striking leg closer to Cadmael's head.

"... is the spot. Lights out, sucka."

Total showboating... and he knew it, but the teenagers were awestruck.

"Once more, Mark," Ian said. "In slow motion. Please."

The man grinned at his pupils.

"The two of you stand on either side of me. Cool. Now, for the sidekick, keep your body in one plane at right angles to your opponent. Yeah, good. Use your arms to balance as you lean down and rise up... yeah, now snap the lower leg and foot at the knee like it's a hinge... yeah, again... yeah. Not bad. Do it again."

A group of little kids had assembled in the clearing below the *Yax Imix Che*. Mark went from group to group, showing them some moves. He had Cadmael translate.

"Remember, it is a sport. Not intended to cause harm. Don't hurt your buds, OK?"

The shot and its aftermath roared, and a flock of roosting birds screamed and scattered between the trees and the sky, enraged at the loud intrusion. The young Ch'ol dropped as they had been instructed whenever gunshots seemed too near. Mark dashed in the direction of the Kapok tree.

Rebecca was in the lift, beginning her descent. The sniper's three shots hit the part of the mechanism that raised and lowered the 4-person compartment of the wooden elevator. The machine's shattered housing supports caused the cage to dangle at a precarious angle just below the tree house supports, 100 feet in the air. The American woman hanging halfway out of the gondola struggled to hold on, reaching with one arm for the lift, one leg uncaught and hanging. Her slippers fell without her.

The rustic structure of the destroyed lift began to disintegrate as the cable fibers began to untwist.

Chapter Twenty-Three: *Max*

Tila, Frontera Corozal, Estado de Chiapas, Estados Unidos Mexicanos

Mark made for a strangler fig, spreading out a short distance from the *Yax Imix Che.* He grabbed a sturdy aerial prop root and pulled himself up, hand-over-hand with breathtaking speed. Higher and higher, he rose into the foliage until he was above the pitching and rocking lift with its struggling occupant.

His climb brought him up to a thick branch running almost parallel to the ground. Mark could stand and travel closer to the space above the destruction. Rebecca was losing her grip, and the basket was turned upside down as it neared the end of its hang-up.

She saw him. They did not have much to say to each other. They were both aware that this was one messed-up situation.

He pulled frantically at a vine and kicked off from his perch. Sailing across the gap between them, he quickly lowered himself, strong arms wrapped in the creeper, coming alongside and a bit lower. Rebecca twisted, reached, and grabbed, falling as the basket broke free.

"Cnuch!"

It was his favorite Welsh curse word.

Her head slammed into his groin. She scrambled to grab him at the waist and made the hold. Rebecca now dangled from Mark's sweat-soaked body, but the vine would not hold the weight of both of them. It began to pull away from its anchorage in the tree's branches. They were set to make a hard landing, 90 feet below.

Rebecca piked her body, and her legs caught an outstretched branch of the strangler fig and wrapped around it. Stabilizing both their descent and precarious swing between the two trunks, Mark switched to a thicker aerial root and began a reverse hand-over-hand descent. Rebecca changed from holding him by the waist to mounting his back. Her beast of burden finished the drop at a reasonable pace.

They touched the ground inches from the destroyed elevator and between a pair of Daniel Green vintage 1950s Boudoir slippers – taupe-colored satin with peek-a-boo fronts.

Rebecca let go of all those sweat-soaked back and shoulder muscles. With one hand on Mark for balance, she stepped daintily into her fabulous footwear.

Mark guffawed and pulled her into a hug up. Holding her out, he remarked, "Only you, Beautiful, would wear poofy shoes in the jungle."

She twirled, " Darling, high fashion is my life."

Mark held her close again, but could feel more anger than fright.

"What?"

"You know what."

He raised his eyebrows – a question.

"I hate the whole 'damsel in distress thing.' Fuck."

They were surrounded by the young Maya who chanted "Max. Max." and "Tarzán." Cadmael and Ian were blown away. They looked like they were in man-crush heaven.

He goofed, "But, you were, Beautiful. Distressed, frail, and in need of a man-save. I mean, but strong in that you managed to hold on and not faint."

Her eyes flashed. She pointed up and said, "Oh, wait, I thought my little acrobatic act saved us in the end. So, as grateful as I am, I will clobber you, Tarzan. How's your..."

Rebecca looked down at Mark's crotch. He turned away from the fans and made an adjustment.

"Yeah, Ow. You came in pretty hard and fast. We can test drive my boys later to make sure no damage."

He winked.

Men! Danger makes them so frisky... and after the bestial gymnastics of last night... honestly!

Elyssa ran up and parted the young folks.

"Are you folks OK?"

"Yes, Darling. So much for closing ranks and hiding out."

Mark asked, "Where was the sniper?"

"On the river as far as we can tell. The border guards took out after them, but their boat was more high-powered. Gone."

"Who spotted them?"

"Mamá Xumucane. She is the village lookout. She saw the boat speeding up the river."

A little boy and a girl rushed up and pointed at the two Americans.

"Max. Max. Max."

"Mark." He corrected with a smile and a head pat. "And that is Rebecca."

Rebecca did a twirl for the fans.

"Oh, my friends. You two are their heroes."

Elyssa chuckled, "In our language, 'Max' is a diminutive for what the ancients called the howler monkey."

Chapter Twenty-Four: The Daykeeper & The Goddess of Discord

Tila, Frontera Corozal, Estado de Chiapas, Estados Unidos Mexicanos

The older woman's eyes glowed with an inner light and urgency of words that had not been uttered for hundreds of years, knowledge handed down by the ancestors. She stopped them as they finalized their preparations to leave Tila.

"You must go to the capital to find that for which you seek. Xelajú. South of here. You must find the Daykeeper. He knows the secrets of the ancients. He will know that you are sent by the child-god, K'awiil. The Daykeeper holds the promise of many generations, like a sack of grain. *Hun k'an*."

She held Rebecca's hands as she spoke in the ancient language, *Lak T'an*. Elyssia translated. Up in the trees, Efraín and his apprentices repaired the damage to the treehouse. The lift and a few wooden images of the sacred animals that hung from the branches were being removed for repairs.

Now, Mamá Xumucane spoke to Rebecca in Spanish as she pointed to the Yax Imix Che, the World Tree above them.

"Ix Tz'akbu Ajaw, I know what he will tell you. "At the rising of the Morning Star, look for the Turtle and the Peccaries. That is where the Ixim God emerges.' Find him. Find the Daykeeper."

She touched Rebecca's cheek and said in English.

"Yes, yes."

She went back to her kitchen.

"Please extend our thanks to Efraín, Elyssa Darling, and to the rest of the folks. I am afraid we made a dramatic entry and are now leaving with even more excitement. Your husband is right. You should remain with your family, Elyssa, until the danger is over. Too many guns. Thank you so much for your help with this project. We have learned so much."

"Let's keep in touch. I want to continue to support your work."

They embraced.

Mark had wandered over and was shaking hands with the two young men with whom he had boxed. They did the man shoulder bump and smiled with affection at the departing.

As they climbed into the SUV, Elyssa said, "Xelajú is the old capital of the Maya in the southern mountains. It is Quetzaltenango in Guatemala."

"What was that your grandmother called me near the end of her conversation?"

"Very strange, even for her. She stayed up all last night, most likely studying the stars. Anyway, she had decided that you are the returned spirit of Ix Tz'akbu Ajaw, the Red Queen of Palenque."

The grandmother hurried back just as they were about to depart. Mamá reached into the pocket of her apron and removed a flat stone and bead necklace.

"*Levántese el pelo*, Señora Rebecca."

Lifting her deep brown hair as instructed, Rebecca felt Mamá Xumucane reach behind. She fastened the teal blue and blood-crimson collar around Rebecca's neck. With wrinkled hands, she smoothed it against the woman's chest near her clavicle.

"*Por protección.*"

***

"Appreciate you driving, Beautiful. I'm going to help us re-focus. So much going on, and I want to make some notes."

"We're heading into the southwestern highlands, Darling. No, Elyssa, so we're flying solo, and I have so many questions. Starting with what was Mamá X telling us besides going to Guatemala? Who is trying to kill us, and why? And finally, where is the treasure of the Maya?"

Mark flipped open his laptop and saw the flashing reminder from his AI assistant.

"Shit. I forgot all about her. Some answers are coming up, I'll wager."

"Turn the sound up, Darling. I do want to hear this."

"Hello, Commander."

Mark was, in fact, a Commander in the Naval Reserves. In addition to war coverage in Syria and Yemen, Mark was respected for his Doctors Without Borders coverage in Rwanda and Libya.

"Thank you for contacting me. This means that you have survived the assassination attempt, and I hope you are not hurt. I wish you had picked up before the sniper hit. I could have prevented…"

"No, I am fine, and so is Ms. Quinto. How did you know of the attack?"

"My monitor on the cell phones of individual members of La Brigada de Salvación is the source. The hit was ordered from Tila. Two gang members used a boat to escape. They used a power launch and abandoned it in Benemérito de las Américas in Chiapas, just south on the Usumacinta River. The police report said it was stolen."

The artificial intelligence superspy continued, "I can see that you and Ms. Quinto are heading south on Highway 307 out of Mexico and into Guatemala. There is a forty percent chance your final destination will be Guatemala City, a twenty-one percent chance that Huehuetenango…

"We are headed to Quetzaltenango, Eris. Stop showing off and tell me more about the brigade guys."

Rebecca heard the sounds of keys tapping. The program simulation was incredibly detailed. It appeared that the virtual associate was correcting her data entry by keyboard entry.

"First, I have nothing to add to Elyssa Trejo's analysis of the astrological messages in the tombs of Palak I or the Red Queen. Her research is grounded in the few Mayan texts on file. The ancient regime attempted to conceal treasure and prepare successive generations for a sociological, religious, and political uprising. There is a seventy-three point six one percent chance that a Savior will deliver the people from their imprisonment. And it is foretold that it will happen in connection with the Pleadies-Venus-Earth conjunction."

"Mark, how would Eris know what Elyssa said to us in the Temple of Inscriptions?"

He held up his smartwatch.

"Not to worry. I take it off when we... you know."

The Goddess of Discord continued through a flurry of fake typing, "Next, it is indeed the La Brigada de Salvación. Their plan started out as an abduction. You both are very high-profile Americans, and the ransom demanded would have been exorbitant. Their other funding sources seem to be drying up at this time. The United States, Mexico, El Salvador, Guatemala, and Honduras have brought criminal charges against more than seven hundred members of cross-border criminal organizations, primarily the Brigade and other gangs. Charges involving terrorism, murder, extortion, kidnapping, money laundering, human trafficking, and human smuggling have been filed. Government authorities in these nations have seized drugs and firearms and filed charges for extortion, illicit association, conspiracy to commit murder, and extortive obstruction."

"So if they are on the run, and they need cash. Eris, why are they trying to kill the golden geese?"

"Commander, leaders of the Brigade, Nelson and Enrique Osterman-Diaz, believe that the U.S Justice Department was spurred to mount 'Operation Regional Armor.' The brothers Osterman-Diaz have sworn to destroy La Comisión de la Verdad -- drug law enforcement for short, and you in particular. Killing you will send a message at the highest levels. I advise extreme care."

"Maria de Flores Benitez Friedman?"

"Mark, Black Gold Commodities, which includes Benetiz Friedman Coffee, Inc., not only represents a great deal of capital, but they are part of an international consortium to end gang violence in Latin America. *La Alianza por la Justicia y la Humanidad*, the group Diego Friedman Cortez and Joaquín Cortez espouse, is funded by Benetiz Friedman Coffee. La Brigada wants that money, and they have offered a reward for the kidnapping of the Cortez couple. However, my data supports the conclusion that your friends will be killed once the ransom is paid. The twins despise homosexuals. Interesting because one of the brothers is rumored to be bisexual."

Rebecca said, "How could she possibly know all of this?"

"There is little that goes on or is said at this age that does not have cyber imprints all over the techno-universe, Ms. Quinto. Emails, videos, committee reports, state documents, criminal interrogation, even Twitter posts... "

Mark interrupted, "Eris is a pro at getting to it all, Beautiful. Encryption and cybersecurity be damned. She gets in and gets out like... "

"*Como mierda a través de un ganso.*"

Mark agreed, "Yep. Like shit through a goose."

"She has a mole."

Eris said, "Your conclusion is obvious, Ms. Quinto, and absolutely immaterial. I will not reveal any more of my sources. Shall I tell you more of the Brigade's plans to destroy you?"

"Easy, Eris."

"Go ahead, Darling. I am a big girl."

The Goddess of Discord spoke.

"T. Jackson Harkness, Chair Emeritus of the Board of the Fritcher Museum of Fine Arts, is one of your harshest critics regarding your human rights advocacy and political support. There is an eighty percent chance that you and he were romantically involved at one time, but we will let that pass, unless..."

"Get to the point."

"He is paying to have you assassinated and is demanding a very public killing."

No one said anything for a few minutes. The road sound under the SUV mingled with typing clatter from Mark's laptop.

"Last issue -- look in your rearview, Becky. You are being followed."

Chapter Twenty-Five: Dark Star

Playa de Santa Caridad, Ocos, República de Guatemala

"Lost them."

"How could that happen?"

"Train barrier came down."

"Our men did not power through."

"No, my brother. The truck stopped running. Just cut out -- no electrical. Like someone or something flipped a switch, and poof! *Nada, Bro.*"

Nelson Osterman-Diaz was furious, "They escape kidnapping and skewer our members. Our best sharpshooters missed shooting them in the trees. Now we've got three *cholos*, paid assassins, and no victims. What do we have to show for this? One dead old woman in Ciudad Guatemala and no money..."

He held up a glass, and one of his girls took it for refilling. The sun glistened on the sensual curves of her dewy body. A mixture of a light sweat and suntan lotion created a sexy sheen on her golden skin. With one hand, she pulled her long black hair off to one side as she did the runway walk away from the brigade's leaders. She set the empty cocktail glass down on the bar, and another bikini-clad beauty replaced it with a full one. They exchanged a sultry look that bespoke their shared bedroom secrets and competition as favorites of the exceptionally lusty brothers.

The seaside estate was far from the *barrios,* on cliffs overlooking the Pacific. Heavily fortified, La Villa El Dorado was as ostentatious as its name. The twins believed in pleasure and power. Built on drug profits and the millions that came with control of human trafficking in four countries, the flashy citadel was the seat of their power. And beautiful women were their enduring passion.

As the young servant brought back the cocktail, "Ricky" stood up and unfastened the top of her swimsuit. He took his brother's drink and handed her his glass.

The statuesque woman let the top fall onto a nearby chair. Lifting both arms above her head, she sensuously lifted her mass of luxurious hair and slowly let it fall back down. She gave a little pout as he said, "Much better, Delia. I just love watching you walk."

She turned and repeated her runway strut. This time, she undid the hip laces of the bottom of her suit as she walked. *It's all about pleasing the Boss...*

"Yeah, so put Ilia Mercado on this, my brother. Hey, you paying attention to me, *esse*? The fuck-ups we have had so far are street-level assholes. And now, four of them are dead bastards. Ilia is a professional."

"Not a bad arse for a *marimacha*,[3] bro. Love some girl-on-girl action in my crib, you know that."

"Serious, Enrique. I want those two. Get it fuckin' done. *No me des excusas. Dame resultados.* Do not give me excuses. Give me results."

***

"She hit 'em from the sky. Tapped into the computers for the train signals and zapped the computer in their Volvo. It's a program called 'Dark Star' that uses the same satellites we have for GPS."

"Mark, we need to swap out this vehicle and move our asses."

"Up ahead. I'm showing a SIXT. I also have a backroads route plotted. It may take us longer, but chances are we will survive the trip."

"Hang on, Darling. We're not waiting around for more shit to happen."

---

[3] lesbian

Chapter Twenty-Six: The Mountain of the Feathered Serpent

La Plantación de la Condesa, República de Guatemala

"The Mexican seeds are for shit. I want this entire section of the mountain terraces replanted with the seeds from Cambodia. The pods are larger, and the latex yield is higher. Take out the cotton on the eastern slope and put in more poppy. Do we have enough cover?"

"*Ay, si, mi General*. The new plastic sheeting will prevent the effects of government spraying. We are painting them to resemble green fields of vegetables. Our crop can grow underneath in this mountain land of the eternal spring."

In fatigues and a mercenary's beret, the woman looked out over the volcanic range and the remote plantation's deep valleys. The landscape rising before her looked as if a crazy quilt of irregular geometric green designs had been thrown up against the slopes of the volcano. Embellished patches of ribbed terraces, furrowed pastures, and corrugated fields crept up from the mountain's base almost to the inactive caldera. The landscape was fringed by the ever-insistent creeping and lurking movements of the jungle.

Workers tilled the acreage and carried precious product up and down the terraces to the barns and warehouses covered by jungle foliage. Guards patrolled the trails, lookout points, and farming sites. Fearful local law enforcement rarely came by land. The natural and artificial camouflage of the terrain kept *La Plantación de la Condesa* hidden from air force patrols. It appeared to be a truck farm — innocent produce and innocuous cotton.

General Ilia Mercado was a thirty-ish, very fit, natural beauty. Her features bespoke a mixed Indigenous and European bloodline. She gave off a serious "don't fuck with me" attitude in a professional setting dominated by men. As Director of Operations, she occupied the top level of the power pyramid for the Osterman-Diaz drug cartel, a secret division of O-D Enterprises. Her ambition was to maximize company profits in the opiate industry.

Her competition was the Mexican cartels just over the border and the criminal gangs throughout Latin America who wanted a piece of the action. La Brigada was their internal terrorist arm.

The Guatemalan government was motivated in recent years to legalize poppy production. It was part of a broader shift in attitudes across Latin America away from the substantial financial and social costs of the U.S.-backed war on drugs. This program was supposed to support the pharmaceutical opiate industry with medical and non-recreational products.

However, Mercado and her bosses knew illegal products equaled more profit.

O-D Enterprises played ball with the drug smugglers on the down-low. Only her best agents ran those covert operations. But she was convinced the Twins needed to come into the twenty-first century. They still operated like fucking Colombian drug lords – sex, excess, gold, and guns. Those days were gone for good.

Play nice with the state boys. Sacrifice a few of the worn-out capos. Emphasize the social economics of the Plantation – jobs, eco-preservation, all that bullshit. "Definitely, Minister. Self-regulation is the way to go."

Smear it all out over a shimmering veneer of techno-terror, corrupt politics, and extreme brutality. It was a game, and Mercado was good at it. She seduced her share of politicians and diplomats from all over the Western Hemisphere. Such brave boys were fighting their "War on Drugs." When the General got them alone, they melted into sexual submission – boy soldiers who wanted to be bad. A strategically placed sharp stiletto heel, a thick belt, a strong rope, and erotic pressure, and they were quickly ready to give her anything she wanted. Blackmail was a strategic device that settled into her persuasion toolbox alongside assassination and torture. Even the gang leaders lusted for and feared her.

Just obey orders, *pachuco maricones*. She hated the street crud that moved the illegal product. Let them all die in the gutter. If they failed her, she turned the government agents on them. The O-D Twins had a powerful force working for them, and they made it worth her while.

142

"I want to see the timeline for this transformation, complete with the financial outlook. We have thousands of acres going from fruits and vegetables to poppy growing, adding to last year's acreage. I want the report to look like a respectable agribusiness prospectus for the Ministry. Do you understand me?"

"*En seguida, mi General.* At once."

"We're not the criminals anymore. We're the industrial backbone of this country. Make it look proper. Pharmaceutical companies – all of that… busted my ass setting up those shells. Right."

She joined her Operations Director in nodding. An immaculately manicured hand patted his cheek with a deadly affection.

"Yeah, baby. That's right, pad the fucking numbers."

She waved him away and said to the other members of her staff.

"The Twins and I will be meeting at the Castillo for lunch. Make sure the airstrip is ready for their arrival. I want to see the Director of Personnel immediately about the stealing situation among the laborers. I hate fuckin' crooks – miserable *ladrones.* Bring me La Princesa and be quick."

The beautiful white mare was led before the General. She let the horse nuzzle her cheek before mounting up on her Princess.

***

"We need to settle a few things, Gentlemen. My recommendation on La Ciudad de Och-Kan is to keep it buried. It has been under these mountains for two millennia. We do not need discovery and the interest that comes with investigation. The Plantación sits on the richest volcanic soil on the Pacific coast. It is remote and difficult to access. All intruders need to be discouraged."

Ilia Mercado unbuttoned the upper fasteners of her uniform jacket – a casual but seductive move. She knew precisely the audience to whom she spoke. Nelson and Enrique Osterman-Diaz watched and listened, sipping brandies in leather Chesterfield chairs in the Castillo's War Room.

The French doors on the west side of the club-like salon were opened to the wonder of the Volcano. The softly smoking mountain seemed to appear out of the verdant jungle and sit on the horizon like a regal deity.

The skirts of her purple and green robes descended in gigantic folds – sky to earth, enfolding the steep hills and lush valleys coming up to the very base of the fortress. The agricultural fabric of the plantation was well hidden in the remote and primitive mountain range.

Nelson lit a cigarette and blew a cloud of blue-gray smoke into the room.

"If I understand you correctly, we have a potential major archeological site beneath our plantation. This is distressing considering our investment in 'La Contessa.' Most distressing."

The general motioned to the Director of Personnel. A portly woman was allowed into the chamber.

"This is Maria Cabrara-Virella. She is a member of O-D's Workers' Relations Team. Please tell these gentlemen what you told me a few minutes ago."

"Your honors, the discovery of the lost city has set the workers, especially those of the Maya community, into a bit of a stir. Legends, myths, superstitions, and taboos have spread like wildfire through the camps. There are tales of a people's cultural resurgence and a turning of the cycle of destruction and creation. There is talk of violence and overthrow, as well as legitimate ownership of the site."

Ilia folded her hands and said, "Thank you, Maria, you may leave us."

The General continued.

"The opening to the ruins was discovered by a few of the children who were herding sheep in the hills and found a cave with these."

She gestured to broken pottery and a few small figurines.

The Brothers examined the artifacts.

Nelson asked, "Did you get them all?

"Yes. We cannot have pilfering and sales to the outside. This would create interest, and we cannot compromise the security of this facility."

"Prevent access, shut down, and discourage all conversation regarding the Lost City. A few examples will keep the workers in line."

144

Enrique waved a hand to indicate his assurance that his suggested solution would work.

"Should government officials become involved, he continued, more drastic strategies will need to be employed."

Mercado turned to look at the fields.

"We have reported that the children who entered the cave have died. Key members of our team have spread the rumor that the cause of death was a very virulent plague sent by divine powers -- Christian, Maya, whatever feeds their fear. The godless believe the area is restricted due to radioactive contamination of unknown origin – a very nice lie."

Nelson raised his glass. He swirled the amber liquid in the sunlight.

"I rather like the divine punishment angle. Excellent as always, Ilia."

Silence filled the room for a brief interval.

"To the next matter. The steps to be taken to increase cacao latex production. The new species will increase current production by fifteen percent over the next two years. With an additional fifty-three acres cleared and planted in the upper altitudes, we will add eight percent more in production totals. Processing facilities here at La Contessa can handle the increase, as those facilities are underused. Our workers will increase their hours or lose their jobs."

She handed each of the brothers a single sheet.

"Projected product output over the next three years and estimated revenues. Of course, this depends on that part of our operation that lies out of my hands– transport."

"The Brigade."

Nelson turned to his brother to make sure he had his attention.

"Our pharmaceutical operations do not realize the profits we see in the street trade. O-D is, in fact, operating on two levels. In confidence, General, we have been discussing the liquidation of our urban gangs. They continue to be a challenge as far as control. If we continue with the traditional transport plan, we will have to install new leadership among the *rateros*. This will amount to a gang war, whatever way you look at it."

The older of the twins continued, "Those sloppy idiots in the Brigade have no comprehension regarding the pushback by the international alliances against drug trafficking in this part of the world. There is a resurgence among the Asian cartels, and the Colombian operations are coming back even stronger. We will not survive with the old ways of mules and fruit truck Trojan Horses."

Enrique seemed to stifle a chuckle.

"Good luck figuring that one out, my brother."

Nelson turned to the woman.

"That is another conversation, Ilia. Because those idiots in the city have a terror approach to enforcement, they have fucked up an assassination. I need you to head up our removal of two Americans who have been sniffing around the Brigade end of our enterprise."

The Chief of Operations for O-D asked, "Capture or elimination? Ransom or punishment – or some combination of both."

Nelson put out his cigarette and said, "Yours to determine. Then convince us it was the correct conclusion to the problem."

The smile that crept across the woman's face as she reached for the brandy bottle was more feral than human.

"Tell me more of these *Americanos*."

Chapter Twenty-Seven: Partners

Eagle's Roost, Aerie Valley, Aspen, Colorado, United States of America

"Ouch, boy. Yo, Kick, pull the drapes. That sun is killing me, mate."

The other occupant of the primary suite did just the opposite -- more drapes pulled and more light. The naked man in the bed flopped over on his stomach and pulled his pillow over the back of his head.

"C'mon, Big Doc. Move that delicious arse. We've got a plane later today."

Mitch relented, coming back around. He stretched his big frame on the bed. Rubbing his eyes, he leaned back on the pillows and patted the empty space for his husband as a sexy look crossed his handsome but sleep-soaked face.

Married life sure agreed with them. They grew up loving each other, and the excitement only seemed to grow through the years. Even during the years when Mitch was working on his graduate degree in Psychiatric Medicine, Kick was his one and only love. But this was a relationship that required a shit load of work.

"Plenty of time for some man time, Hot Mess. Your man can still party into the wee small hours and be ready to rock out at the dawn's early light. Bring that sexy arse over my way, Lad."

Kick pulled off his running shorts and gear and flopped next to his husband. Mitch watched with his arms behind his head. He had learned a while ago to observe with care and caution. Kick's antics were multifaceted and exciting as Hell, but needed to be taken with a grain of salt and some correction on occasion.

"They're wrong, Mitch."

Used to his spouse's quick change-ups in his thinking, the combination older brother, husband, accomplished jock (one has to be some kinda sporty as a kid growing up in Australia), corporate executive, and noted psychiatrist asked, "Who are you talking about?"

Kick pulled in close and whispered into Mitch's ear. He made sure his tongue made suggestive overtures in his husband's ear. "Your admirers..."

Mitch grabbed a fist full of the teasing naked man's hair and pulled Kick's head down into his lap, face up.

"Of which I have oh so many, right?"

Kick interlaced the fingers of his right hand with Mitch's. He made like the imp that everyone knew him to be.

"Ummm, yeah, lots... I'm talking about the ones who think you are a dead ringer for Chris Evans." He twisted his left finger between and along Mitch's scruffy chest muscles. The game was on, and the man's body was responding to each and every play.

Kick was one beautiful man/boy, stretched out across Mitch's thighs. The older man often recalled their childhood in Australia and how Thomas Michael Sorenson, aka Kick, the youngest of the triplets, struggled with bipolar disorder. Only Kick's older adopted brother, Mitch, could get the lad to take his medication by sheer force of will and strong unconditional love. They had come through some dark periods over the years.

"So, yeah, they're wrong. You are much more handsome and have more muscles than Captain America. But, he's probably a lot better in the sack."

Mitch loosened his grip and dropped an arm down to Kick's butt. He tried to sound sincere as he said, "Yeah, I think I hit my peak as far as sexual performance is concerned. Nothing seems to get me excited anymore. Guess you may as well be resigned to live the rest of your days with a celibate monk."

He stroked his husband's glutes and sighed.

"It's a shame. Maybe I should take up Jesus."

Kick shifted and groped in the covers. Finding what he was looking for, he grabbed somewhat earnestly.

"Yeah, right. Doc. This monsta says you're about as chaste as..."

He didn't get a chance to finish. Mitch was headed for the big score.

"No. Stay right here. We have enough time to shower, dress, and have breakfast with our guests."

"OK, just make it quick. I want to squeeze in round two."

"You're killing me, Mess.

"OK, the meeting at the Lodge – are we gonna do this?"

"Yes, Mitch. I vote we get involved. People are on the run from violence and persecution. The incident last year with the internment camp right in our own backyard... shows that the federal government has a way to go in the remediation of the asylum issue."

The older man shifted in the big bed as the sun made its full illumination through the eastern windows of the primary suite. The Main House of the estate had been rebuilt and renamed "Eagle's Roost." It was an architectural wonder in the Western Prairie Style. Lofting up four stories under pitched roofs and sloping eaves, each floor boasted of broad balconies for entertaining and meditating on the Rockies' ineffable beauty.

"I'm with you, Lad. Kids in cages. That has a profoundly damaging psychological effect on children and their parents. That policy has to end."

Kick sat up and responded. Mitch loved how the expression on his husband's face illustrated the determination to focus on the issue and stave off all distractions. This "little kid" look of concentrating over a difficult math problem, Mitch found incredibly endearing and a holdover from their boyhood.

"I thought the former head of the Department of Homeland Security's remarks were right on target. There are many dimensions to this issue. The home countries need strengthening – their economies, criminal justice system, and youth programs..."

"You're right. I believe that's precisely what the Alliance for Justice and Humanity stands for, Kick-- the big picture solution."

He folded his arms and looked at the naked back of his husband. The passionate Kick seemed to be addressing an invisible audience somewhere off the foot of the bed.

"So, as Vice President of Aerie Industries, what do you propose our involvement, Mess?"

Kick turned. His blue eyes sparkled with excitement.

"Come on, Doc. I can see Diego and Joaquin on the breakfast terrace. I want to run a few things by them."

The young jock bolted and made for the door.

"Hey, I thought you wanted more of a little somptin' somptin'."

"OK, so later. I thought about all of this when I was riding this morning. I think it's a great plan.

He turned to leave the suite.

"Kick!"

The man turned in the doorway.

"Huh?"

Mitch pointed.

"Clothes, ya brogan."

"Oh yeah, right."

***

"We try to make the best use of our assets. It started with a program right here at Aerie. I mean, first, the youth equestrian program. So, we combined youth camps sponsored by agribusiness and the equine breeding industry and created a not-for-profit group. City kids get taken out to the country to learn the sport, and we slip in some character instruction."

Diego said, "Careful, Kick. That gets into some areas that may be political – whose character, whose moral character."

Kick smiled and pointed at the artist.

"Right, Aerie's. We got tons of character here, guys. Seriously. Next asset, the Ute, their land is just northeast of us. Joshua Walker Strong Bear, a Ute, is the Master of Horse for Aerie Stables. They love the opportunity to have their youngsters mix with kids from other backgrounds."

Mitch said, "We'll show you the program in action when we tour the Horse Palace this morning. Think you'll like it. Kick has done an excellent job making our breeds some of the finest lines in the country."

Kick continued, "The world, Doc. OK, so the kids get to learn the ways of honor and truth from one of the indigenous communities that we put into the field, like a culture sharing program."

"I advise you to bring some of the community leaders together and get their ideas on this part, Kick."

"Good idea, Doc, yeah. Last...."

Joaquín interrupted. He nodded to their hosts. "This all sounds like a wonderful program. You are members of a very elite group here in the West. We encourage you to tap your partnerships to advocate for systematic change in the governments to the south. I am talking about human rights advocacy and crime prevention. The business leaders you know can invest with a proviso that resources for change are part of the deal. There are many models of that kind of social capital advocacy with mutual benefits on both sides."

"I remember that particular call to action from the Human Rights Conference. I have been thinking about that," Mitch said. "Some of our business colleagues have a lot of clout on the world stage. It is a matter of convincing them that the immigration issue holds a lot of influence on international economies, and together we can work for positive outcomes."

Here in the mountains, the early winter morning air seemed iridescent on the second-floor balcony. It was jacket weather, but the temptation to dine *al fresco* could not be resisted. Not too far away, a large hot tub simmered, occasionally sending wisps of steam into the ambiance.

"Yes. You have the beginnings of a plan here. We would love Aerie Industries Inc. to commit to the networking it will take to create an international advocacy group." Joachin said.

"We have a Board meeting in three days. I will call for consideration on this, but my friends. It will take time. Will you make a presentation?"

"Of course."

Mitch refilled coffee, serving the decaf to an already excited Kick. He said, "Kick is leaving for El Paso later today, but I will be around. I took the day off, anticipating the chance to show you around.

"Cool, what's in El Paso?"

Kick beamed.

"Horses."

Chapter Twenty-Eight: The Barbarian Lord

The Horse Palace, Aerie Valley, Aspen, Colorado, United States of America

"Scott Iverson, Mitch."

"If the intelligence that has been shared with your office, Matthew, comes from Aerie's Directory of Technology, it is reliable. What do you think, Gints?"

The murmur of voices in the stable indicated that the Miami guests were excited about the upcoming afternoon ride. The Master of Horse, Joshua Walker Strong Bear, was showing them the herd's pride.

Back in the *ex parte* discussion at the front of the Palace, the hulking figure of Gints Bergovic, Security Director, spoke up.

"Police would be no help on this, Boss. No offending to you, Matthew, but is true. Scott obtains FBI profiles and sends them to each of you. They are evil men among us, like secret police back in Latvia in old days. They want your two visitors. We must close ranks and be in the alert."

Captain Matthew Strong Bear said, "The technology of my operation is minimal, but I have surplus staffing, Gints. Things are relatively quiet on our lands. What if we assign a couple of my braves to be bodyguards while the Cortezes are here?"

The big Latvian added, "Gints will meet with Security Force Aerie and work up best protection plan. Send to you ASSP, Doctor Mitch."

Neither Mitch nor the Police Captain was in the habit of correcting the hunky security director's spoonerisms. His skill at protecting the lands and personnel of the corporation belied his *faux pas* with English.

Laughter came from the trio as Joshua Walker Strong Bear showed Diego the proper way to mount a horse. Mitch said, "I will explain the situation to your husband, Matt, and the guys from Miami. Get us those bodyguards. OK, Gints? This is Need to Know only. Scott is fine with this and your squad, but I do not want the resort guests, management, or staff to be aware that a problem exists.

153

Matthew nodded and stepped slightly away to make a call to his office. Likewise, Gints nodded and walked back to his SUV, his cell phone to his ear. Joshua was leading the mounted Cortez guys in Mitch's direction. A woman employee followed, leading Mitch's stallion, Atilla. A breathtaking thoroughbred and a gift from Kick. The beauty flared his nostrils and snorted as he recognized his master standing in the stable's massive doorway.

Before the encounter, Mitch turned to the Ute Police Captain and said softly. "Matt, please send someone to El Paso. Scott will give you Kick's information. I will let him know what is going on, but not just yet, I think. It's always better to warn my husband of danger face-to-face."

He took the reins and nuzzled the equine Barbarian Lord. Swinging into the saddle, Mitch said to Joachin and Diego, "You greenhorns ready to get some saddle sores. Teach you how we ride like real men here in the West."

Chapter Twenty-Nine: The Galiceno

Ciudad Juárez, Estado de Chihuahua, Estados Unidos Mexicanos

"I'm interested in three mares and a stallion. American Azteca, yes. That's right. Please show me what you have to offer."

What Kick did not say was, *Impress the fuck outta me, mate. My sources in the industry tell me that your ranch has the best bloodlines in Mexico.*

The rancher bowed and said, "Señor Sorenson, we at Establos Cirollo are pleased to be of service. Please allow me to bring forth our best."

He hurried away, speaking on his cell.

The woman in the serge suit with the cigarette leaned in and said, "Ask them to show you some of their Galiceno stock. Cirollo is world-famous for that breed. That is what I am here to buy."

"Don't know the bloodline, to be honest, Ma'am."

"The Galiceno is a horse breed developed in Mexico, bred from Spain's horses brought by the conquistadors. They are small-around horses used for riding, packing, and light draft. They are often used as mounts for younger competitors. They came to the indigenous communities of the American West via the Spanish missionaries. They are the ancestors of the American Indian Horse."

"Hey, wow. You made me think of something."

Kick stopped talking and pointed to the woman's face. She was attractive and brown-skinned with slightly almond eyes and straight black hair, falling just past her shoulders.

"Classic. Hey, I know you, but..."

The woman offered her hand. "I am Daniella Lamb. My Ute name is 'Brave Horse.' I retired from Washington to live and work on the reservation two years ago. I help out a bit. You and your husband are the white guys next door. You go by 'Kick,' I hear tell."

"Yeah, that's it. My nogging sometimes goes into a stall. Sorry. Now I remember — Special Forces in Afghanistan. You took out one of the big-arsed Al Qaeda dudes, right? Awesome hand-to-hand. Fuckin' hero goes to Congress – Colorado Representative Daniella Lamb... now I remember."

The hacienda was a gleaming white pueblo-style building going back to the 1930s. The building consisted of three low-slung, flat-roofed stories framed by dark wooden rafters that supported balconies, patios, and walkways. The house was framed with a riot of bougainvilleas– blood-red blossoms and emerald green leaves. Three enormous stone chimneys were also cloaked in billows of the tropical vine.

The Mexican royal ebony beams were carried over into the interior rooms. Decorative ironwork in the owner's suite added a flair to the showroom's appointments on the purple-black wood pillars and ceiling beams.

As he acknowledged his companion, Kick's smile was broad and sincere. He resumed his seat and indicated the club chair next to him. Establos Cirollo's executive showcase room in the main hacienda was appointed like a luxury club, featuring trophies and portraits of the estate's champions going back to the 1900s. Prospective buyers were positioned on stylish seating a few feet above a large lower section.

As Representative Lamb settled next to him, Kick raised his glass of Perrier and lime and said, "So what's up, hero gal?"

Daniella saluted with her tequila on the rocks and said, "Just here on some business for the Nation. Interested in the Galiceno for our stock. Funny running into you."

"Hey, it's great to be with someone from the home spread. Aerie Industries and the Nu Ci Nation are excellent partners. Many of your guys and gals work for the Resort and..."

"... your equine industry. The Nation is so happy to partner with Aerie and its youth equestrian programs. At some point, I would like to offer my services as a member of your youth project board."

"Wow. So great to hear you say that. Never saw a kid who didn't love horseback riding. So much to be learned. It's like a school for life's lessons – respect for nature, self-confidence, collaboration... a great sport."

"Pardon me, Mr. Sorenson."

The company representative had returned. He handed Kick a prospectus in a tooled leather folder. The breeding lines and registry of the horses to be shown were printed on gleaming vellum.

Kick turned to his new friend and whispered, "I just love the kiss-my-arse service."

Daniella said with a wry smile, "Money talks. Nobody walks."

With a showman's flair, the agent gestured to the large double doors at the rear of the lower section of the spacious showroom. Attendants theatrically opened the gates as a classical guitarist played soft music in the background.

A white stallion was led into the carpeted show space. The majestic animal was 16 hands high at the withers and was probably around 450 kg. The beauty was followed by a black, a roan, and a grey. All three had straight facial profiles and slightly arched necks. With long sloping shoulders, broad croups, and chests, they were brought forward by livery-dressed attendants.

They never got to the viewing platform. Kick was off like a shot. He leaped down to the lower level and then adjusted his speed to a slow stroll as if remembering.

The agent was reading, "Our first offering is 'Aztlan Tlaloc' sired by Macana del Castillo out of..."

 The black was misbehaving. He was rearing up on his hind legs while his companions flashed annoying looks and stomped forward. As the black horse screeched and pawed at the air, the young handler lost control, nearly catching a front leg and a deadly hoof. The young man dropped the reins, and the horse went into a bucking fit. Other attendants rushed forward as the horse lowered his head between his front legs and raised his hindquarters into the air while kicking out his hind legs. He began to take over the show space with his wild display, and the other two stallions moved into a panic as they attempted to get out of his way.

The agent stopped speaking.

The guitarist stopped strumming.

Daniella poured herself another Calle 23 Blanco on the rocks.

Kick held up his hand. And the attendants backed off. He signaled for them to close the back doors. The reins of the frightened horse flew free. He snorted and kicked, eyes full of fire.

A clear tenor rang out in the hall.

> Once a jolly swagman camped by a billabong
> Under the shade of a coolibah tree
> And he sang as he watched and waited 'til his billy boiled
> "You'll come a-Waltzing Matilda with me."
> Waltzing Matilda, Waltzing Matilda
> "You'll come a-Waltzing Matilda with me."

Kick moved forward slowly as he sang, hands at his side, making eye contact throughout the careful approach.

The crooning had no effect on the raging animal, but the steed circled and turned so that he could keep seeing this new thing coming at him, making those strange sounds. He continued his fit.

> He sang as he watched and waited 'til his billy boiled
> "You'll come a-Waltzing Matilda with me."
> Down came a jumbuck to drink at the billabong
> Up jumped the swagman and grabbed him with glee
> And he sang as he stowed that jumbuck in his tucker bag
> "You'll come a-Waltzing Matilda with me."
> Waltzing Matilda, Waltzing Matilda
> "You'll come a-Waltzing Matilda with me."

Now the steed slowed his turning and jumping. Kick softened his voice with each verse, and the animal stopped. He stared at the goofy human moving slowly toward him. Another snort and head lowering, but his circling stopped.

Now, Kick was softly speaking the lyrics in a lilting voice. He reached into his jacket pocket and took out a small apple.

> And he sang as he stowed that jumbuck in his tucker bag
> "You'll come a-Waltzing Matilda with me."
> Up rode the squatter, mounted on his thoroughbred

Up rode the troopers, one, two, three
"With that jolly jumbuck you've got in your tucker bag,"
"You'll come a-Waltzing Matilda with me."
Waltzing Matilda, Waltzing Matilda
"You'll come a-Waltzing Matilda with me."

The balladeer took a bite and hummed the melody. He held it out, and the horse sniffed, snorted. The stallion turned away, shaking his big head.

Kick continued the approach, the song, and "The Temptation of Eve."

The horse came close, snorted, and took the fruit. Kick slowly raised a hand to stroke the cheek while touching the reins. Matilda was still a-waltzing.

"Ahhh, you are sure a fine one. Yesss... good boyo. That's it. Just a bit of the Andalusian temper of your ancestors."

The horse swished his tail with excitement, but the frenzy was gone. He huffed his new friend and stared with calmer eyes. Throughout, Kick murmured to the magnificent steed.

Now nuzzling the beauty, Kick turned to the startled agent.

"I do not need to see the prospectus, mate. This one for sure."

***

"Well, that obliterated the new acquisitions budget for this year. My husband will be on my arse for that... three and three. I was just so impressed by the line. They have such spirit and visual appeal. I think this will boost our stock considerably."

"Plus the Galicenos."

"Yes. Aerie Stables has been involved with the Interscholastic Equestrian Association through our membership in the United States Equestrian Federation. We teach kids from grade three to high school equestrian sports and competitions. The Galicenos are just the right size for the little shavers."

They watched the sunset on the Chihuahuan Desert Resort's patio, seventy miles northwest of El Paso. Kick had come back from the ranch,

159

changed, and had gone for a run on the Chihuahuan Desert's dry roads and rocky hills. Now, as twilight turned the desert sky to dark purple, the two neighbors shared some evening reverie. They listened for the night sounds, roosting birds, and an occasional howl of a coyote.

"Ok, 'Waltzing Matilda,' where did that come from?"

Kick laughed despite himself.

"Yeah, so not bonkers, really. Back in the Outback, growing up with my three brothers, Da hired a series of tutors. I say a series 'cause we went through them like shit through a kanga's arse, and they quit. One actually had a busted ankle."

"What were you guys, the Trapp family children? So, then an ex-nun comes along and teaches you to sing?"

"Oh, fuck no, we were three deadly bushrangers – four counting Mitch, truly. There were many trips to the tack room carrying Da's discipline strap. My arse still smarts.

"Anyway, this geeky professor type actually taught us one piece of music before we threw him in the billabong, clothes and all."

The fascinating boy/man grinned and treated the deepening desert shadows to...

"You'll come a-Waltzing Matilda with me. It became a family meme."

"Music hath charms to soothe the savage breast. To soften rocks or bend the knotted oak. William Congreve."

"Yes, true, most likely... this case anyway. Poor boyo was frightened, is all. That was probably his first time in that setting, and my being so frantic at the start... horses can sense that. I have learned that my manic energy swings can set them off. Just some lovey-dovey and it gets 'em right."

"And an apple."

Kick nodded and smiled.

"Yeah, always carry a spare around the equines.

Four waiters from the resort brought their dinner, and they moved to one of the patio tables. The space was warmed by a crackling fire pit. Kick pulled a vial from his pocket and took his meds before sitting down. Daniella threw the front panel of her woven poncho over her left shoulder and accepted another cocktail from the server.

As the staff left covered dishes for their enjoyment of Southwestern fare, she said, "Kick, I have a favor to ask."

"What's on your mind, girl?"

"I want to check out the Olivado Sands Detention Center. It is southeast of here, near Brownsville. It's the illegal immigrant kids in cages thing. I'm no longer a Congresswoman, but I want to report what's going on to some of my contacts. The truth, these days, is so tough to determine.

"Will you come with me? I need a fake entourage, and you and your family are among some of the most influential folks in Colorado."

"Sure. I'll be glad to help. I've faced down with the immigration guys and gals before. As a matter of fact, some of us talked about this issue over the last few days with some plans to help. Hey, on one condition, you help with this project I am working on to bring equestrian sports to the barrios of Central America, like an advisor... deal?"

They shook on it.

"Hey, look at that star on the western horizon – so beautiful."

Daniella drew a four-pointed star with a cross in the center on the tablecloth with her fork.

"That is the Evening Star. For my people, it is a sign of hope and guidance. It brings courage of spirit and purity of spirit."

They both looked up as the Native American Woman added one word,

"Venus."

Chapter Thirty: Caged

Olivado Sands Detention Center, Brownsville, Texas, United States of America

"I said, I don't need a bodyguard, Mitch, I... Yes, Doc, I realize that. That's awful about Diego and Joaquín. Excellent. Ran 'em off, eh? The big bads should never mess with the Gints. Haha, wish I were there. Those blokes wouldn't know Christmas from Bourke Street. The Cortezes musta got a bit of a scare... glad they are..."

Kick listened for a bit.

"Yes, but Mitch, I can... No, there has been nothing suspicious in the last few days. Yes, I have been across the border, El Paso, and over this side to the Chihuahua Desert in New Mexico. If anything... Been quiet and empty as a tomb."

Kick paused and listened again to Mitch. He did an eye roll and pointed at Daniella. She flicked her cigarette butt.

"OK. OK. I will... yes, count on it. Thanks for understanding about the horses, Doc. You are gonna love them. See you in a few days. I love you."

Kick ended the call.

He grumbled a bit as he turned to his new friend.

"Let's go. I'll drive if that's all right with you, bodyguard."

***

"It's not summer camp by any means."

"Well, we do the best we can for families. I'm happy to show you around," said Albert Matthews, U.S. Immigration and Customs Enforcement's director for the Olvidado Sands Detention Center. The facility was a family detention center, but one section was for children who had been taken from their parents. The sixty-acre campus was home to about one thousand mothers and children awaiting immigration or deportation hearings.

"We have a dental facility with dentists and clinicians, and free toothbrushes. In here is the cafeteria. We are serving hamburgers, chicken, tortillas, and potato salad. It's all you can eat – three meals a day."

Kindergartners sat at colorful tables in a classroom and colored. American patriotic themes covered the walls of a recreation room. There was a small computer lab.

Outside, both boys and girls gathered to talk or play games. Soccer was popular.

Daniella said, "It appears to be rather cramped, Director. Are the children detained indefinitely?"

"Not under this administration, no. We hope to hold them no longer than fifty to sixty days, enough time to deport those ineligible for asylum and release the rest. The trouble is, appeals take a long time. With more right-wingers in the government, all of this will only become more draconian."

He pointed to a few outbuildings. "Those are our dormitories."

Kick asked, "How many beds?"

"Close to three thousand. Bathrooms are shared. Can you excuse me, please? I want to introduce you to Susan Delborn, our head of Security. She will continue your stay with us."

The woman was the serious type, immaculate ICE uniform, and a by-the-book attitude. Sergeant Delborn had an honest face, making Kick and Daniella feel at ease. They walked in the play yard as they talked.

"Our critics call our facilities concentration camps, calling for an end to Olivado Sands. I hope you are seeing quite a different picture."

Kick said, "Isn't locking up children in large crowds dangerous, Sergeant Delborn? Diseases can spread quickly. My husband is a psychiatrist. He has often voiced his concern regarding stress levels incarcerated families have to endure, as such conditions often lead to suicide."

Daniella chimed in, "Lock-ups are bad for children, the research shows. They do not have coping mechanisms. They want to go home and be with their families. One report from UNICEF talked about detained children experiencing long-lasting harm to their well-being, safety, and development."

"Our guests move around freely. The children play and attend school. They receive medical treatment. We have had only one child die, and it was shortly after she was released.

"Deported?"

"Yes, the family lost their asylum case."

"May we speak to the children?"

"No, Ma'am. I am afraid that is against regulations."

Near the outer fence, a girl of about six sat crying. Through her sobs, she called for her mamá.

Chapter Thirty-One: Meeting Jack

Quetzaltenango, República de Guatemala

"Be careful of the Tumi, Darling. A whole lot of elegance in those ten pieces of luggage. Oh, yes, and that knapsack is Mr. Gadarn's."

The lobby of Casa De Flores Tikal was bright, airy, and filled with Western Guatemala colors. Indigenous artwork filled the walls, woven, painted, and ceramic. There were flowers everywhere – a preponderance of orchids pervaded the cream-colored room.

A massive White Nun Orchid dominated the registration counter. Rebecca was fascinated. The hotelier, Rosalina Ochoa De Leon, smiled as she took Mark's credit card. She nodded to a massive epiphyte near the stairway.

"My late husband, Alejandro, raised them. The bright yellow one is a Spotted Coralroot Orchid. He won a prize for that beauty."

Rosalina hit the bell.

Immediately, a little dog ran from a back alcove, yipping. She was followed by a hurrying boy of about eleven, who tugged at the belt of his uniform pants with a stripe down the side of each leg. He straightened his pillbox hat with a chin strap. The kid came to an attention stance, shoulders back, chest out, and arms at his side. He broke form to push a swatch of black hair back off his forehead and out of his eyes. The boy also tucked in his sky-blue uniform shirt with the hotel logo on the right and small yellow epaulets on each shoulder. The little dude looked like a miniature Roxy Usher.

The three-legged dog sat in front of him between the boy and the Americans. She looked up at their faces and sniffed the air between them.

"Bellboy DeLeon, Hotel Service is not permitted to bring their pets to work. You are familiar with the regulations."

"I'm sorry, Mamá. Oops, I mean, Señora DeLeon. Cauli was just wanting to help out. I'll send her in the back."

His mother handed him a key and said, "Three O Seven. The luggage is over there. Use the bigger Bellman's cart."

Jack spoke to his pal, and the dog slowly exited to the back, tail slunk low. Two-handed, he rolled over pieces of Rebecca's red luggage collection and stacked them on the cart. Mark walked over with his backpack on his shoulder. Jack attempted to push the filled conveyance in the elevator's direction but could not get sufficient traction on the tiled floor. His running shoes spun on the ceramic as he remained in one spot. He puffed.

Mark placed his backpack down and picked up the boy. He placed him on top of the hard-side cases and handed Jack the rucksack. As he stepped to the rear and pushed, Mark said, "We need a navigator, Kid, and you're it."

But apparently, he wasn't. Cauli reversed her travels and scooted ahead of the parade, taking the point on the way to the elevator.

Rebecca brought up the rear. As she walked, she said to no one in particular. "I believe I will take the stairs. Too soon to get my adorable ass on another elevator."

***

"Yes, I am eleven, and that's almost a man. My friends call me 'Jack.' My mother calls me 'Jacinto.' When she's angry, I am 'Jacinto Davide, *Ven aca*!' Like if I break stuff or feed my dog table scraps."

Rebecca said, "I see. And are you the *capitán de campana?* The bell captain?"

"No Señorita, I am just *botones* – the bellhop, 'cause I am in punishment."

"My goodness, Darling. What did you do?"

"Forgot, Señorita."

Mark watched the two of them get acquainted. Jack took the luggage off the trolley and placed it next to the end of the bed. Neither of the two Americans assisted him, even with the big pieces. Cauli was sizing up the tall journalist but keeping one eye on her boy. Rebecca was seated not far from the little lad.

Jack finished and now stood at a little soldier's parade rest, chin up, shoulders back, and hands behind his back. He continued his narrative, "I go to San Cristobal's School across the plaza, and Señora Fernanda is my teacher. I got an A+ in maths."

"That's great. Math is a tough one."

"Yeah, only my friend Rafaela is better, but not Carlos. He is a jock like his brother. You're pretty."

"Thank you, Darling. You have exquisite taste."

The boy addressed Mark, asking, "How tall are you, Señor?"

"Hey, Bud, I'm 6'1."

"My Dad was not that tall, but he could've taken you. I bet."

Mark started to put his hand on Jack's shoulder, but a soft growl began inside the little three-legged terrier. He dropped to Jack's eye level, stopped, and said, "He must have been a great guy, Bud. But folks are meant to get along, don't you think?"

Jack wrinkled his nose and tilted his head, something he did when thinking something over. After a bit, he said, "Yeah, I'm not allowed to fight."

Cauli came over to monitor the action. She pushed off from her sitting position with her one hind leg. To walk, she shifted her weight forward onto her remaining limbs. This changed the dog's center of gravity to a more forward position. Her back end seemed to bob and push ahead as she walked. Cauli was very good at it. Even running was not a problem.

As she approached the trio, her head was slightly down, but her eyes were bright and watchful. Cauli's forehead was wrinkled in deep thought. Her pointed, triangular ears signaled the alert.

No tail wag.

"It's OK, Pal. They are nice people."

Tail wag.

"Tell me, Jack, how did Cauli lose her leg?"

"Oh, she was born that way, Señorita."

The boy stooped to give his buddy some loving.

"No one wanted her, not even her Mom. Dr. Ajurño said she would not live to be a growed up dog. She is a Xoloitzcuintli, not the ones with no hair, though."

Jack petted her bronze, short coat.

Mark said, "I was in the Syrian war. I reported for TV – stories about the people in the war. The soldiers had a K-corps. The soldiers called the dogs their partners. They were outfitted with collars that helped us locate them when they went into the front lines. They also put tiny cameras on the dog soldiers to identify the enemy even at night.

"My dog, Cauli, could do that. She is real good at getting through tight spaces. Sometimes, I sneak her into places in my backpack, too. We can be very sneaky."

"You are just adorable, Darling." Rebecca held out her palm, and Cauli first sniffed it before giving it dog lick-kisses.

Jack squatted next to the dog.

"Yeah, and you know what? Cauli can track real good. I taught her some, but I think she was born with that, too. Once, she found Señora Rivera's runaway cat. Went clear to the next town. We let Cauli sniff the cat's play toys, and off she went. That kitty was stuck up in a drainage pipe, but Cauli found her. Pulled her free too. Didn't hurt that kitty at all."

The little boy's expression seemed to glow with pride.

"Tell me, Jack, is your family Ladino? Do you know what that is?"

The boy thought hard with a pensive frown and an index finger to his cheek. "Yes. People here in Guatemala who are Spanish."

"Well, Darling, yes. It also includes those of German and Italian descent."

"Like my friend, Gretchen Keeler..."

"Most likely, yes."

"Mark's people came to the U.S. from Wales..."

"I know where that is. Wales is in the UK."

Mark said, "Good for you, Tiger. And Rebecca's family is from Puerto Rico. In fact, she was born there."

Jack switched to a recitation tone.

"The Island of Puerto Rico is a territory of the United States. The People of Puerto Rico are citizens of the United States."

"Many people do not know that, Darling."

"They should have studied geography with Señora Fernanda. She raps knuckles for wrong answers."

"Ouch." Mark comically rubbed his to make Jack smile.

"So, I am whatever my mother is. Ladino, 'cause I am adopted. Yes."

He reached for an ear scratching on his best friend.

"I'm like Cauli. No one wanted me when I was born."

"Oh, Darling, I know someone who did. Very much, I bet.

"Who?"

"Your Mamá Rosalina. She and your Papá even gave you their name, De Leon."

"Yeah, I guess. Anyway. Did you want to know about *Los Indios* around here?"

"Yes, the Maya."

"Like the K'iche people. My dad was one. And my Auntie knows lots. She is married to one, as a matter of fact. He works in Honduras. That's another country. My Tía Carmen used to work for the UN. You know what that is?"

Mark scratched his head, "Yeah, Bud. I think I remember."

She helped me with a presentation on Jewish people in Guatemala last fall. I got an 'A' in that too."

"Keep getting those good grades, Bud."

"Not much else to do but school and working here at the hotel. Mamá says it is too dangerous to play outside most times.

"Anyway..."

Jack opened the door to the suite.

"C'mon, pal. We need to get back to work."

Downstairs, the proprietress repeatedly slapped the top of the bell, but no little bellhop answered the constant ding.

The boy and the dog exchanged a worrisome look. Jack shrugged his shoulders and sighed.

"Oh, great. In trouble again."

Chapter Thirty-Two: Wash, Peel, Chop, and Grind

Quetzaltenango, Repúblic de Guatemala

"Make yourself at home, *amigos*, but if you are going to stay in my kitchen, you must work."

She held up a thick vegetable.

"This is yucca. Peel it like you would a potato."

In a white restaurant apron, Rebecca took the knife and propped herself up on a stool with a pile of freshly washed white roots.

"There, *Chico*. Jalapenos."

Mark said, "Yeah, chop'em up. I got it, Ma'am."

As Mark picked up the knife, Carmen Varela-Garcia placed one hand on her large abdomen and the other hand on his. She shook her head as she gave careful instructions.

"No, Señor, you must wear an apron and these plastic gloves. Fold the apron and wear it like an *el camarero*, a bartender. At the hips. Right. All those layers protect your *cojones. Mira.* Even through your jeans."

The cook made a hand wiping motion just at the level of her loins.

Mark did an involuntary shudder and donned the protective gear. He chopped.

"No seeds and stems."

The journalist did an eye roll in the direction of his gal. *Pulitzer fuckin' prize my ass… now I'm a sous chef for Qutzaltenango's own Julia Child.*

"No, Señorita, you are not carving salad tongs. Like this."

Carmen demonstrated. Wack. Zip, zip, zip. Toss in a bowl — five seconds in total.

Now assigned to sink duty, Jack stood on a low stool and washed pots, pans, and utensils. The suds covered him to the elbows, and his own apron went from under his armpits down to touch the tops of his running shoes. From her bed in the corner, Cauli supervised, never taking her eyes from the boy.

He was grumbling.

His Auntie checked on her firstborn, asleep in his cradle, and leaned in to her grousing nephew.

"What is troubling you, *mi hijo*?"

"Shouldn't make men do women's work, is all." He nodded to Mark. "Me and Mark are manly men, is all."

"Hold on, *macho*, no such thing as woman's work and man's work, Tiger. You see that Vanderbilt's woman field goal kicker? Her name is Sarah Fuller. She was the first woman to score in a college football game in Tennessee. Equality rocks, kid."

"Yes, Jack Darling, countless men, many of them famous, do astonishing kitchen work."

"I guess. But they don't have to wear *el delantal* with ruffles on it and *flores*."

"You'd be surprised, Darling."

Rebecca added one more peeled yucca root to the pot and asked, "You worked for the UN, Señora Varela-Garcia?"

"*Hay, sí*. Before I became a housewife, I was a professional." She stopped grinding the corn and threw up her hands. "Men. You can't cook'em, you can't eat 'em." Her hands came down over her swollen abdomen, and she smiled.

"My parents had no boys – two daughters. I went to college, and my big sister Rosalina went to work, cleaning hotel rooms with our Mamá. Rosita became a big shot innkeeper, and I got a job with the United Nations Division of Statistics department. I worked for the director of the Cultural Commission on the Indigenous Peoples. Hand me that big bowl, Girl. Thank you."

Carmen emptied the mortar contents into the container and stripped kernels for more grinding.

"Our offices were in Ciudad de Guatemala and right here in Xela."

The former diplomatic assistant used the ancient name for Quetzaltenango, derived from the old Mayan name for the city, Xelaju.

"That is where I met my Sachi."

She suddenly pointed with the pestle.

"No, no Señor Mark. If your nose itches while you chop chilies, let it itch."

Mark was dancing.

Carmen grabbed the hunky man and a hunk of bread and, with one hand behind his head, pressed the chunk to his nose, pushing his head back like she was staunching his nosebleed.

"What I tell you? Men. Such little boys."

Rebecca laughed.

"Darling, touching places that shouldn't be touched again? Not good."

Mark's eyes were red and watery. He said, "*Cnuch*! This stings."

"You will live, Macho."

Even Jack was sniggering.

Rosalina came into the kitchen. She looked askance at the Americans but addressed her sister.

"Carmencita, if you are finished with Jacinto, may I have him for upfront? By himself, Avram cannot handle this group that just came in."

Not waiting for an answer, she made "Let's go" motions to her son as he dried off his hands.

Jack stepped off his box and undid the apron. As he passed, he handed the frilly apron to Mark. Back walking out the door, the boy made a two-handed point to the soapy pots in the sink.

Mark shook his head, saying, "Ok, now I see how you are, Tiger. Gonna get ya."

"Carmen, we are trying to solve a mystery."

Rebecca explained their adventures in Ciudad Guatemala, Chiapas, and Tila. She recounted their explorations of the Maya civilization and its expansive culture, the enigma of the two royal tombs at Palenque, and the Brigade's violence.

The cook stopped her work and stared at the narrator as the tale continued.

Rebecca spoke of the riddle of Mamá Xumucane.

"She said we must come here to the capital, Xelajú, and find the Daykeeper. She said he would know the Creator's secrets, the Maize God. And something about some sacred animals."

Now Carmen watched the fall of the ground corn through her fingers. She said, "The mating peccaries and the turtle."

"That's it."

She wiped her hands on her apron and picked up a squash, and began to cut it into chunks.

She spoke to the squash.

"There are about eighteen million Guatemalans, of whom about half are under the age of fifteen. Forty-two percent are Maya, K'iche, Kaqchikel, Mam, Q'eqchi', and other Maya people. My husband, Sachihiro, is Mam.

"These communities have twenty-three officially recognized indigenous languages. There are many self-titled Daykeepers, Rebecca, crazy men and women who believe they are channeling the ancestors."

Mark shook off suds and turned to face the two women. "One of them holds a generational secret. That's the guy we are looking for."

"My sense is that it is some kind of eschatological treasure -- something that will bring about the next cycle of rebirth of the people. Something..."

"Or someone."

"A messiah," Mark said.

Carmen chopped.

"What oppressed group is not looking for a leader who will lead them from misery and bring back their former glory, restoring greatness?"

"Look at the rise of the autocrats, Darling, the strongmen, the despots. Washington, DC, all the way to Beijing."

Now the woman looked intently at the Americans.

"Necahual Ahau-Kin, he goes by 'Señor Balam,' the Jaguar. Sorta looks like a spotted cat. Anyway, the old man sells fruits and vegetables just outside in the plaza."

Carmen stopped, put one hand on her hip, thought, and said, "I often wondered why. The larger markets nearer to the City Center would bring him more customers. The Jaguar is very old. It is said he is descended from the priests of Tikal. His ancestors go back more than a thousand years. Sometimes he goes up into the hills near Gagxanul, the volcano, Santa Maria. It is said he has visions there."

Now, the chef intensified her gaze and lowered her voice.

"From what you describe, the crime syndicates do not want you meddling in their territory. They are most likely familiar with your adventures and are up to something that brings you and them together. They will not tolerate interference in their finely woven web of terror and crime. Like the spider's web, they conduct their deadly business reaching far into the land and its people."

She pointed to each of them with a dire warning.

"Walk away from this. The Brigade is not something to be taken for granted. They will kill you or worse. Every day in Xela, we must fight them and their gang violence. First, the Spanish, then the *Federales* in the civil wars, and now the youth gangs — our own young people.

She pointed with her knife.

"And the people on both sides of this war are losing hope."

Thomas Paul Severino

Chapter Thirty-Three: The Jaguar and the Mule

Quetzaltenango, Repúblic de Guatemala

"Buy some fruit and leave me alone."

"Señor Balam, we mean no harm. We are seeking empowerment for the Maya."

Rebecca used the Maya word for Jaguar to gain his attention. She calmly looked over two mangos, one in each hand, as she spoke.

The vendor sniffed.

"More trouble. Things best left alone."

Mark added, "Our intentions are to help the people and end the victimization of the indigenous people of your community."

The old man blinked. Mark had momentarily forgotten himself and used some big conceptual images. He went for the money shot.

"The Brigade is after us, Señor."

The older man sniffed and said nothing. He looked at the Americans. He scanned the Plaza. He brought his attention back to the fruit stand.

"Aapo, I will not be long. Sell something."

The boy continued to pile up the oranges and nodded. He had the look of a child who had already seen too much of life.

"The Jaguar" motioned for Rebecca and Mark to follow him. They walked among the trees and sat on a low wall. The sounds of the evening settled over the garden-like plaza. Flowers that had spent all day nodding in the bright sunshine began to close up as the darkness came on.

Some vendors were closing up while others, like the food trucks, stayed open for the early evening customers. Scents of sizzling deliciousness wafted on a soft breeze.

"They are after all of us, the Brigade. They will not stop, nor will their greed. In their hunger for wealth, they destroy our children."

He pointed to his assistant, who was making up a package of beans for a woman carrying a child in a baby sling.

"He was a mule."

Mark and Rebecca looked away toward the boy.

"Almost killed him… they did kill his parents. The boy was forced to swallow envelopes of the drugs, then starved and sent north. When he was rescued, it took many doctors and weeks in the hospital to save him from death."

"No one wanted him. He has bad dreams, still."

Somewhere, a nightingale called for its mate. Four bats swooped up towards the church steeple, where the bugs were swarming. Lights began to come on in the houses and buildings surrounding the plaza. People moved in the shadow and soft light, hurrying home.

"Doesn't the government do anything?" Mark asked. "The police, the courts? Why are they helpless to mount an all-out effort to rid the country of these criminals?"

"They do some things… not much. It is overwhelming to be at the mercy of these crime lords. They kill your family. We are in the grip of great evil and the destruction of the people."

In the soft lights of the evening, the old fruit seller seemed to transform into Necahual Ahau-Kin, the Daykeeper. He gazed up at the stars.

"Make no mistake, *Señor, Señorita*. They do not fear the government. La Brigada holds the local municipalities prisoner with assassinations, kidnappings, and other crimes. Last year, a police officer, a very good man, disappeared. He was never found."

Necahual Ahau-Kin flashed his black eyes, sparkling in the ambient light of evening, and continued, "They do not fear religion. They make a mockery of the Church and crush those bishops and priests who speak out against them. Over in Chichicastenango… that convent of nuns… horrible. They spoke out and organized resistance.'

The older man shook his head.

"It was La Brigada. No one doubts it."

He crossed himself and muttered a quiet prayer.

Now he seemed to take on an otherworldly expression, and his voice seemed to take on a sing-song-like chant. Most of what he said next was in an ancient language. What was recognizable was. "Only one thing will overcome the evil from the realm of death – the last Ajaw."

Rebecca asked, "An ancient Maya lord?"

The shaman/fruitseller stood up and stepped into the plaza under the open sky. He pointed up.

Seven stars in a cluster now twinkled in the western sky above a cone-shaped mountain dominating the city's horizon.

"We come from there, my people do. It is that one, Maia – that star is our birthplace. Soon we will celebrate the New Fire Ceremony – the fifty-two-year cycle is coming to an end. And so, he rises."

Rebecca said, "Mark, it's the Pleiades."

He took her hand and whispered, "In alignment with Venus."

In the darkness, they heard the old man say, "I will meet him on the mountain, and he will save the people."

Chapter Thirty-Four: Minerva

Terminal Minerva, Quetzaltenango, Repúblic de Guatemala

"Stay close, Jack. It took a lot of convincing to get your Mamá to agree to let me take you with me to *el mercado*. I sometimes wish you could go out more, niño."

She shifted her market basket.

"Yes, Tia Carmen. I will be right next to you. Cauli and me are on the lookout for trouble."

The boy held the dog on her leash and stayed close to his Aunt as they made their way through the bus terminal, buzzing with travelers and the commotion of selling and buying. The Minerva Market was huge, with vendors making competing prices for just about everything. Carmen steered them through the crowd to the food area.

"*Oye chico*, three hundred for the dog. She looks like a fighter. Is that how she lost her leg? I need a winner."

Jack said nothing. He set down his backpack and scooped his angry little buddy into one of the bigger compartments. He then flipped it up and onto his back. Cauli still yapped at the sketchy guy, growling through bared fangs.

See, I get to ride back here, Jackass, and protect my boy. So, back off.

Carmen took Jack's hand as they passed alongside rows of brightly colored umbrellas and tarps sheltering baskets and crates of fruits, vegetables, and other foodstuffs. No placards or signs suggested prices. All transactions were arguable.

A woman in traditional garb moved deftly through the crowd, one hand balancing a basket of oranges on her head. One vendor held up a large stalk of green bananas like a prized trophy. He sang out a low price as a farmer pulled a loaded hand cart almost too close to three women with large sacks hanging down their backs to butt level. A boy in a striped shirt pulled hard on a stuck hand truck loaded with water bottles. Masses of flowers, bunches of sugar cane, sacks of spices, baskets of rice, and net bags of potatoes were like obstacles on a racetrack, confining passersby and tempting conscientious shoppers.

On the cross streets, buses and jitneys crept through the bustling crowds. At the end of the concourse near the zoo entrance, the strangely out-of-place Temple of Minerva presided over the city's hive of transportation and commerce. Built in 1900 by the dictator Estrada Cabrera to honor the Roman goddess Minerva, the Doric-style building symbolized Cabrera's plans to modernize the country and promote it as a Central American cultural heavyweight.

In her maternal condition, Carmen Varela-Garcia had no intention of lugging produce back to the hotel's van through the retail citizenry of Quetzaltenango. She would simply place orders. She stopped at a supplier of food delicacies.

"*Hola*, Manuel. The plantains last month were overripe. I fed them to the pigs and not the guests. You must send me another two weeks' supply quickly as a replacement. Teresita Paudak's at the end of the block has a fruit selection looking to me to be much better than what we are getting from you."

The fruitier spread his arms wide and shrugged. He said almost to himself.

"Ten years, I supply La Casa De Flores…"

Now, to the complaining cook, he said, "And you will pay a higher price for a mealy selection. Plus, her growers use chemicals. You will grow an extra nose on that pretty face. I'm telling you, radioactive."

He picked up a piece of yellow-orange fruit and polished it with a white cloth before offering it to her. He pointed to the delicacy.

"*Caqui*, Señora, persimmon. Seedless and pleasingly sweet. I get these from Israel. My Brother, Escamillo, will be growing them next year. He is putting in a grove of trees. You put Paella Stuffed Persimmons on your menu, and you will have to drive them off. My sister-in-law also makes an appetizer with *caqui* and cured tuna belly… or chutney… *ay, Dios Mio*."

He kissed the tips of two fingers and a thumb, opening them as he brought his hand away from his mouth like a French chef. His large brown eyes sparkled.

Carmen took the tomato-shaped fruit and tasted it. She inspected it a second time.

"Not too bad. Give one to my nephew."

The little man looked around.

"Who?"

***

"You got PS5, right? I like the version in English better. I am going to the U.S. one day, for sure. Live the good life, kid..."

Jack picked up a set of discs encased in a plastic sleeve. He crooned, "Cool. 'The Lost Kingdom.' My friend has 'Horizon Zero Dawn.' I did not think this was out yet. I wonder how much."

Jack was mesmerized by the variety of games in the kiosk. Many were out of production.

"Take it, bud. I will distract the guy."

"Oh no. That's stealing."

Cauli agreed by yipping just over his shoulder.

"No guts."

The street kid stepped between the display case and the proprietor and snagged the game with his hands behind his back.

"Hey, no dogs in here."

The owner moved towards the boys. Jack put down his backpack, and Cauli jumped out of her compartment. She snorted at the owner, sat, and looked up at her boy. Street Kid picked up the haversack and slipped the stolen game into one of the slots.

Jack took the carrier and said, "I gotta get back to my Aunt."

"Hey, you little thieves. Something is missing from this pile. Come over here."

"Run."

He was not fast enough to follow his new buddy out into the street. The angry man nabbed him by the collar. Cauli went into attack mode. The game booth owner reached in and almost grabbed "The Lost Kingdom" while positioning the battling boy between him and the enraged dog.

"Lemme go. I didn't take it."

"It's in your bag, Thief."

Cauli got a clear shot at the man's ankle but was pushed aside by the returning *ratero*. The raggedy pickpocket shot both hands through a piled-up display. Thin plastic blue boxes flew into every open space. Jack stumbled and slid on the cases, but got free. Boy, thief, and dog dashed into the street.

"Come on this way."

Jack made to follow but stopped in the crowd. He pointed over the head of his best friend.

"Cauli, Tia Carmen. Go. Go."

The dog looked at the situation as she heard the command. Street Kid was looking back as the owner tumbled out of the makeshift shop and began to run after them. He grabbed Jack's arm to pull him away.

This is not good. My boy...

The little dog shot back in the direction of the fruit stand and the pregnant cook.

***

"No, no, you don't understand. They tried to take him once before... Look, there is his dog. Cauli. Cauli. Where is Jack?"

The excited animal barked at his boy's distraught aunt. The woman called for help to find her nephew, and a few of the market workers and customers came to help her. Pregnancy often brings instant assistance.

Most were disinterested, however. The Minerva Market was full of unaccompanied children.

Cauli pivoted on her three legs and raced between, under, and around market-goers, moving in many directions. A fast-moving three-legged pup was something to whom folks gave a lot of deference.

"Señora, get on."

Carmen hoisted herself on the back of the Vespa, gripped the young man and her abdomen simultaneously. The driver, using the horn, attempted to follow the frantic dog. People scattered.

"There. Ahead, on your left."

Near the Temple to the Goddess of Wisdom, Cauli was just off the curb where trucks unloaded their produce for the market. She was barking like a fiend. Ahead, a white and green truck, a *camión*, surged up the street. A confluence of traffic prevented them from following or getting the license plate.

Carmen began to cry.

Chapter Thirty-Five: El Esquivador

Quetzaltenango, Repúblic de Guatemala

"Stay behind these boxes and keep quiet."

"Please, I want to go back to my dog and my Aunt. Who are you, anyway?"

The Urchin drew himself up straight and tall in the moving truck.

"I am Domingo Diaz-Sandoval. I am called 'the Dodger,' and you can see why. I am a regular escape artist like the hero in 'The Forbidden City of Gold,' a very cool game. El Esquivador... I get in and out of tight spots."

The boy sat down next to Jack and said, "You owe me, bud. And I can get you outta this fix."

Jack reached into his backpack and pulled out the stolen video game. He looked at it for a moment and said, "I did not steal this."

"Then how did it get in there?"

Jack looked at his captor and at the blue box. He tossed the stolen property and started to stand up.

"Not so fast. Kid. You're staying with me."

El Esquivador nabbed the boy by the back of his collar.

"Ever jump from a moving truck?"

Chapter Thirty-Six: Rebecca and Mark on the Case
Casa de Flores Tikal, Quetzaltenango, República de Guatemala

"It was bound to happen. When the Brigade puts its mark on you… They have been tailing him for weeks. There is no doubt it is their doing. He is lost. Lost. That is all there is to it."

Rosalina sat staring into the inn's small courtyard as if transfixed by the disappearance of her son. She wiped her hands on a towel and surrendered to a place of shock and despair reserved for the hopeless. The police had just left.

Rebecca asked, "Carmen?"

"She is lying down. The doctor gave her something. She told the police everything she could. I fear now for her baby. All of this… excitement."

The innkeeper and mother tried to keep her thoughts and speech cogent. She nodded as if in a dream.

"Yes… complete rest. We will await the police and their…"

Mark came into the room.

"Senora, I gotta say that my confidence in the local authorities is not good. That guy's either an idiot or on the payroll of the crime bosses in this town. I asked him five basic questions concerning child abduction in this city, and he doesn't know shit. "

It was then that Rosalina dissolved in grief, fear, and anguish. Her voice went from a plaintive cry to a wail.

"My… *mí hijo*, my boy. Jacinto…" She tried to staunch her keening and tears with the hand towel. Her body rocked with sobs. Rebecca leaned in to embrace the desolate woman. The woman cried out as Rebecca held her, "He is the light of my life… and so small. Why would anyone want to steal a child?"

Both Mark and Rebecca knew, but it remained for another voice to answer.

"They want to use him to transport, Señora de Leon. They will pack him with drugs and force him through the border to *El Norte*. Cash for the parcel will go through an international banking connection. After that, they will not care about him. But then he will be a risk. He will know too much."

The soft voice continued. It was an attempt to be truthful but empathetic.

"If he is picked up by the American agents, he will be put in a detention center. There are many children in those places. They are camps for the lost."

The waif from the fruit stand – the boy with the deep-set eyes, leaned on his crutch and continued, "We heard the outcry out in the plaza. I am sorry to tell you this, but it is true. If you interfere, they will come for you."

Rosalina pressed her towel to her face, trying to blot out the anguish. She rocked back and forth, trying to close out the world that had taken her child.

The boy, Aapo, nodded to the older man who came into the small parlor from the kitchen holding the very irritated Cauli. He handed the pup to Rebecca.

Old Necahual Ahau-Kin said, "The beast will lead you to the boy. She is wise and fearless. This animal has been sent by the gods so that no harm may come to the boy. She will keep the evil at bay and bring him home to you."

Rosalina touched the head of the squirming terrier. Rebecca held her, but Cauli seemed to want only to race back to the Minerva and await the return of her boy.

Rebecca spoke gently to the distraught mother.

"The three of us will find him, Rosalina. Carmen said it was a truck, white and blue, leaving from the market's north side. Mark?"

"Leash in the kitchen, Señora? C'mon, Beautiful. We got some catching up to do."

Aapo said, "I will get you a cab, Señor."

"Wait."

They looked back to see Rosalina standing and reaching out to them. She handed Rebecca a black plastic disc with a gold star on it. It was about the size of a peso. Rebecca turned it over in her hand while showing Mark.

"Mark, it's a kid's Com-Con thing. Captain America's shield in miniature.

Mark turned the disc and held it to the light.

"It's a tracker."

Rebecca looked at Rosalina with curiosity.

"Jacinto gave you this?"

"*Sí*, Señorita Rebecca. Jacinto loves tech gadgets. He told me he could find me with that black button, but I do not know how it works. And anyway, I am not the one who is lost."

Mark held it up.

"It works with your cell phone. Does Jacinto have one?"

"*Sí*, Señor Mark. His backpack is a very unique creation. Many secret compartments and hidden things, with decorations and superheroes all over them. His... whatever this is... is pinned to the back."

Rebecca took the tracker and bent over Jack's best friend. She fiddled with the dog's collar a bit before standing back up. She gave Mark a wink.

The man grinned and looked at this woman in the eyes. He gave Cauli full rein as they headed out to the street.

"To paraphrase something I often heard in Afghanistan, Beautiful, 'No one's getting lost on this mission.' That includes the pooch."

Chapter Thirty-Seven: The Parish Boy's Progress

The Barrio, Quetzaltenango, Repúblic de Guatemala

"*Mi querido,* welcome to our little home. I presume Mr. Diaz-Sandoval has helped you to find your way here. Our little clubhouse is just right for boys like you. Mind the fallen beams. Our band of warriors will make you feel at home."

The speaker was anywhere from twenty to forty, the kind of person who showed few age marks. His wrists were loaded with rubber and leather bracelets, peppered with metal grommets and bedazzles. He wore a denim vest over a blue and black T-shirt with Adam Levin on the front. The singer was shirtless, smeared with stage lights, and leaping forward, howling a savage lyric into a microphone during a Maroon 5 performance. Sweat and colored lights accentuated the singer's many tattoos, somewhat mimicked on the wearer — bodies inked with the spots of a contemporary panther.

Through fingerless leather gloves, the street denizen scratched a kneehole of lacerated jeans. He continued, "I am your *Maquinista,* the Engineer, the Mechanic. You call me 'Sir' like the rest of the boys. Marco, my lovely boy, beans and rice for this one."

Jack was frightened. Although the man was slight of stature, he moved with the grace of the lean and wiry. A hunting knife was strapped down into purple and red high tops. The goth makeup on his eyes and lips accentuated the bizarre cut of his jet-black hair. It was razored to the skin up to the temples. A forest of black sprouted above this line, tumbling onto the left forehead to below the cheekbone. An artful barber had carved three curves and the word *Alboroto,* "Rampage," into the shaved hair of the back of his skull, curling up and over his right ear.

Without saying another word, "The Engineer" carefully lifted the backpack from the grip of the petrified boy. He examined its contents, replaced them, and handed back the piece. Jack's eyes were as big as saucers in the dim light of the tumbledown building. Although it was mid-afternoon, the thick walls of stone and adobe, combined with the caved-in wooden ceiling, created a darkness that seemed to hold danger close by. In the shadows, the faces and voices of other boys filled in around the piles of rubble.

Someone near a fire handed Jack a pie plate with some food. He looked at it for a long time. The food seemed to run together and be all the same gray color. Jack set the plate on a broken chair. A pair of dirty, greedy hands made it disappear.

"No, thank you."

Jack turned in the space to face the way they had entered. El Esquivador blocked the way. Other openings were blocked by the residents of the Club House. The Mechanic looked at their most recent acquisition. He smiled.

It was then that Jack began to cry.

"Take him upstairs, Domingo."

***

"We work these produce trucks all the way north to Ciudad Juárez. That's on the U.S. border with Mexico. Three days total. Then we turn around and come back."

Jack said nothing. He was tired of crying and being sad. The group of ruffians in the rat hole was far from friendly, yet no one gave him trouble. It seemed the plan was to move him out before the authorities searched for him.

The Dodger never left his side. They went into the street just once to do some stealing, but Jack never saw a chance of escape. It all happened before the boy was even aware of the thievery. Dom was slipping stuff into Jack's backpack like a magician.

"Just run and don't ask any questions, *chicito*."

The older boy turned over his take to a crooning Mechanic, whom Jack thought might have been a girl in disguise. The evil leader of the young band hugged Domingo, examining each piece of stolen goods.

"You are the best of all the *rateros*. I am going to promote you soon."

The Chief of the Thieves looked carefully at the little boy.

196

"How did he do?"

"Good, Boss. The people think he is cute. One guy gave him an apple."

Jack looked down at his shoes and made a wet-sounding sigh. He desperately wanted to go home to his family, his friends, and his dog. He even wanted to go to school and study more with Señora Fernanda.

"Here, *Chico*. Save this."

Jack looked at the ten-centavo piece like he was staring at a spider. He slowly put it in his bag.

"The Dodger will show you how to earn a quetzal in no time. Now, you boys get some of those sausages before they are all gone. We are going to move you out early tomorrow – a bit of a vacation, my dear."

***

"What's that one for?"

Maria touched a pin on the front of Jack's backpack.

"I got that online, also. Cost a lot. It is a badge for Aquaman."

"He looks like a... a... whatchamacallit... a...."

A little urchin in the back of the pile of debris called out, "A mermaid like that Disney movie. You are so stupid."

Sancho defended his sister.

"Shut up, La Shuka. We have never been to the movies, is all."

"Don't call me that, Pig Boy. My name is Lena."

Jack jumped in.

"Lotsa these badges and stuff are about heroes who defend us against the bad guys and evil things... women, even."

He hoped to calm the angry little outcast as he drew attention to one of his badges – a pair of golden, winged W's, nestled one on top of the other.

"This is for Wonder Woman. I got a comic about her, see? She is beautiful and really strong. Got a golden rope and an invisible plane. She's not one of the Avengers like Thor and Iron Man, but she is powerful like Superman, Batman, or..."

He touched another embroidered badge depicting a bolt of lightning.

"The Flash."

The dirty little child paged through the magazine. She touched the superhero's long, luxurious hair, pulled back by her golden headband/crown in one of the panels. Maria pulled in to look over the girl's shoulder. Lena's eyes were wide despite her attempt to act cool in front of the others.

The boy called Tucki said, "I know that one. He's Nick Fury. He is the guy in charge of the Avengers. I watched one of those movies over at the game store near the train station."

"Yep."

Jack handed the boy another one of his comics.

After a few more pages, the girl handed back the Wonder Woman comic. She settled back but kept her eyes on Jack's treasures. Lena indicated a red, white, and blue shield pin just near one of the straps.

"What's that one for?"

"Captain America."

Chapter Thirty-Eight: La Shuka and Her Hunger

Terminal Minerva, Quetzaltenango, Repúblic de Guatemala

"Rebecca, this is Bartolomé Cabrillo, a former CIA. Bart and I served on assignment in Saudi. He is part of a multinational task force on drug and human trafficking."

"I thought there was no such thing as a former CIA member. Don't you guys and gals have to go into hiding when you leave?"

The dark-eyed investigator had an easy smile and a continental bearing. He shrugged and said, "Some of us have a reason to disappear. In my case, it was my opposite numbers among the rogue nations that seemed to have vanished. I just switched jobs."

Cauli anxiously pulled at the leash, unable to contain her excitement at returning to the Minerva, where Jack was last seen. She made it clear that whatever these humans were up to, she had some tracking to do. She jumped and pulled as Mark took a knee to calm her.

As they made their way through the stalls and carts, Rebecca and Mark brought Bart up to speed on Jack's disappearance in the crowded markets.

"I know this barrio. I grew up here. It is infested with thieves and criminals, many young ones. See there...."

Three children dashed into the street, colliding with a couple of elderly shoppers. A passing policeman was quick to jump into the fray. One of the tiny thieves broke free of the tangle and collided with Rebecca.

"*Fácil mi hijo.* Go easy now."

The kid fought her captor, but Rebecca prevailed. The police officer chased the other two urchins into the market's confusion. Cauli barked at the little stranger, and the child's cap came off. Long, scraggly hair tumbled over the face of the girl. Dirty face and hands, about twelve, she broke loose, but this time Mark stopped her attempted escape.

On the tatters of her torn shirt, she had pinned an embroidered badge of Wonder Woman. She wiggled like an eel in a trap, twisting and kicking into the space between them. The little hairless barked on high alert.

"Mark, something set Cauli off. She recognizes this kid."

"It's the logo, Rebecca. Keep her tight."

Cauli had indeed recognized the insignia and continued her growling and yapping.

"It's Jack's. I remember it on his backpack." Mark was convinced.

Rebecca continued to soothe the frantic girl and asked her name.

Big pout and head shake – the urchin was frantic.

"Lena, calm down."

Mark looked up with a questioning expression. Rebecca turned the inside of the collar of the child's t-shirt. A Sharpie mark identified her.

"Raised in a commune – secure what's yours, most likely."

The girl hollered, "You suck. Let me go."

Mark picked the dog up under one arm and took a few steps to a food cart.

"*Por favor, El Chuchon. Sí, uno. Gracias.*"

Lena stopped her resistance at the sight and smell of the combination hoagie. The cart chef put together a mix of carne asada, a beef frank, chorizo, guacamole, and boiled cabbage. Mark nodded to the raised-up squeeze bottles of mayo, ketchup, and mustard.

She held out both hands.

"*Ohh, por favor, asada fries, asada fries.*"

She got them spilling over in a paper cone. Rebecca held off some of the food -- too much for little hands. The hungry girl went to town on the feast. Cauli got a snack, gulped it as if to say, "If it will make you happy. But we've got work to do. Gotta find my boy."

Rebecca pointed to the image of the superhero.

"¿Lena, donde esta el? Where is he?"

Bart returned.

"The police have the other two. They will end up at the SOS Children's Village, where they would be smart to stay and not run off." He pointed at the gorging child.

"No te escapes. And slow down on that food. *Despacio."*

He continued, "She is known as 'La Shuka,' the Dirty Dog. Also, she is deaf, but she reads lips and signs."

Lena gulped and stuck her tongue out at the investigator. He leaned forward and wiped a smudge of dirt on her cheek. Then handed her his handkerchief. The Dirty Dog pocketed the linen and wiped her mouth on her sleeve. Mark gave her a milkshake concoction.

Bart looked her in the face and said, *"Ahora será enviado a la cárcel a menos que nos lleve a su casa club.* Take us there..."

Brown eyes as big as saucers, Lena looked from adult to adult as she finished her dripping sausage roll and fries – a little more slowly as requested. Cauli stopped her fidgeting and sat next to Rebecca, her canine eyes on the child.

Bart mused, "So many of these *rateros* are malnourished. This kid needs some real care."

He stepped back and made a call.

The girl held up her hands, about to wipe them on her vest. Rebecca knelt and intercepted with a couple of paper napkins. Lena lightly touched the American woman's hair with one clean hand. Rebecca returned the contact by wiping hoagie sauce from the girl's face.

The gentle exchange triggered something. Lena pulled at her vest and looked at The Warrior Princess, then at her captors. Cauli jumped up on all threes.

Rebecca said, *"Lenita, vamonos. Es bueno."*

The ragged little girl slipped her hand into Rebecca's and turned into the crowded market. Two men and a dog followed.

***

Speaking in Spanish, after a short hug up, Rebecca said, "Lena, you go with this nice woman. There will be food, nice, clean clothes, and someone to wash and make your hair nice and pretty."

The wide-eyed little girl seemed to understand the potential consequences of leading these folks to her rat hole. She brought her small right hand up to her face and extended her grimy fingers. The child touched her chin twice while putting a questioning look on her face.

"*Sí. Como una madre* – like a mother, like your mother, sweetheart. We will come and see you soon."

The Children's Services Officer took the child's hand and started back up the alley. The urchin broke loose and ran to her new friend, clasping both of Rebecca's legs. She stopped after a bit and stepped back. She reached over to her vest's left side, took the badge off, and handed it to Rebecca. She pointed to her beautiful American superhero and nodded to complete her identifier.

As Lena turned to take the officer's hand, Rebecca felt two things: tears and Mark's comforting touch. He moved a strong arm along her shoulder, under the fall of her hair, to caress the back of her neck.

***

It was as if a bomb had gone off.

As Bart, Rebecca, and Mark (holding a squirming Cauli) ducked low and entered the Hoyo de Rato, Children from seven to thirteen streamed from every opening in the crumbling ruin into the grim and narrow passageway, overturning heaps of junk and garbage. From as high up as three floors, it rained very ragged juvenile thieves and pickpockets. The mosh-up of the leaning building seemed to suggest there was no rear exit.

Bart grabbed a fleeing boy.

"¿El Jefe?"

The lad wriggled free and pointed up a broken set of stairs. The invaders climbed upward.

The Maquinista had partially fallen through a hole in the second floor. One leg was trapped. He could not seem to decide whether to use all his might to free himself or to secure the sacks of assorted valuables pulled from their hiding places in the panic of his crib's invasion.

He flopped like a fish on the deck of a dinghy – lots of frantic twisting. Bart extracted the thief and held on tight. Cauli went insane with fury.

"The police are on their way, my friend. It will go better with you if you help us find this boy."

Rebecca showed the thug a picture of Jack given by Tía Carmen.

The man pulled a no-fuckin'-way expression while struggling with the burly investigator. Mark came closer and lowered the fierce dog into the space between them. He held the leash just tight enough to keep Cauli about an inch from the legs of the panicked bandit.

The Maquinista freaked, struggling against the body of his captor. It appeared as if the terrified man would climb up on top of the hulky Bart to escape the vicious little canine. Mark restrained the excited dog.

Rebecca said, "If you tell us where this boy is, we may be able to persuade law enforcement from locking you up forever, although your crimes would appear to include human trafficking, thievery, and most likely murder."

"You do not know with whom you are messing, my beautiful, *Señorita*. The Brigade will have its revenge. Of that, I am very certain."

Arms bound at the wrists, the Prince of the Hoyo de Rato pointed with his chin at Jack De Leon's photograph. "That baby is lost. The Americans will get him and put him in a cage. Might as well be dead."

It was then that Cauli snapped her leash.

Chapter Thirty-Nine: Slicing

Highway 190, República de Guatemala and Estados Unidos Mexicanos

"Jack, stop whining, Buddy. We will get you back. Just keep that backpack close, little Dude. That's all we have between us and a whole mess of trouble. You know, you even cry in your sleep?"

"I do not. Don't say that, Dom. I'm not a baby. I guess I'm trying to be tough."

The Dodger pulled his little pal closer to him behind the crates of vegetables. He adjusted the wide belt with the nine wide and flat plastic packages that encircled his torso from his waist to his chest. Thin strips of cloth held the vest in place, attaching to his shoulders.

It was sweltering and uncomfortable in the rocking vehicle. The van had very little ventilation. Four other children rocked along with the crates in the tight spaces. Their expressions were like those of sleepwalkers, thin, stunned, and aimless. They were silent, sweating, and quite listless.

"Have some water, Jazz Bow." Domingo passed a canteen to Jack and the others.

"Why do you call me that?"

"You look like a buddy I once had. A dead ringer, in fact."

Jack waited for the rest of the story.

"'Bout your age, too. So, yeah, he died. They used to make us swallow this crap. The trouble is the packets were for shit, and they busted inside most times. Most kids died after two trips. I was lucky, I guess. They changed it all when they started running out of mules. They do not care a bit about us kids. They just want the money."

"Mules?"

"That's what you are, Jazz Bow. You are carrying big drugs. Worth a lot of *dinero*. I'm glad we transferred it to your satchel, and man, El Maquinista would have a shit fit if he…"

The older boy slapped his forehead and said, "I am so fuckin' dumb."

The Dodger stood up and raised his shirt. Handing Jack his pocket knife, he said, "Cut this off me, Jazz Bow. Be super careful not to slice me or the packets. That stuff in a cut is deadly."

Jack was the right man for the job. He had been deboning chickens in his mother's kitchen since he was seven.

"*Oye,* Maria, Teresa, Sancho, and Tucki, get up, get over here, and lift up your shirts."

Jack worked like a surgeon, skillfully and quickly. Dom stuffed the raw cocaine into the superhero backpack, replacing a bundle of comic books. The children, relieved of their strappings, stretched.

"This stuff can buy us a lot of happiness and freedom, *mí amigos.* Time things got better for us. Here, wad these up."

The five mules began to tear up Iron Man, Black Panther, The Scarlet Witch, Thor, and Hawkeye into colorful paper balls. Jack was not worried. This actually was fun. Domingo used his knife to pry open a crate of peppers and tomatoes. He handed the food to the children and replaced the vegetables with crumbled comic pages. He adjusted the contents before resealing.

"Almost forgot I am an amazing thief."

The *rateros* ate greedily, with extras going into pockets. The backpack rocked between them like a treasure sack.

"Hey, we're coming up on a truck switch. I can tell."

As they gathered up what little they had, Dom entrusted the satchel to Jack. The truck slowed.

The older boy skated on a bit of self-satisfaction. He said, "You know, before my buddy Jazz Bow died in that fuckin' awful way, I used to think I wanted to trade up to La Brigada. Riding on choppers, guns blazing, and causing a shit load of trouble. Getting rich and feared. But... that shit is just wrong, ya know? I don't want to kill nobody. 'Sides. I can really play football. I would like to someday do that. You know, professional. International star and shit."

Jack asked, "How old are you, Dom?"

"Thirteen."

Thomas Paul Severino

Chapter Forty: Cauli

Highway 190, República de Guatemala and Estados Unidos Mexicanos

"Grab him or shoot him, you idiot."

A white streak shot out of the van, turned, shot an angry look at the humans, and ran among the other trucks sniffing and searching.

Stupid and slow.

"I don't want no dogs in the produce."

"You know I don't even have a gun, *Cholo*."

"Then use a rock. Where's his other leg anyhow? Stupid freak dog."

"How the hell did he even get in there?"

"What do I know? I'm the driver, E*sse*."

"Drive my ass, bitch. Help me change the cargo."

Neither of the men bothered with the hitchhiker who scampered in and around crates, tires, and hand trucks. She avoided the workers and focused totally on her sole aim in life.

Wait. Is that a piece of a chicken sandwich? Wow, I thought so. Hold on a second. Why would anyone throw that... gulp, gulp. Gone. Water... there, that pipe. Yeah, good. Water, yeah.

A woman shooed her away, but not after the dog had taken a good drink. She hesitated in her roaming for just a minute.

My boy! Yes, yes... this one.. this one...

She jumped up through the open door and made for the back behind sacks of beans. While the workers finished the loading, Cauli hunkered down and peered between the parcels.

The doors were slammed shut, and the bolt shot in place. It was dark inside. Jack De Leon's best buddy sighed deeply. Her big brown eyes were blinking every so often, but sleep would have to come later.

Let's go.

Chapter Forty-One: The Executioner

Quetzaltenango, Repúblic de Guatemala

"I sent you the coordinates of the dog, Mark. She is moving quickly. I have her in Veracruz State moving North. Highway 180 -- so the conclusion is she is a stowaway or a captive on a truck. Her recent activity would suggest, however, that she is not restrained but is free to run.

"There is an eighty-five point zero seven percent chance her destination lies north of Tampico. This is a photo of the truck, white panel, green logo-- Jardines de América. They are a fleet of produce vans out of Santa Ana, El Salvador."

The AI techy tapped her virtual keyboard. She had taken the appearance of a British codebreaker a la Bletchley Park, but in the uniform of a member of the Women's Auxiliary Corps. An army cap posed at a jaunty angle completed the outfit, featuring a white dress shirt under a belted wool jacket above a knee-length skirt. The avatar's hair was tucked in a snood, and she wore black sling-back heels.

Rebecca did not get the WWII connection.

You would have thought the cyber bitch would have been rocking a Katy Jurado "boobalicious" peasant blouse, fringed shawl, and fiesta skirt. Fuckin' nut job.

"The satellites over Mexico's eastern states are sketchy at best. It may be that the tracker on the dog's collar is wet or malfunctioning. I will revise my data every twenty-three point three minutes. I sent you an app for one-click updates, Mark."

Rebecca asked, "Eris, what about the boy. Where is Jack?"

"One moment, please."

The simulated sounds of techno-research as the image shifted at her desk, crossing her shapely legs.

"In sum, you are aware that the boy, Jacinto Davide De Leon, has been kidnapped by La Brigada de Salvación. I can provide archival data on the group. The boy is in possession of a significant amount of raw cocaine. The most recent image shows his satchel has increased in size by fifty-seven percent, indicating that the child is smuggling more than his original amount."

Mark's artificial intelligence hacker and super spy paused to analyze. After a moment, she continued, "He is traveling with five juveniles. Their destination is any of seven locations along the Rio Grande in either Tamaulipas, Nuevo Leon, or Coahuila States."

She tapped animated keys.

"Revision to the data – Restaurante El Lino in Aguila, Mexico. Seventeen kilometers north northwest of Matamoros, but the information is unclear."

Mark said, "Drug smugglers head for the border, and these days their crossings are through very sophisticated tunnels."

Rebecca said, "By the time we locate the boy, Mark, he could be arrested by the United States patrols. These days, children do not do well in the refugee camps with or without the contraband."

Mark snapped his fingers.

"Yeah... this is where we call in our marker with Diego and Joaquín, right, Beautiful? Remember, they were decrying the children in the cages atrocity. Trouble is, with what he's carrying, Jack may not live to see..."

His voice faded as he looked into her eyes.

Rebecca said solemnly, "Yes... the light at the end of the tunnel."

Eris interrupted, "Something else is coming through, but I cannot make much sense of it. It is very scattered. There is talk, chatter on the deep net. Very strange."

Mark asked, "What is it, Eris? Do the best you can."

"I am operating on the assumption that the criminal underground in the region has a price on your respective heads, but the reason is unclear. Revenge? Possible. Ransom? An equal probability. Wait. You have a treasure... no... they believe you have a treasure, something very valuable. The data analysis supports the conclusion that for what seems to be a variety of reasons, you and Ms. Quinto will be eliminated and the treasure stolen."

Rebecca said, "Old news. They have attempted and failed a few times."

The fingers of the image moved over her keyboard with lightning speed.

"I recommend you keep a very low public profile. There is an individual... *un insano* v*erdugo*... and a city... the beautiful serpent in a lost city...."

Eris stopped typing, turned, and looked directly into the portal. The pupils of her virtual eyes were a deep, ghastly red. She did not speak, but Rebecca did.

"It would seem there is an insane executioner in El Dorado."

Chapter Forty-Two: Boy and Dog Dreams

Near Tampico, Estado de Tamaulipas, Estados Unidos Mexicanos

"Cauli, look at what I got. Gonna fetch the baw-ball, Girl?"

The boy threw the tennis ball as far as he could. He watched it bounce on the freshly mowed grass of the large field.

"There. Go get it, Cauli. Hurry, and bring it back. Good doggie."

The white, three-legged hairless was sitting at his feet when he extracted the tennis ball from his backpack. She wagged her tail in anticipation of their favorite game. Her eyes were riveted on her boy.

Sometimes he did a fake throw, and she came out at a fast run only to realize in about five seconds that the ball had disappeared. Her boy would smile at the joke and wave the ball again. Cauli would sit back down at his feet in anticipation of the real throw.

This one was real, though.

She shot out into the field, eyes on the yellow-green orb. She could hear him giggling behind her and calling out to encourage her. When she clamped it in her mouth, it smelled and tasted of him — the same sensations she got when they would snuggle up to sleep at night.

He always settled her in her dog bed each night, but she would climb up and snuggle against him after a short time. As they both hovered close to sleep, his arm would come up around her. Sometimes, a licking dog kiss, and they both would fall off to dreamland.

The scent and the taste of her boy, like the sound of his voice, meant comfort. Home.

Cauli turned to run back to her boy, but the other end of the field was empty. Was he lying in the grass and just playing with her? Ball in mouth, she investigated.

Gone.

The frustrated dog dropped the ball and barked. Every direction she looked appeared to be the same – no distinction and no boy. Not even his scent.

Gone.

She twitched in her sleep.

***

He watched his best friend race after the tennis ball and just kind of fade. She disappeared. One minute there and the next, gone. Like the armies of the Thron in "Ancient Kingdoms at War." Jack rubbed his eyes in disbelief.

He hit a run in the lost dog's direction, but it was just grass, grass, and more grass. The edges of the field were blurring as if the meadow were surrounded by fog. The further he ran, the more confusing the landscape became, just yellow-green grass and pale blue sky. It was hard to tell one direction from another.

"Cauli. Come to me. Cauli. Where are you, Girl?"

He ran and called more frantically as his search continued.

No Cauli.

Jack called.

"Come to me. Cauli. Come to me, Girl."

The boy sat up, awake and startled.

***

"You were dreaming, Bud, talking in your sleep. Yelling, really."

"Yeah? I was dreaming about my dog, Cauli. I sure do miss her."

"Go back to sleep, Jazz Bow. I think we will just about be there in the morning. This guy is driving through the night. We will talk about what happens next when we get there."

"OK."

Jack wiped his runny nose on his sleeve.

Dom realized that Jack was not going to get back to sleep. The boy with the backpack needed to be fully rested for the last part of the trip. He pulled the kid closer to his shoulder and put an arm around the boy.

"Tell me about Corey."

"Cauli. What about her?"

The truck rocked to the rhythm of the road. Nearby, three sets of eyes blinked in the darkness. Tucki continued to sleep undisturbed. Two of the children who were listening had silently begun to weep. They also wiped noses.

"How did you come to own her?"

Jack sighed wet and deeply.

"There was this man who lived next to our inn, Señor Verte. He had a Xolo, a female. She had puppies behind a shed in his yard-- seven of them, some white, some black, and some mixed. My mom said I could go and see them right after they were born.

Someone nudged Tucki.

"Wha'?"

Teresa nodded to the little narrator as if to say, "You don't want to miss this."

"So, anyway, Cauli's mom had six of those things on her belly that give the milk for the babies, and Cauli couldn't get to one to get some milk on account of she was born with only three legs. She could not even stand up and walk. She sorta dragged herself.

"Her mom just kinda looked at her. Her mom would nudge her every once in a while, but Cauli could not balance. She just flopped over, and I knew she was very hungry.

"Oh, yeah, Señor Verte said he was probably gonna drown her cause she was misformed."

Now, Jack was not crying. He continued in a soft, storytelling voice.

"So, I ran home. My Tia Carmen had a small, plastic baby bottle on account of she is 'spectin', and I swiped it, microwaved some milk so it was warm, not too hot. I went back.

"I fed her a little and then teased her. 'You gotta stand up, girl. Come on, and you can get more milk.' I remember my Mom and Señor Verte just shook their heads."

Now the boy sat up and spoke with more excitement.

"Check it out. So here's what I did. I had in my backpack, that one right there, a very hard-to-get comic book, my Mom let me buy that very morning. It was *Adventure Comics #210.* I'm not kidding.

"On the cover was Superboy's dog, Krypto. Pure white, just like my Cauli. So, I said, 'That's you, Girl. You gotta be like this here super dog — just like Krypto.' And you know what? He can fly. Yes, see?' And I showed her."

Jack got even more expressive as he reached the end of his tale.

"She stood up. Yeah, she did. She was real rickety and stuff, but she took a few steps over to me and the bottle and the comic.

"Anyway, my Mom said I could keep her, and I worked with her over the next few weeks, but I never helped her or forced her or anything. She did it all on her own. Even stairs, yeah..."

Dom said, "It's kinda funny. Her front end goes on ahead, and her back end kinda bounces up and down like *el saltador* – a pogo stick."

"Yep, and she can run too..."

Jack gulped. He was crying again and was very embarrassed. The others were snot-sniffing as well.

Dom pulled him back down.

"I guess she's your Superdog, Jazz Bow. And she'll..."

"Yeah, she is coming for me. Cauli is gonna find me... and then we'll go home."

***

She twitched again.

The dog's close-fitting skin rippled a few times along her torso, and her forehead wrinkled above her closed eyes. The lower joints of her three legs paddled slightly as she ran in her dream. The white Xolo's bat-like ears turned in her sleep like radar dishes attempting to hone in on a beam.

Her dream continued for a few minutes.

Without raising her head or moving her body, Cauli opened her eyes in the darkness of the rocking truck. She stared and then blinked twice.

He is out there. I hear him.

I'm coming, my Boy.

Chapter Forty-Three: The One Who Cleans Up the Dead

La Plantación de la Condesa, República de Guatemala

"Thirty-three of those orphans, that's how many. With the raid on the other two rat holes, another fifteen. Eight were picked up by the Federales. The rest are on the streets. It's just a matter of time."

General Ilia Mercado spoke into her cell phone.

"I want them brought here. Why? They know too much. Most of them have gone on assignments. That's right. I am glad you understand. Also, they are a valuable asset to the organization. Remember, the company bought some of them. No one wants those little thieves. We will put them to work on the plantation."

She paused and listened to the question.

"The authorities will look the other way. Believe me. The pictures... the threats... yeah, they don't want to get involved."

The woman did a take-her-to-the-barn wave to the stable boy holding La Princessa. She walked across the courtyard in the direction of the main house. As she talked, she tapped her riding crop against the right leg of her cream-colored jodhpurs.

"But, the Engineer, I think..."

Ilia stopped on the veranda of the big house and knocked the dirt from her boots. A woman in a servant's livery approached with a towel and a water basin. The General wiped dirt from the trail from her hands and face while keeping on the call.

At the other end of the line, Nelson Osterman-Diaz said, "No. *No te preocupes*, Ilia. If that *puta's* not dead already, he will be. He's also a security risk. I took care of it. You focus on Quinto and Gadarn."

Mercado froze. She was unable to respond.

"Are you there? What's going on?

Her voice was toneless as she continued, "I'm heading there in about an hour. Nelson, I have to be honest. I'm not sure how this will go down with those two. They are very well-connected. Also, they are very smart, not some local civil ruffians we can pay off and then....

He dropped the call.

Chapter Forty-Four: Bath Time

Restaurante El Lino, Aguila, Nuevo Leon, Estados Unidos Mexicanos.

"Sit at the table at the back, near the door with the sign that says '*Ducha,*' Showers, and wait."

The girl in the worn apron was about fifteen. She was holding two platters of food at shoulder height. She gestured with her chin. The restaurant was practically empty due to the lateness of the hour. Two other family members waited on the few customers who sat near the bar. The patrons seemed deliberate in their attempt to ignore the newcomers – the kids with the big eyes. The place smelled wonderful.

Their van driver had sped off as soon as the children got out. The Dodger led the way, weaving between empty tables and chairs. He kept one hand on Jack with his very important satchel.

"Do not look at anyone's face," he had warned.

Their waitress brought a large platter of black beans and rice with a stack of corn tortillas. Passing out plates, she stepped back to let the five hungry minors dig in.

"¿*Baño*?" Teresa asked.

"Through that door, but make it quick. You guys are leaving very soon."

She brought another platter.

Jack made some provisions, rolled up in paper napkins, for the journey and stuffed them in his backpack. He ate a few in between. Dom stepped to a side table and retrieved plastic glasses of water for the young "tourists."

"In pairs, like we practiced. Count one hundred between teams. Me, Jazz, then Sancho and Teresa, then Maria and Tucki. Remember, count to one hundred. And stop looking scared."

"Dodger, if you and Jack have the bundles. Why do we have to go also? The kids who go to the U.S., if they get caught, are put in jail."

Sancho said, "Me and Maria just want to go home, Dodger. We don't want to get put in cages and like that. My friend Jolo said he was locked up for three months, and it was very bad. In the end, they sent him back to Mexico. He had to walk back to Guatemala."

Maria started to cry quietly. Dom thought a moment.

"Change of plans. Tucki is right. Our ride home will be out in the parking lot..."

Dom looked at the old clock on the wall.

"... in two hours, as soon as the driver unloads in town."

Teresa returned.

"So you guys' job is to just cover for me and Jazz Bow until we get back. You got that?"

The older boy looked at Jack and lowered his eyes. The Dodger then said, "Better yet, the truck guy comes back, and you go. Just go."

The six sat in silence for a bit.

"Let's move."

***

The shower room was dirty and wet. The Dodger opened a utility closet door. He rolled out a bucket and mop and carefully positioned it against a nearby wall. Reaching down, he lifted a trap door and hit a switch just beneath the opening. The boys descended a wooden ladder and followed the chain of dim bulbs.

Some of the lights were out, but the stone floor was dry as it slanted down and down. When the pitch leveled off, the tunnel's dirt walls transitioned to a large-mouthed cement culvert, thick and crusty. It dripped down the rounded sides. The crud they would have to walk through was black and muddy.

The view down into the passageway was gruesome and foreboding. The Dodger tried to sound reassuring as he said, "We are under the river, Jazz Bow. How cool is this?"

Jack was petrified. He pointed into the tunnel.

"There's probably monsters like Orcs down in there, Dom. Let's go back."

"It's OK, Jazz..."

The sound of Domingo's voice caused Jack to stumble. The Dodger pulled him to his feet. He paused them both at the mouth of the wide passage.

"OK, lemme go first. Take my hand and hold on to that backpack."

A rat passed them, going the other way. Someone had forgotten to retrieve a dropped ragdoll. Somebody's toy baby was now muddy and wet, sitting below graffiti–chalked words that said: "*El Norte*" and an arrow pointing forward.

It seemed like the trip into the gloom was endless and scary. Finally, the string of lights began to angle upward. The concrete ended, and the stretch continued into a dirt and rock shaft that stopped at another ladder.

"Up. You got it?"

"Yes."

"Just like in the comics. We escaped!"

***

"Who else?"

Jack was silent. He was doing his best not to cry. The Dodger pretended he did not understand English. The younger boy saw that his "guide was about two sniffs away from crying also. The boys pulled on their clothes, even shoes and socks.

The agent held up the now drug-less shoulder bag like a bribe. The last of the comics had not been confiscated. The back room of the KFC smelled of cooking grease. The American agents had been waiting as the boys emerged from the janitor's closet.

Jack reached out to take his satchel and said, "Just me and my brother, Señor."

The agent slipped plastic ties around their wrists and spoke again. "Get in the van, Kid."

Jack held on to his backpack and their small trove of comic books as he shuffled into the vehicle. He did not look at Dom, who was, in fact, now snot-crying.

As the boy lifted himself into the van, he passed his hand over the back of his knapsack. His fingers touched the round plastic button, the red and blue with the white star.

Chapter Forty-Five: The Stars of Myth and Time

Parque de las Flores, Quetzaltenango, República de Guatemala

"This is not turning out as I planned, Mark."

The waxing moon, newly risen, created puddles of soft light dripping through the darkened trees onto the small park across the lane from La Casa De Flores Tikal. Somewhere, a father called for his children, a guitar sounded from a balcony, and two voices were raised in disagreement. The aromas of the evening meal wafted from the surrounding buildings as night came on.

Back at the Inn, a mother tried to focus on running the small hotel. Just a few hours ago, the visit by the police brought little reassurance that her child would be found. And now his dog had run off.

"You mean the trip?"

He pulled her closer as they strolled. In the shafts of moonlight, night moths swirled in a dance of feeding and egg-laying in the open flowers. Now and then, a gecko would soundlessly make a swooping grab for a tasty treat.

"Yes. A simple expedition to create an international collaboration for an exhibit of ancient cultural wonders has turned up a hornet's nest of crime and murder. Now kidnapping and drug trafficking. We have been on the run, and lives all around us are in danger. My Board of Trustees is gonna love this. Mark, I will get the evidence on my Board chair. His ass is mine."

Mark sat on a low wall surrounding a raised bed of roses beneath a canopy of Ya'axché trees. He held her hand and looked up, saying, "One of the things I love most about you is your fearlessness in the face of injustice.

"Art often is a cry to the world for justice by the artists. A work of art tells the world, 'This is us.' We created this, here, in this time, and in this place. And we are a rich and blessed people, divinely created, worthy of personhood, and the acknowledged good that rightfully belongs to every human. You may starve, enslave, exploit, and take our lands, women, and children, but we will endure. Humanity's dignity is ours by heaven's mandate, bestowed on our ancestors and bequeathed to our children."

"So eloquent, Darling. Yes, Mark. I strongly believe in what you say. These ideals are the basis of a people's self-determination."

Here they were again at the intersection of two lovers' hearts and minds. It was a familiar place where passion arose and forged a bond, where words gave way to meaningful caresses and fiery intimacy.

As she spoke, Rebecca reached forward and ran a hand through Mark's brown-gold hair, pushing it back on his head. He was achingly handsome, a night satyr — the strong planes of his handsome face, the contours of his muscles that seemed to rebel at having to be clothed.

Damn. The open shirt... the sexy mouth. Yeah, and those stars reflecting in Mark's upturned eyes...

She struggled to focus on what he was saying. A warm breeze lifted some of the overhead branches. The sky was clear and star-studded above Rebecca as she looked down at her man. As if he could tell of her reverie, he shook her hand, continuing his soft serenade.

"I have tried to convince the Board that uncovering the glories of a people's past is an act of resistance. An act of liberation."

Mark gently pulled her next to him. As she sat, he asked, "How?"

"Our work is an educational enterprise with treasured artifacts. We... endeavor, I guess you would say. We endeavor to free people from the ignorance of thinking that the way things are today is the way things always have been. Ignorance and lies are the evils that we confront for the sake of the folks who speak from the past so that those who come after may thrive."

He moved aside the hair on the right side of her neck and shoulder and began to nuzzle. As he spoke, he added just a little bit more huskily, "Ummm... you and your little museum are not about creating fascinating pastimes for sophisticated urbanites. The Fritcher, Fort Lauderdale, isn't just a tourist attraction. With your leadership, that institution has brought the world's attention to the plight and dignity of suffering folks worldwide."

Philosophy, politics, and making out... one amazing evening. Mark nuzzled

"Ummm... beautiful, you taste delicious."

"My little museum?" She pushed against his shoulder.

"Ya, big lug. The Fritcher is one of the leading..."

She could not finish as his mouth captured hers in a passionate kiss. Rebecca made what was an automatic move. She drew him closer, arms around his torso as he entwined around hers.

When they came up for air, Rebecca pointed to a patch of sky. She said, "Look, Darling. That is Taurus, and that group is the Pleiades, the Seven Sisters."

Mark paused his romantic arts a bit to star-gaze with his love.

"I read somewhere that we are close to a fifty-two-year precession of the Pleiades. A cycle of new birth and prosperity is on its way for the Maya. This one is predicted to be a big one."

"I wonder..."

"Yes?"

Mark attempted a make-out resumption combined with an interest in her remarks.

"When we were in Tila, the folks were doing some kind of ceremony around fires – fire pits, at night. Elyssa said it was some kind of prayer ceremony connected to the Maya calendar and the dawn of a new age. Something about the Pleiades and the Golden Gate of the Ecliptic... "

"I think I remember something about that," Mark said. "Anyway, the Earth is moving through the constellation, between two clusters of stars in the constellation Taurus."

"Yes, Darling. Supposed to bring a cataclysm of fortune and destiny for the people. In ancient times, the priests were sacrificing to save the sun, and the people were awaiting the fate of the world."

She pointed up.

"They timed the New Fire Ceremonies with the appearance of those stars."

Rebecca stopped and looked down at her hands.

"Mark, what can we do about the boy?"

He raised her chin.

"We will find him, Beautiful. Bart and his buddies are on it. If you and I become too visible in this, La Brigada will strike. We wait. We hope."

She wanted to believe this star-studded night would send down positive energy to bring the boy and his dog safely home.

"Hey, Beautiful, let me change the subject here."

"Mmm. I know what's on your mind. Enough with the ancient history. All this talk of fires and stars…"

She pulled him closer.

Mark asked, "How did Jack's father die?"

"Oh. Mob hit. Alejandro De Leon was mounting a grassroots campaign to run for political office. The focus of his campaign was ending corruption in this state. Carmen told me all this. He was run over by a truck. He was a big loss to the anti-corruption movement."

"Damn. Poor Rosalina."

"Jack's father was of Maya blood. He advocated for the rights of the poor and disenfranchised in addition to running his family's hotel."

Rebecca's pocket started to chime.

As she picked up the call, she said, "This better be good, Darling. Your girl is cueing up a huge romantic make-out, and hunky Mr. Gadarn will not be put off."

She listened and said, "Call you back in ten."

Chapter Forty-Six: Añejo

Casa De Flores Tikal, Quetzaltenango, República de Guatemala

"So, if I were there, Mark would..."

"Don't you even start with that, Kick Darling. Mitch is right. You are such a Hot Mess."

"Hey, Kick, you're on speaker. How yer going, Mate?"

Kick Sorenson practically purred as he said, "Hello Marko, you, you, you man, you. What's up?... Opps, sorry Rebecca, I will be good."

"Right. And we will see the Second Coming first.

Mark asked, "How is your husband? Dr. Sorenson's good?"

"Mitch is sensational, thanks. Left him in Colorado running the place."

"So, I'm checking in. I'm in Texas buying horses for Aerie with a new buddy. My brother, Kayne, said that you and Mark were in Mexico. We are just across the border, as a matter of fact."

"A little further south, Darling, Guatemala, but we have a situation, and I think you could help... Hold on..."

She tapped the screen and flashed a look at Mark, who sat next to her on the edge of their bed.

"I was just thinking of you guys, Diego darling."

As she spoke, she undid the last three buttons of Mark's shirt with her free hand. He slipped it off.

"Hey Rebecca, Mark. We're at Mitch and Kick's place, and all is good. We were notified by *Les Gardiens* of a situation that... "

"My woman's intuition tells me that we all have the same issue, Darling. I have Kick on the other line. We need a meeting. Hold on."

She tapped. Mark poured them a whiskey glass of Añejo for post-meeting relaxation and various activities. The amber liquid seemed to glow in the soft room light.

Yes, it was about the kidnapped boy. Kick added Daniella Lamb to the call. Diego and Joaquín received information that a pair of boys had been apprehended carrying drugs through a tunnel near Brownsville. One matched the description given by Rebecca of the boy from the Inn. For the next fifteen minutes, Rebecca and Mark fill in the gaps of the story of the little and very reluctant drug mule, Jacinto Davide, aka Jack De Leon.

As everyone was brought up to speed, Daniella said, "The boys will be incarcerated at Olivado Sands Detention Center, just west of Brownsville, Texas. It is right near the river."

Rebecca said, "I am not crazy about going the legal route on this one."

Joaquín said, "Correct. That could take months, and those kids will be incarcerated — pens. We need some options."

Mark said, "So we rescue them."

Kick said, "I hear you, Bad Arse -- guns blazing!"

"Okayyyy. So we outlaws need a plan, Darlings. Let's think this one out carefully. Next call, we refine the details."

***

"It's a good plan, Beautiful."

Mark dipped his fingers in the Añejo and let the rich tequila drip between Rebecca's breasts. As he brought his head forward, tasting the smokiness of the liquor blended with the smooth tanginess of her hot flesh, Rebecca ran one hand down his naked back, pulling his body closer to hers. The touch of his tongue and lips over the curves of her body triggered a whole set of sensual sensations. She sipped her whiskey and kissed him in a series of arousing places. The result was a simmering of passion driven by their bodies' heat and fueled by the sensuality of their minds.

Rebecca gasped but said softly, "Yes. It will work. It's just such a wild collection of characters, Mark. A real challenge to... ohhh, Darling, do that over here... yes!"

The night turned hotter.

Chapter Forty-Seven: Jack and Cauli

Olivado Sands Detention Center, Brownsville, Texas, United States of America, and the Brownsville & Matamoros International Bridge

"This sucks major, Jazz Bow. We are in jail."

"I think it's gonna be all right, Dom. Those guys who questioned us know that the bad guys put us up to this. We get to go outside again today."

"Yeah, and we're minors, so that's gotta count for something, right?"

"I guess so. I sure do want to get back home."

Jack pulled on a set of clean clothes, pants, shoes, and socks. The showers had to be taken fast, and breakfast was next, in the big hall with the picnic tables. The guards encouraged them to hurry along.

"You didn't cry much last night, Jazz."

"Neither did you. Guess it makes no sense."

"Dude, those blankets are made of aluminum foil. That little guy next to me cried for his Mamá all night. This place sucks."

"My Mom and my Auntie will get us outta here. They just gotta find us. It's not like we wanted to stay here in the United States… unless you…"

The Dodger finished toweling off and slipped into a pair of clean underwear. He sat to complete dressing.

"No, I changed my mind again. But I'm afraid to go back. We could be in big trouble with the Brigade. Hey, what's that?"

Jack pulled his shirt down.

"It's a birthmark. My Mom says it's a star thing on account of I am a superhero in real life."

"That's bull shit. How can you be a superhero? You're just a kid. Those comic books are making you *loco*, Jazz."

The guard walked over and said, "Let's go, you *hombres*. What are you doing, planning the big breakout? We gotta get you guys fed. Hurry up and get in line."

As the man turned his back, Domingo Diaz-Sandoval, the Dodger, flipped him "the banana."

***

"You were too busy eating your lunch, Danny. How could you not see that dog? The pup had three legs and bobbed up and down like a jackrabbit as it ran over the bridge."

The big customs officer finished his lunch and asked, "Did the guys on the Mexican side say anything? Are we supposed to let dogs cross?"

"You got me. Anyway, I don't see it now. Musta gone into the brush on the riverbank."

The Brownsville and Matamoros International Bridge routine kicked back in as another train approached the Mexican side's American checkpoint. Below, the Rio Grande made dozens of twisting meanders as it proceeded to the Gulf. A small white, three-legged dog scurried upriver through the bushes and trees. Cauli stopped for some river water and then trotted up the bank, avoiding any signs of interfering humans. She seemed to be guided by an inner force.

My boy is close by now.

Chapter Forty-Eight: Superboy and Krypto

Above Brownsville, Texas, United States of America, and on the Ground

"Rebecca, Eris' app for the trackers shows them converging. Daniella was right, Olivadado. That little dog made it, Beautiful. Holy shit."

"Mark, this pilot just said we are landing in Brownsville in ten minutes. Kick and Daniella are meeting us at the airport. We are rounding up at the Hilton. Diego and Joaquín are snowed in at Denver — huge storm."

"We can do this."

"Yeah, we can."

The private plane began its descent.

***

"Sneaky little fucker."

"What are you talking about, Jim?"

The Center's guards were kicking back in the break room. Security Officer James Riser of the United States Department of Homeland Security turned a comic book page. He chuckled.

"Deadpool, Sue. He's some crazy-assed dude, let me tell ya."

"Jim, you're pushing fifty, man. What are you doing with a comic book? Homeland Security will…"

"I took that kid's backpack. He's got comic books – had anyway. Mine now. Oh, yeah, and he had this."

The guard held out a disc-like Captain America insignia and said, "I do not like the looks of this."

He dropped it to the floor and crushed it with his heel.

"Stop messing with these boys, Jim. They are kids, you asshole."

Sergeant Susan Delborn snatched the Deadpool mag and the backpack. She left the breakroom and a very surprised Private James Riser.

***

"Here."

"Thanks."

Jack let his hand slide along the contours of his satchel.

No tracker. That's bad.

"You behave yourself, *Chico*."

Jack's eyes welled up.

"Can I go home now, please, *Señorita*? Me and my friend, I mean? We didn't do anything, and we were kidnapped. For real."

Sargent Delborn felt a lump in her throat as she looked over the twenty-three boys with soulful brown eyes in confinement pen #14. Most were just sitting and waiting, watching.

"It takes time, Kiddo. Maybe you guys need more exercise. I think we got some new footballs."

She left.

I hate my fuckin' job.

***

Jack sat up and listened.

The entire hall was asleep except for a few guards who monitored the dormitories. He nudged Dom.

The boy was still groggy as he said. "Whoa, Jazz Bo. I was having a ..."

"Shhh, Dom. Do not ask questions. Just go along with this."

Jack walked over to the chain-link fence that surrounded his confinement area. He was careful not to disturb the other kids. Most were asleep, but some watched in the darkness, big round eyes full of sorrow.

Tilted against the cage was a guard's chair. The man was dozing. Jack stuck an index finger through the fence and nudged the guy.

"Permission to use the bathroom, Boss. It's my friend. *Va a vomitar*."

The big man yawned and looked at Jack. He said, "OK, Buster, but make sure you use the mop and pail in there in case he pukes on the floor."

"Yes, Sir, Boss."

Jack had read about his comic book characters in prison a few times, and he was good at aping the lingo and the patter between inmates and guards. He went back and got the Dodger and his backpack.

"Hold your stomach like you're sick, Dom, but don't make any sound. Bathroom." He pointed to where the cage was attached to the wall of the building.

The guard was not looking as Jack closed the door.

"What's going on, Jazz?"

"*Estamos reventando fuera de este porro, amigo*. We're busting outta this joint. Boost me up."

A dog barked again off beyond the play yard. No animals were allowed in the compound.

Jack used his satchel to push against the wire mesh screen on the bathroom window. It gave way easily. He pulled himself through. The Dodger followed.

Scooping up his backpack, Jack said, "It's her, Dom. Krypto... my Cauli."

***

She saw them coming and stopped barking. She was so excited, she wagged the entire back end of her body. They were sneaking across the soccer field to the perimeter fence, avoiding the sweeping security lights. The only sound was the wind sighing in the trees in the surrounding blue-black forest of the night.

The dog ran along the fence line to a thicket of bushes, doubling back twice to ensure they followed her on the other side. They ducked into the undergrowth and found the hole she had spent most of the day digging.

The bigger boy first, her boy's backpack was pushed through next, then her boy.

Cauli went nuts. She jumped onto him with tiny yelps and smothered Jack with dog kisses. He hugged her and lovingly spoke to his best friend as Dom watched and surveyed the surroundings.

"Good girl. I got you, pup. Yes."

Don't ever go away, my Boy. I always want to be with you.

He whispered. "We gotta move, Jazz Bow."

Jack got up, and the dog sat attentively, looking at him. He pointed into the woods.

"Go, Cauli. Home."

Chapter Forty-Nine: The Great River

The Rio Grande

"Any word from the Cortez guys?"

"Kick, they are still waiting to leave Denver. I hate winter, Darling. God only wants humans to live in the tropics. She told me so."

About one hundred yards to the southeast, the riverbank shone in the light of the full moon. Here, the river was narrow but swift.

Daniella leaned against the truck. She was on a call. Mark tapped his smartwatch.

"Captain America is toast. The tracker is offline. I do have the dog, though. Just as Rebecca predicted. Holy shit, Cauli is headed this way."

He pointed to the edge of the forest.

"So are the Po Po, Mark. Look."

She pointed to the flashing lights higher up on the road.

Kick looked at his bud and said, "Let's go, Maverick."

Mark kissed his lady love and said, "Meet you on the other side."

***

Cauli growled.

"The lights, Jazz. We've been spotted. It's the guards. Shit, Dude."

"No, Dom. Look."

Through the brush, two horsemen came riding towards the three fugitives. The moonlight seemed to reveal spectacular mounts and mythic riders. The black steeds were breathing steam in the crisp night air.

"The fuckin' cavalry, man."

The Dodger was three seconds from panic. He looked in the direction of the river.

Shoulda learned to swim.

"No, wait, I know that man."

Jack went down on one knee to scoop the excited Cauli into his satchel and called, "Señor Mark. Over here. It's Jack from the Inn."

Mark and Kick reined their Galicenos and approached. In the background, the patrol cars got closer.

"Let's go, guys. Mount up. We're gonna take these horses to water."

Using one arm, each of the men pulled one of the boys onto the saddles so that the youngsters were behind them. The horses danced a bit in a circle until all four humans, one with precious cargo on his back, were settled. Kick could tell that Dom was petrified.

"It's gonna be OK, Kiddo. Just like in the movies, Mate."

***

Patrol cars, marked with "Olvidado Sands Detention Center Security," pulled down the dirt road to the river. Their blue and red lights gave an eerie luminescence to the riverbank. The officers approached on foot. Daniella and Rebecca met them between the horse trailer and their cruiser.

Before anyone spoke, Daniella held up an index finger and handed Sargent Susan Delborn her mobile. She addressed the other law enforcement officers while pointing off to the southeast and the string of lights that spanned the two countries' edge.

"Just taking the scenic route to the border bridge, fellas. Such a beautiful night, I wanted my friend, Ms. Quinto… "

Daniella nodded to the officer inspecting their IDs.

"To see the river in the light of the moon and by starlight. It's beautiful, isn't it?"

"Horse trailer?"

Another officer with a flashlight came up and said, "It's empty, Sir. The SUV also. They must be going to the horse auction in Matamoros."

Rebecca said nothing. She mysteriously raised her eyebrows.

Could be, fellas. Could be.

"We're looking for a couple of kids who… "

Susan Delborn interrupted, "Forget it, Hank. Call in the search. Let's go back to the Detention Center. The situation has changed. "

The officer handed the phone back to Daniella.

"You are very well connected, whoever you are."

Daniella smiled and said into the mobile.

"Thanks again, Doctor. I'll be in DC on Thursday. Lunch sounds great. Good night."

She winked at Rebecca.

As they got into the SUV, Daniella said, "It's all about who you know, Girl."

Thomas Paul Severino

Chapter Fifty: Dark Water

The Rio Grande

"Hold on, Kiddo. The horse will do all the work. Grip me tighter."

The stallion snorted as the waters swirled around her chest. Man and boy leaned over, held on, but let the horse lead into the swim. Dom held tight to Kick at the man's waist. Kick felt the boy's legs scrabble for purchase, tucking around his.

Between the rushing sounds of the water, the horse heard the gentle voice of the man singing.

> I've been a wild rover this many a year
>
> And I've spent all my money on whisky and beer
>
> But now I'm returning with gold in great store
>
> And I never shall play the wild rover no more

Dom squirmed. Behind them, Mark and Jack followed as their mare took to her swim. Jack had zipped Cauli into the backpack with only a small opening in the enclosure for air. She knew to be still and be a good dog. She felt the heartbeat and smelled the scent of her boy.

> And it's no, nay, never
>
> No, nay never, no more
>
> Will I play the wild rover
>
> No, never, no more.

The river was swift. A few miles downstream, it would broaden as it passed Brownsville and fanned out into Mexico's Gulf. As they forded the current, the far riverbank was revealed out of the darkness. The horses pulled hard at the swirling water.

Kick's horse saw the tree branch just before the collision. It was big enough to cause the horse to turn in his swim. The Galiceno stallion snorted and shifted in the water.

Dom slipped off.

The water shot over the struggling boy and pulled him under.

Kick dove.

Mark managed his mare so that the horse pulled closer to her riderless swimming mate. He tried but could not reach the dangling reins. The riderless horse continued to the safety of the bank alongside her *compadres*. He saw Kick sounding in the churning water, the tree branch sailing down the current.

The Galicenos' hooves hit the underwater scrabble of the riverbank, and the steeds climbed up and out of the water. Mark dropped and got Jack to the ground.

"Stay here with the horses, Jack."

The boy pulled the mare up the rise and managed to snag the stallion's reins to lead them both to a dead tree on the bank that would serve as a hitching post. He let Cauli out and huddled with her, watching the dark waters.

He looked for the spot where Mark had run back across the bank and dove into the river.

***

"They should be coming up just over there. Mark and I parked the rental just over that crest."

Rebecca eased the truck and trailer down the embankment and onto a dirt road. Daniella saw them first.

"There."

As they got closer, Rebecca heard Cauli announcing their arrival. She pulled over. The woman ran to the boy, the dog, and the two horses.

Jack pointed to the dark water. He made every effort not to cry.

***

He could not see. It was black beneath the water. He surrendered to the current and reached out in as many directions as possible. Legs pumping. He knew the boy went down here, but the current was strong. The kid could be anywhere in the watery hell.

He is here... I have him... Reach, human... do not fail...

Now he was out of air. Up!

Just as he was about to return to the surface, Kick touched an outstretched arm. The man's body reacted in an instant. He gripped the boy's wrist and leg-pumped them both to the surface. As he breached, Dom grabbed him around the chest and neck. He coughed up air and water. Kick's strength was ebbing, and they were both in danger of drowning.

The athlete tried to settle the lad against him and turn in the current toward the shore. As he spoke, his voice showed no gasping sign but took on a note almost like crooning in Spanish.

"Breathe, yeah, I got you. Now kick your legs, Kiddo. Swim with me."

Another set of arms reached, pulled, and turned them in the water. The underwater scrabble came up against their feet. The two men shifted the boy so that his head was well out of the water as they climbed against the current. Dom was coughing but conscious as the three collapsed on the shore.

***

Mark called. "Hey, are you our Uber Driver? You're awful pretty."

"Darling!"

Dom was walking between the two men. Somehow, Rebecca had a blanket and wrapped the shivering boy in its folds. Jack, Cauli, and Daniella brought up the rear.

Everyone hugged everyone. Rebecca's Outlaws all got cold McDonald's breakfast sandwiches, except Kick. He passed, saying, "Body softener. Just the orange juice, thanks."

He moved the horses to a thicket of grass nearby. He thanked them in whispers, murmuring and stroking their heads.

Jack said, "Hey, bud, I thought you said you couldn't swim."

Dom smiled and said, "That stupid guy in your comic book, the shiny dude with the surfboard."

Jack said, "The Silver Surfer."

"Yeah, well, the story said you hold your breath. So, I did. Then this big singing dude here grabbed me. But he can't sing underwater."

Rebecca and Mark seemed to communicate the gratefulness of the situation with their eyes and not words until she threw her arms up and hugged him.

"Such a hero, Mark. I am overwhelmed."

"Yeah, your plan worked, Beautiful. We all make a great team, especially the advance gal here."

He gave the little dog a head scratch.

"Super pooch here sprung these guys."

Mark tossed Cauli a sausage biscuit.

Jack said, "Krypto!"

Kick came back.

"I put the Galicenos in the trailer. Best purchase I ever made. I gotta tell Mitch..."

He was unable to finish. Dom had run over and grabbed Kick in a surprise hug up. He cried softly into the man's chest.

"*Muchas gracias, Señor. Muchas gracias.*"

A bewildered Kick raised his hands and said softly, "*De nada, amigo.*"

He took a knee to come face-to-face with the thirteen-year-old.

"Listen, bud. Gonna pull some strings, Kiddo. I think you belong at our place, Aerie, up in Colorado. We're hiring. We can finish your swimming lessons."

Daniella said, "Kick, we should head back. I'm thinking the *Federales*, you know? Right this moment, you are here illegally, a literal wetback. The horses too... Let's see how we do with this one at the crossing."

The man nodded. Goodbyes were said with hugs and kisses.

Kick said once again to the Dodger. "Seriously, Dom, I know people. We'll meet again soon."

Rebecca looked at Daniella and said, "And speaking of..."

She pointed to the opposite bank and made a phone sign with her hand to the side of her head.

"The President? No way, Darling."

Daniella smiled, "Ahhh, college sororities... University of Delaware, 2006. No, Babe, not the President... his Boss. School teachers rock."

Thomas Paul Severino

Chapter Fifty-One: Ilia

La Plantación de la Condesa, República de Guatemala

"Abduction done right. What can I tell ya?"

Nelson and Enrique Osterman-Diaz were impressed.

The CEO asked, "Where?"

Ilia Mercado smiled and said, "Near Tuxtla, Chiapas state, close to the border. The four of them decided to stop for the night on the way back to Huehuetenango."

"How?"

"My little network of associates, Boss. To reveal more would risk slipping my aura of mystery and power. It's done. They're here. They are being kept securely."

"What's next?"

The woman known as "The General" signaled to the staffer who refilled glasses and left the Great Room.

"So, it's time they disappear. Señora Quinto has an avid interest in pre-Columbian ruins, and coincidently, we have some."

This time her smile was devious.

Enrique said, "That one is a beautiful woman. Do you know she already has a rep with the peasant scum?"

He waved his cocktail glass.

"They call her *Ix Tz'akbu Ajaw*, the Red Queen. Some reincarnation shit. How fucked up is that?"

"What my brother is suggesting is removing those two for a weekend at our place down at La Playa. Some extended interrogation at La Villa El Dorado, yes, my brother?"

With a leer, Enrigue said, "Oh yes, and the man is just your type, Nelson man. You love breaking those hero types. So persuasive, my brother can be, Ilia."

The woman gazed out over the planting fields and up the volcano's slopes. She sighed, "No, Gentlemen. I suggest maintaining your distance from these two. There will surely be an investigation."

She added, "I understand the *Nido de Ratas*, the Rat's Nest in Quetzaltenango, has been liquidated."

Ilia turned from the window to face them. Her eyes took on a look of steel as she spoke.

"*El Maquinista*. Now, tell me about the Engineer."

Chapter Fifty-Two: Into the Mountains

Tila, Frontera Corozal, Estado de Chiapas, Estados Unidos Mexicanos and Casa De Flores Tikal, Quetzaltenango, República de Guatemala

"Do not question me. We are going."

The older woman wagged a finger and reached for her cane.

Elyssa Nájera Trejo and her husband, Efraín, looked at each other.

What now? More of the unexpected...

"A few days... no more than a week. The mountains to the west... We will come right back. It is time."

Mamá Xumucane looked at her grandchildren and gave the remaining orders.

"Cadmael Santana will go with us. Tell him to put the wooden crate from my room into the truck."

The old grandmother moved forward on her walking stick.

"We will go now."

***

"Your friends are not here. Last night, I got a text that they were coming today from Mexico, bringing my son home to me. So far, they have not arrived."

"Señora De Leon, we are Diego and Joaquín Cortez, friends of Rebecca and Mark. We were supposed to... anyway, the snow in Colorado... "

"You have a car, a big one, *sí*? It will take five?"

The intervening voice came from behind them.

Rosalina said, "Señor Necahual Ahau-Kin, you surprised me."

"We do not have much time. The stars call us to the mountain."

The old jaguar pointed to young Aapo standing in the doorway with a sizeable crate.

"Ask your sister and your staff to watch over the Inn. It will take three, possibly four days."

The Americans were amazed.

"You will find your friends there, *Señores*... and the boy."

His pale eyes searched three faces.

"*Apurarse.* We must go."

Chapter Fifty-Three: The Lost City of Kukulkan

The Mountain of the Feathered Serpent, La Plantación de la Condesa, República de Guatemala

X Ciichpan Ek

hohopnan yook kaax

cu butz'ilan ca lamat lamat

u taal u cimil u

yook yaxil kaax.

Ilia Mercado turned to her Labor Relations Officer and asked, "What are they singing?"

"The chant is from the Songs of Dzitbalché, the only known ancient Maya lyric poetry."

Maria Cabrara-Virella listened a bit and said, "The Beautiful Star shines over the woods, smoking as it sinks and vanishes; the moon too dies over the forest green."

"It is an ancient song of renewal."

Cauli sounded the alarm from her backpack compartment. Jack stepped forward and took in the vast cavern.

"It's OK, Girl. This is... It's OK."

He seemed lost in the moment. From her place on his back, the dog rested her head on his shoulder. They both peered wide-eyed into the valley inside the foothills of the volcano.

Rebecca reached forward and held the boy back. Dom took up next to his buddy.

"Damn, Jazz Bow, where are we? Inside the mountain?"

Mark tried again to struggle with the guards. He was the only one tied, hands behind his back. Nelson Osterman-Diaz hissed, "Slow down, muscle boy. Do not make this easy for us." He signaled to the guard to put Mark on his knees as they stood on a broad landing just inside the destroyed portal. There were stairs carved into the rock leading down into the lost city.

Ilia said, "I gave orders that no one was to cross that opening."

"Since word of the discovery, they have been coming at night, climbing up the mountain, my General. They are here to pray. Those fires you see are part of their religious ritual. But..."

"What?"

"We need to get closer, but I think that many of those people gathered around the fires are not our laborers. See there, others are still arriving through that lower entrance."

"What are they carrying?"

"I do not know, General. I would say ceremonial jars. This seems to be some sort of religious ritual."

Geologically, the gigantic cavern was created by the exit of an enormous amount of lava when the volcano last erupted. The expanding lava flowed down the mountain, leaving behind a vast domed amphitheater of rock. Ancient people had turned it into a treasure city.

The sides of the rock cavern stretched wide and dropped from a roof nearly two hundred feet to the cave floor. Terraces were cut into the sides. The openings of ancillary chambers appeared at every level — living quarters, armories, storage chambers, and royal apartments.

Frescoes adorned the walls, and gigantic statues of the gods watched over a central space dominated by a round, raised ceremonial platform—the Royal Dias. There were stone stairs everywhere, linking the chambers and terraces. The feathered serpent motif was featured as the decoration on the stairways' sides, along the walkways, and spiraling up the lost city's dome. An opening pierced the stone ceiling directly over the center dias. Its twisting stairway coiled against the dome suggested total sky access—an opening for the astronomer priests to view the heavens.

Rebecca whispered, "Kukulkan."

She felt hands on her lower back. A rasping voice muttered, "Gold. There's a ton of it in here. The walls... the pillars... have you ever seen such beautiful gold, my Queen?"

Fingers found their way to her neck and fingered the necklace Mamá Xumucane had given her in Tila. Rebecca turned to Enrique Osterman-Diaz and shoved him back.

"Pig! Keep your hands off me."

He was not pleased, but she did not care. She stepped over to the kneeling Mark and lifted him to his feet. The guards stirred but backed off as she touched her necklace and shot them a challenging look. Looking at Nelson, she ordered. "Take them off. Now. Do it. You are on holy ground, *esse*. Do not mess with the gods. They will kill you where you stand. Listen to me, your Red Queen."

A cry rang out from below.

"Jacinto Davide, *mi hijo. Ah, Dios mio.*"

Rosalina emerged from the murky shadows and bonfires. She rushed up the stairs to the entry platform. Behind her came the Cortezes as if trying to keep the distraught mother from doing something rash.

Ilia Mercado seemed to snap out of a trance from taking in the lost city's magnitude and splendor. She turned and shot the Osterman-Diaz brothers each in the chest. The chanting stopped.

Rebecca grabbed Jack and turned his face so that it pressed into her. Mark pulled Domingo into an embrace that kept him from seeing the assassinations. Ilia's guards were stoic and immobile.

The twins struggled in the dirt, their faces a combination of pain and confusion.

"Why? I will tell you why, you pieces of shit. That is for my brother, *El Maquinista*, your Engineer. You enslaved him with drugs and made him a corrupter of children. I found out that you paid the authorities to shoot him with some others and burn their bodies up north in Mexico."

She took aim and fired again and again.

"Die, you miserable fucks."

The brothers stopped thrashing and closed their eyes.

Now, the General turned the gun on the Inn de Flores' proprietor and the two Americans, who had stopped climbing when the killing started.

"No."

She waved the gun and indicated that they should go back down. A hand in the air was a signal to her two guards to force the captives down to the cavern floor with her. Ilia mounted the ceremonial stage in the center and motioned that her entourage of death should follow her. Fire pits at the base of the Dias illuminated the deadly performance.

"This is exceptional. Diego Friedman and Joaquín Cortez. You two seem to have walked right into my spider's web. Friedman Coffee's money has supported the dissolution of our cartel for two generations. And you, Señor Joaquin, shall I send your head to *Les Gardiens*? They are such meddlers."

Ilia threw a glance at Rebecca and Mark.

"You two, I will kill as a warning to others who would seek to destroy Osterman-Diaz Enterprises."

Rebecca started out softly but raised her voice as she continued.

"You are at the end, General. You are no match for the force of the divine or the will of the people. You are simply one of the thousands who have stood with a foot on the neck of the Maya. The gods will not have it so."

She pointed up to the Oculos. The full moon's light streamed into the domed cavern and hit the ceremonial platform and the twelve-year-old with the backpack.

Jack stepped away from the clutching arms of his mother into the moonlight. He slipped his satchel and let Cauli out to sit beside him. As he did, the right side of his T-shirt lifted up.

It started near the edge of the stage where the people could see.

"Ajaw! Ajaw! Ajaw!"

"Ahau, Pakal, Ahau."

Ilia became somewhat disoriented as the chanting echoed to the point of thunder in the chamber. Rebecca stood next to the boy, the light beams illuminating the necklace of the Red Queen. In the crowd, Mark recognized Necahual Ahau-Kin, Aapo, Cadmael Santana, Elyssa Nájera Trejo, and her husband, Efraín, and Mamá Xumucane moving to the front and the foot of the Royal Dias. The elders, eyes shining, approached the stairs and climbed up.

Efraín and the young men stoked the fires so that the people could better see the birthmark on the boy. Rebecca kept Jack's shirt from covering the Pleadies. The shaft of light seemed to intensify. Motes of gold dust swirled in the beam. Onstage, the prisoners and their captors were transfixed.

Ilia struggled to understand.

"They are calling him 'The Shield of the Sun,' General. The descendant of Pakal the Great," Rebecca said over the cries of adulation. "He is guarded by the Feathered Serpent, by Hunab-Ku, who is the Sole God... by the Divine Twins, who are the Sun and the Moon..."

Rebecca raised her arms like an ancient priestess. She pointed to the Maya elite in the surging crowd.

"The Jaguar and the Daykeepers foretold his rising. They know the secrets of the universe revealed to them by Kukulkan."

The stucco figures on the walls and doorways seemed to throb with life as she continued her litany. She was shouting now.

"The Turtle and the Peccaries... See, the Maize God emerges. He is the child-god, K'awiil, bringing prosperity. The cycle is ending with the destruction of great evil. Now is the rebirth of the Maya. He is the last... the last, and he is under the protection of..."

Rebecca put both hands on the boy's shoulders.

"The Lady *Ix Tz'akbu Ajaw,* the Red Queen..."

The assembly was thunderous.

The General's fearful guards backed up to a rear opening in search of an escape. Ilia Mercado turned as the list of deities echoed through the chamber, and the crowd started up the stairs. Now she stopped and leveled the gun at Jack and Rebecca.

"Enough."

Cauli jumped as if weightless and hit the woman dead center in the chest with a flying springboard leap. The dog caused the woman to fall back and off the platform's edge. The pair tumbled into a blazing fire pit, thirty feet below.

Jack screamed.

Chapter Fifty-Four: The Ways

The Mountain of the Feathered Serpent, La Plantación de la Condesa, República de Guatemala

"In the Maya belief, every day has its own energy, and this energy will either aid or hinder one's journey on a given day. The Ways are any one of a class of protector spirits whose energy aids and directs someone through the course of a day and in life.

"Every person has a Way who tends to that individual spiritually. A Way may manifest itself physically as an animal that helps guide someone. In this aspect, they would be recognized as Totems. The Ways may also communicate through dreams. A dreamer is brought to the Dreaming Place, where the individual soul may commune directly with their Way. Even the gods have a Way attached to them, guiding and directing the deity's energy if that god is open to such guidance."

Now, starlight replaced the moon's beacon coming through the Oculus. Necahual Ahau-Kin, the old fruit seller, the Daykeeper, continued to speak directly to Jack.

"She is your Way, Jacinto Davide de Leon. She will never be parted from you. You are hers, and she is yours."

Cauli looked over Jack's shoulder from her place in the superhero backpack. Jack was sitting on the stage's floor, receiving the people. Cauli eyed each of them. Efraín, Dom, Cadmael, and Aapo were ushering and doing crowd control. Rosalina was hovering behind her boy.

Mark held close to Rebecca and said softly, "Damn, Beautiful. If I hadn't seen it... three legs, and she flipped off of that evil bitch at just the last second. Not even singed. Unbelievable."

"Makes you just want to believe, I guess, Darling."

Elyssa Trejo came over to the Americans. She was ecstatic.

"You two have got to see this."

As they mounted the steps to the platform, Diego was on his phone.

"I am telling you, we need secure transport, and the Guatemalan Ministry of Cultural Affairs needs to be in on this ASAP. Yes, I am telling you. I am watching it happen in front of me."

Closer to Jack, Mamá Xumucane and Joaquín were receiving what appeared to be a tribute in the form of urns made of obsidian.

"Each of these had been handed down in the families of the Maya for hundreds of years. The families guarded them with their lives and passed them on to succeeding generations."

Elyssa continued, "Each sealed urn contains a scroll. Maya books, histories, literature, scientific treatises, genealogies, sacred texts, legal renderings."

The archeological researcher seemed to just about fly off the platform and up to the ceiling.

Rebecca and Mark were speechless.

"The codices appear to go back to the time of K'inich Janaab Pakal I."

Rebecca gasped as she carefully examined one urn. The illustrated texts could be seen through the dark glass. They were bright and colorful, curled in their sacred clay vessels.

"Pakal the Great. His treasure and the legacy of his people."

Jack, looking on, nudged his bud, the Dodger.

"Look, Dom, ancient comic books. How cool is that?"

Epilogue: The Glory of Gods and Kings

Eagle's Roost, Aerie Valley, Aspen, Colorado, the United States of America

"Arf... arf... arf... arf..."

"Hello, Cauli. Am I on your contact list, Darling?"

The FaceTime image on Rebecca's mobile slid away from the dog, wobbled a bit, and picked up another cute face – brown eyes, black hair, a big smile, and a crooked bellboy's cap.

"*Hola*, Rebecca. Cauli and I wanted to call you and say 'hello.' Is Mark there too? Sit, Girl."

"Jack. How nice to hear from you, Darling. Yes, I will get him."

Mark and Mitch Sorenson, enjoying the sunshine in the last of the wintry days at Aerie, were discussing America's changing foreign policy in the Middle East. One of the house staff was refilling coffee on the spacious balcony of the Main House, The Eagle's Roost. The view of the Rockies and the snow-filled valley was spectacular. Skiers tumbled and soared down the mountain that reared up behind the Aerie Lodge directly across the valley.

"The pressure is on the Saudis, Mitch, now that the Americans are not backing them in the war. They need to pull out of Yemen and end the genocide of the Houthis. Too many have died. The next caldron over there will be Gaza. Only a matter of time. Hey, Beautiful."

Rebecca was holding her phone.

"Someone and someone's dog want to say hello."

"*Hola*, Mark. *Que tal, amigo*? Thank you for the comic books. I did not have those."

"Jack! You're welcome. How are you, Kiddo? And hello, pup. Mitch, meet our best buds in Guatemala, Jack, and Cauli, total badasses."

"Wow, you guys really do look like some real superheroes," Mitch said. "Rebecca and Mark told me of your adventures. Great going, Jack."

Rebecca took back the phone. "Mitch is Kick's husband. We are staying for a while with them in Colorado before going on to Fort Lauderdale. I see you are working. Is everything going well? How are your Mom and your Auntie?"

Jack pushed back his hat and said, "Oh, yeah, Tia Carmen had a baby. It is a girl. I have a cousin. They named her 'Rebecca,' like you."

"Darling, that is so cool. I'll bet you are still getting good grades in school."

"Yes, I am. Hey, Rebecca, can you do me a favor, please?"

"What is it, Darling?"

Jack looked from side to side and lowered his voice to almost a whisper.

"So, could you talk to my Mamá about me having to do chores and stuff? I mean, I don't think someone who is a King like me should have to mop the floors and push luggage carts, do you?"

Before Rebecca could suppress a laugh and respond, the visual changed again. The mobile was the victim of a hand grab by Rosalina.

"Break time is over, Your Highness. Roberto needs help with the new arrivals. They are up on four. I'll give this back to you later. One more thing. Jacinto Davide, Superdog belongs in the kitchen. You know the rules. You can call Rebecca back when your shift ends."

The boy waved and scampered off-screen.

"Bye, Rebecca."

"Hola, *Carida*. I hope you and Mark are getting a well-deserved rest."

"Congratulations, Auntie. Please kiss Carmencita for Mark and me. How fantastic, Darling. Yes, we are with our friends near Aspen, Colorado. No more work chasing the bad guys."

"Update time. The Inn is doing well, thank goodness. Apparently, law enforcement got pressure from the people, and local governments collapsed in this region, with big demands to arrest members of the youth gangs. But the best news is that the new folks in charge of Osterman Diaz Enterprises are taking responsibility for the sins of the past and retooling their company. It means many more good jobs for the people. The citizens are getting control of many of their operations. Also, a company known as Black Gold Enterprises is investing in youth programs across the state. And speaking of Diego and Joaquín, the Cortezes bought Jack this phone before they went back to Miami."

Rebecca said, "Rosie, I recently learned that the UN is declaring the Mountain of the Feathered Serpent a World Heritage Site. Diego and Joaquín pulled some strings and got that fast-tracked."

"Yes, there is a foundation that is building a museum for the manuscripts — the treasure scrolls. El Universidad San Pedro in Ciudad Guatemala is behind that. I think Elyssa Trejo is heading that one up."

"Rosie, they are going to ask you and Jack to be honorary members of the Board for that museum." Rebecca looked at Mitch as she spoke and gave him a wink.

"I'm going to be a Trustee of the Museum — essential steps in a cultural Renaissance for the Maya."

Rosalina did not reveal that there was talk behind a gift from a private American donor, to name part of the Museum after the late Alejandro De Leon. She would leave that surprise for another time.

"We will talk again soon, *Carida*. I have guests who want all sorts of things. Please give my love to Mark and your dear friends.

"Likewise, Rosie. *Adios*."

Mark and Mitch were watching two riders arrive in the broad porte-cochère one floor down. Mark's phone pinged.

Rebecca walked over and put her arms around her man.

"All seems well with the De Leons."

She smiled as she added, "I also just of word that my Board chair for the Fritcher resigned. One does not mess with the Red Queen, Darlings."

Mark read his latest email and said, "Hey, Beautiful, listen to this. Bronson Chambers, my boss at CBN World-Wide, loved my piece on the resurgence of the Maya, 'The Glory of Gods and Kings.' They pitched it to the History Channel, and, long story short, they want me to be in on the writing and the narration of a series. It is to be based on our adventures and the social issues we encountered."

"Mark, let's tie it into the Fritcher Museum exhibit. The agreements are in process. My curators are working on the list of artifacts. The designers are creating the atmosphere and physical dimensions of the experience. I imagine graphics of the City of Snakes– the Pyramids and the Palace complex floating across the Fritcher's exterior. Darling, am I sounding like an executive producer?"

Mark listened but scrolled.

"Holy shit! Chambers' investors are sending a sizeable contribution to the Thomas M. Sorenson, Jr. Inner City Equestrian Fund."

He showed Mitch and Rebecca his phone.

Mitch whistled.

"Rippa! Kick is gonna love all those zeroes."

Rebecca placed a hand on Mitch's shoulder.

"While we are talking money, Darling, I want to thank you again for The Aerie Corporation's investment in the youth programs. Putting Daniella Lamb at the head of that effort is genius. She knows everybody."

Mitch smiled, "Yeah, tell me about it. As for our support, we are happy to do it. The Board was wowed by the presentation made by the one and only Hot Mess. The equestrian program will start near Quetzaltenango in three months."

The handsome man added, "Back to the opening... tell us more."

"This is the part of my job I love best, Darling. Guests of honor include the folks from Quetzaltenango, the De Leons, including Cauli, the Day Keeper, and young Aapo, the Tila folks, Mamá Xumucane..."

Mark added, "Elyssa, Efraín, Cadmael, and... and...

"Ian, Darling."

She was speaking into the Notes function of her iPhone, creating the opening's invitation list.

Mitch added, "Include my Board – oh yeah, the hotties from Miami, the Cortez boys."

She spread her arms up to the beautiful blue sky – drama personified.

"It will be a grand gala like the world has never seen, Darling. 'The Glory of Gods and Kings.' I love it."

As she figuratively descended to earth, Rebecca said, "How will I ever keep the South Florida gays off you and your divine husband?"

Mark said, "And speaking of…"

Kick and a young cowboy stomped up the stairs from the ground level and shook off the snow.

"He rides like a pro, mates – a natural. We went to visit the Nu Ci on the Ute Reservation. They love this guy."

The enthusiastic rancher/corporate VP kissed his husband and two friends. The youngster lagged a bit behind.

"I will admit, this young brogan had the best teacher when it comes to horsemanship. And when the snow fully melts, I'm gonna teach the lad to swim."

The new ranch hand pulled off his hat and gloves and used them to dust off the snow and ice accumulated from the wintery trail up the foothills. The four friends watched as the lad joined their group.

The boy raised his handsome face and nodded a greeting. Rebecca noticed that the biggest grin of all that morning came from Aerie Stables' new hire, Assistant to the Master of Horse, Domingo Diaz-Sandoval.

The End

Thomas Paul Severino

Author's Notes and Acknowledgements

For non-English words, I used Italics for sentences and phrases, e.g., *mi hijo*. Name prefixes (Señora Fernanda) are not italicized unless the prefix is used without the surname. (*La Señora*) Likewise, the names of places are not italicized (Plaza de la Constitución).

Locations after each chapter title are as the people of Guatemala, Mexico, or the United States title them, e.g., Ciudad de Guatemala, República de Guatemala; Frontiza del Sur Highway, Estado de Chiapas, Estados Unidos Mexicanos; Aspen, Colorado.

I use "Maya" both as a noun and as an adjective. I found that convention is preferred by indigenous people when I was researching online. I do not use "Mayan."

The children and adults who are fluent in Spanish are captured in the text as if their dialog were translated to keep matters simple for the reader. I have attempted to include authentic titles, words, and phrases in Spanish or the Maya language to honor these cultures.

I would like to thank my copy editor, Keith Hickman, for again supplying excellent subediting skills. He makes me a better writer and encourages my efforts.

To my husband, Tony Wallner, and my dear friend, Gerry Iacullo, I extend my thanks for insightful editorial assistance and valuable comments.

To my biggest fan, Janet Severino Neary, who has read and delighted in all of the books in both of my mystery series, I dedicate this book. Like the heroine, Janet is giving and fearless, generous, kind, and beautiful.

I love her dearly.

Thomas Paul Severino

Afterword:

Thank you for reading <u>The Amazing Adventures of Rebecca Quinto: The Last Maya.</u> I hope you enjoyed the story.

Rebecca will be back soon, and the adventures will take her to breathtaking heights and spellbinding exploits. As usual, she and Mark will be doing unheard-of things in parts unknown.

In the meantime, what's happening with Kayne Sorenson and Nick Sechi, heroes of the Kayne Sorenson Mystery Series? All signs point to a new and terrifying whodunit, <u>The Crystal Orb</u>. Coming soon.

Here's just a little taste....

The Crystal Orb

A Kayne Sorenson Mystery

Thomas Paul Severino

Thomas Paul Severino

Prologue: The Workshop

Il Monastero del Santissima Annunziata, La Repubblica di Firenze, Italia

1500 CE

"I cannot tell if he is looking at me or through me and into the distance."

"Ah, Most Gracious Majesty. Even Christ himself would be stunned by your sublime beauty. No one could ever ignore the loveliness of the new Queen of France. He is transfixed. Surely."

"Well spoken, Master Boltraffio. Voiced like a true diplomat. When you pay such homage to my wife, you honor me."

Giovanni Antonio Boltraffio did his best courtly bow to the two visiting French monarchs, Louis XII and Anne of Brittany.

The Queen continued her meditation on the portrait of Christ painted on the walnut plank, mounted on the easel in the center of the studio. Her words seemed almost prayerful.

"I find as I gaze upon his countenance, my emotions shift. The almost smokiness of his features... His mouth is quite enigmatic. Does Our Lord smile or... The color of his lips – perfect."

The Queen turned from the painting and took her husband's hand. Her smile held a smirk as she recalled his remarks.

"I fear that our reputation as patrons of the arts has brought on this effusive flattery, has it not, Signore? This Master Giovonni would like a commission from us, My Lord, that would rival our sponsorship of his master, the great Leonardo."

Near the portrait, twenty students stood beside their easels around the trio at respectful attention. Each was a bit nervous given the royals' surprise visit. Their attempts to copy the portrait of the Saviour were in various stages of completion. Louis waved them back to their labors as he strode through the studio donated by the monks of the Monastery of the Most Holy Annunciation to the Medici's "Universal Genius" and his pupils.

The King took a moment to discuss a few of the interpretations of the Master's rendition of the Saviour of the World. Anne also did a sweeping appraisal of the attempts. She paused at an empty station – only the easel and painting – no artist. Her pointing hand and raised eyebrows were a question.

"Andrea Salaì, your Majesty. The young man has accompanied the Master to the meeting of the Platonic Academy this morning."

Anne looked again at the rendition. She summed up her appraisal in a single word.

"No."

The Queen reached again for the King and said, "I want the original for the chapel at the Château de Blois. He must finish it by my coronation day, Signore."

"And finish it, he will. Majesty!"

The last word was an exclamation from the artist who did a sweeping bow upon entering the salon. The younger man who accompanied the very robust Maestro also swept the floor with his hat while bending low at the waist. At twenty, the dashingly handsome Andrea Salaì was twenty-eight years younger than his lover. He sported the brashness and overconfidence of the exceptional and the favored.

"Signore Leonardo, only you could keep us waiting and not feel the signature impatience of the French Throne. The Queen and I are delighted to see you and your... ahh... your protégé."

The Monarch extended his hand to the artists, each of them in turn.

"How fares *Le Père du Peuple?* What says his beautiful Queen?"

"So very tired of the Italian Wars, Master Leonardo, my husband just loves his new toy, gunpowder. Invincibility is not all that it is fabled to be."

She faked a theatrical yawn.

Queen Anne was delighted to be in the presence of the incredibly handsome and talented Leonardo. The promise of the Christ painting was a fitting tribute to the new Masters of Italy. She loved the little intrigues connected to art's politics, a diversion while her husband sought to be the lord of Europe.

Louis suddenly became cordially insistent.

"Listen to me, Signore. You must defy the Borgia and become my military engineer, Master Leonardo. My troops have set our sights on the Kingdom of Naples now that we have secured a foothold in Italy. The future of the peninsula lies in the grasp of the House of Valois."

The King pointed to his chest.

"With respect, Majesty. My defiance of the Pope comes with excommunication and…"

He shot a secret glance at his paramour.

"Even though I have been accused of even more heinous sins, I fear risking the wrath of Alexander VI."

He slyly winked at the Queen Consort.

"My art will suffer."

She waved at the men and their banter, turning the group's attention back to the unfinished masterpiece.

"I thought it was to be just the head and chest, Signore. This is different. I will say, though, the lightness of the beard has my favor."

Anne touched the smooth cheek of her husband.

"Much more appealing."

Leonardo stepped up to the center display and motioned for Boltraffio to come forward.

"Giovanni Antonio, this is a good start with the blessing hand. Consider…"

With a piece of white chalk, the Master redrew the thumb. He stepped back to Salaí's place in the semi-circle and pointed to the boy's painting.

"Andrea has it correct. Yours is too curved. We want this straight up. You understand?

"Also, please observe. The colors of the hand are lighter, and the hand itself must be clearer in its rendering. It is in front of the body. The observer must get the optical effect of the hand coming forward."

"In addition…"

He marked again.

"Refer to the drawings of the drapery I have posted on that wall. In attempting to suggest the wound beneath the tunic on Christ's right side, you have reversed the garment flow. Correct it or allow me to."

Leonardo turned to another student.

"Giorgio… no, no, boy.. *sfumato, sfumato*. Remember the 'Virgin of the Rocks.' Use the heel of the hand and… that's right, boy, blur the hair. You are softening the transition of the colors. See how it seems to go out of focus and moves the head further back in the painting? Yes, yes, but carefully. Leave the detail sharp in the curls. They cascade over his shoulders above the chest and, therefore, forward in the optic plane. Go into the hills and study a cascading stream. There, there. See. Tomaso has it correct. Help your cousin, boy."

The royals were fascinated.

Andrea sat at his place and picked up a paintbrush. He asked, "Master, the left hand. Have you decided?"

Leonardo directed his response to the King and Queen. He was excited and talked with passion about his work.

"A problem. The left-hand demands the *globus cruciger*…."

Anne explained to her husband.

"The gold and jeweled orb topped by a cross– very popular in the Northern European paintings."

"I think I have a few of those myself," Louis replied. "The symbol of global authority. Most fitting."

Leonardo shook his head.

"No. The 'Salvator Mundi' is at once reassuring and unsettling. While in harmony with the blessing gesture, such an orb would throw the painting out of balance. It is the face… haunting and mysterious — evocative of the divine…"

As he left off speaking, he looked closely at the Queen's chest in a way that almost unnerved the woman.

"*Signore…*"

Leonardo ignored the moment of royal modesty.

"Bernardino Luini, sketch this if you please."

Anne brought her hand up to her breast.

"No, Your Majesty, I mean no rudeness. The knot pattern on your sash- - *exquis, ma Reine.*"

He gestured to Giovanni Antonio Boltraffio and the crossed trim of Christ's tunic.

"Gio, replace that design with the beauty before us. Yes, such divine loveliness."

Anne, Duchess of Britany and the soon-to-be crowned Queen of France, was pleased.

***

"Who are you?"

Leonardo da Vinci sat on the workshop floor in front of the 'Salvator Mundi.' He leaned against the seated figure of Andrea Salaí, who gently stroked his Master's hair. A single candle was placed on a stand in the space before the painting, illuminating the room. The artists shared a glass of deep red wine.

"I am no one, Master Salaí." The figure lowered the hood of his cape and shrugged. "A writer of sorts…"

The man who spoke in the darkness was tall and very well constructed, as revealed when he moved into the pool of candlelight. His eyes sparkled in the reflected flame, caught as he bowed.

"I beg your indulgence."

Leonardo was languorous but somewhat alert. He pointed at the specter in black and rose from the floor as he spoke.

"Signore, I am still sober enough to recognize the Republic's esteemed Secretary of the Chancery, Niccolò di Bernardo dei Machiavelli, Master of Political Philosophy and member of the Signoria. Good evening to you, Sir."

The figure advanced further into the light, which highlighted the sharp planes of his patrician features.

"I am your servant, my artistic friends. I come on business."

Salaí sought to lessen the strange and somewhat foreboding elements of yet another surprise visitor. The minister was known to be a rather peculiar and very powerful man, albeit incredibly intellectual.

"Wine, *Signore*?"

Machiavelli declined with an open-palm gesture. He spoke with the sonorous tones of an oracle.

"Master da Vinci, I am under the assumption that you are unaware that you are being caught up in the ongoing clash of a mighty political game. The rules you will find are steeped in violence, deception, treachery, and crime. The field of play is Italy, and great and talented men like you are expendable collateral to be bartered and exploited."

The minister walked within viewing distance of the Christ portrait. Machiavelli studied it assiduously as he continued.

"Ahhh, the great evils men do in the name of the people, in many cases, are most necessary. Quite heinous, nevertheless."

He brought his face close to the painting as if scrutinizing each brushstroke.

"The players are the Borgias, most notably, Pope Alexander VI, the Medici. Oh yes, they will return, Signori, have no doubt. His Most Christian Majesty, Louis XII... I have it on the best authority that you met with this Prince as late as this very day. The French King's newly acquired ally,

Ferdinand II of Aragon, and Emperor Maximilian I of the Holy Roman Empire. All of these for the Italian lands."

Machiavelli turned to da Vinci. He pointed to the Saviour.

"Astounding. But, where is Christ's other hand?"

Leonardo shrugged.

"Unfinished."

"Yes. I have heard that of you... unfinished... revised... continuing. Your artistic sensibilities are organic and unresting. Unconventional. Even highly unusual. Almost forbidden. I believe it was you who so famously rebuked one of your latest critics, saying, 'Not unfinished, Signore. Abandoned.'"

The younger man addressed the diplomat, "You make a sport of collecting your spies' reports on us, Signore Machiavelli? How soon are we to be arrested for...?

"Indecency? For that which is unconventional? This is neither my purpose nor my interest, boy. Not when a man like this regularly touches the divine, as with..."

He gestured again to the Christ.

"But, my leniency is not marked by others, Master Andrea. It has not been all that long ago that we Florentines incinerated the fanatic priest, Savonarola, in front of the Signoria. Those others, I have mentioned, will not hesitate to use you for their own nefarious ends or burn you with impunity."

The dark man shook his head.

"Not your art, Leonardo. Your machines. Your machines of war. You cannot be allowed to remain unfettered to a prince. No, no. The trouble is not your sodomy. It is your genius."

He paused to let his words sink in.

"I am here to urge you to leave Italy. It is that simple."

Niccolò Machiavelli seemed to pirouette in the chiaroscuro atmosphere of the workshop. He flipped up the hood of his cape but hesitated. From within its folds, the minister drew forth a crystal globe about the size of a small melon. Returning, he handed it to the painter, designer, and illustrator of the hidden wonders of creation.

"Perhaps a paperweight for your notebooks, *Sì?*"

With a swirl, he was swallowed up by darkness.

Leonardo held the crystal ball between them and marveled at its purity in the flickering light.

"A masterpiece!"

www.ingramcontent.com/pod-product-compliance
Lightning Source LLC
Chambersburg PA
CBHW071128200626
46817CB00018B/2474